Alice could scarcely believe her eyes. It was Nicholas Tennent.

Was her memory playing tricks on her? Surely the distinguished gentleman looking at her was not the same man she'd given her heart to so long ago.

Nicholas Tennent. The name evoked pain and longing. For a second she thought she would faint. But she clamped down on her emotions. She had come a long way from the innocent girl she'd once been.

What was he doing here in London after all these years? Had he always been in town? Wouldn't they have run into each other?

She began walking toward him. Did he remember her at all? He must _____ way he was looking at her. His _____ ____ ____ oved from her face.

They re_____ ut her hands, h_____ she spoke. "M_____ ___?

"Miss She_____ he bowed, taking both her hands in his. "Would you care to dance?"

Books by Ruth Axtell Morren

Love Inspired Historical

Hearts in the Highlands
A Man Most Worthy

Steeple Hill Single Title

Winter Is Past
Wild Rose
Lilac Spring
Dawn in My Heart
The Healing Season
The Rogue's Redemption

RUTH AXTELL MORREN

wrote her first story when she was twelve—a spy thriller—and knew she wanted to be a writer. There were many detours along the way. She studied comparative literature at Smith College, taught English in the Canary Islands and worked in international development in Miami, Florida, where she met her future husband.

She gained her first recognition as a writer when her second manuscript finaled in the Romance Writers of America Golden Heart Contest in 1994. Ruth has been writing for Steeple Hill Books since 2002, and her second novel, *Wild Rose* (2004) was selected as a Booklist Top 10 Christian Novel in 2005.

After living several years on the down-east coast of Maine, Ruth and her family moved back to the Netherlands to the polderland of Flevoland, where she still lives by the sea. Ruth loves hearing from readers. You can contact her through her Web site, www.ruthaxtellmorren.com.

RUTH AXTELL MORREN

A Man Most Worthy

Steeple
Hill®

Published by Steeple Hill Books™

STEEPLE HILL BOOKS

Steeple
Hill®

ISBN-13: 978-0-373-82797-8
ISBN-10:   0-373-82797-0

A MAN MOST WORTHY

Copyright © 2008 by Ruth Axtell

www.SteepleHill.com

Printed in U.S.A.

He shall receive the blessing from the Lord,
and righteousness from the God of his salvation.
—*Psalms* 24:5

Chapter One

Richmond, England, June 1875

The numbers wouldn't add up. Nick ran his ink-smudged finger up the neat column of figures and back down again.

A smothered giggle disrupted his concentration. With a frown, he glanced up from his desk, irritated that he'd have to begin adding for a third time.

He stared.

The most exquisite creature stood in the doorway to his small office, a finger to her lips. In her navy blue pleated skirt and sailor blouse, she appeared no more than sixteen.

Before he could do or say anything, she moved into his space, bringing with her a vitality the dusty nook had probably not seen in a decade.

Her eyes were wide, pleading, yet with a touch of mischief. "Shh!" she whispered. "Don't tell them I'm here."

He almost jumped out of his seat as she came around his desk and crouched behind it at his feet.

He drew his legs in, his eyes drawn to her slim, pale hands

clasped over her knees. She lifted her head. "You won't give me away, will you?" Her sparkling deep blue eyes looked up at his in a conspiratorial smile. They must be what the poets called violet. Another part of his mind noticed the coppery shade of her hair. It was worn down, as befitted a schoolgirl, with a deep fringe across her wide forehead, and drawn away from her face with a wide blue bow in the back. Her hair was very straight but its toffee-colored tones glistened in the bit of light from his small lamp.

A noise at the door caused him to look up again. A youth and another young lady stood at the doorjamb, their faces peering doubtfully in.

The young gentleman ran a disdainful eye across the room. "You don't think she came in here, do you?"

The young lady, also pretty, but nothing compared to the one crouched at Nick's feet, put her hands on the hips of her similar schoolgirl outfit and took a slow turn about the cramped space, her slim nose wrinkled. "I daresay not. There's not space in here to hide a pin in!"

Nick couldn't help glancing down at the girl at his feet, and experienced once again a moment of shock at her loveliness as she glanced up at him, her finger to her lips.

"I say, you haven't seen a young lady run by here, have you, my good fellow?"

Nick immediately took umbrage to the young man's tone. Instead of replying, he picked up his pencil and pretended to go over his figures again.

The young man cleared his throat. "See here, I'm addressing you."

Without straightening from his work, Nick's gaze flickered up. "I beg your pardon?"

A look of annoyance crossed the young man's fine

features. "Never mind. I shall look for myself. Come on, Lucy." He beckoned to the young lady standing at his side.

"Alice wouldn't hide in here," she said with a toss of her head. "Why are we wasting our time in this stuffy hole? There's nothing but dust and paper in here." As if to prove her point, she sneezed.

"You're right." With a sniff, the young gentleman backed out the door. The girl followed after him. Their voices faded down the corridor. "We shall find you, Alice. You can't hide from us!"

Silence descended once more in the office. Before Nick had a chance to move, the girl stood in one quick motion, smoothing down her skirt. "Thank you ever so much, Mr.—"

"Tennent," he said without thinking, pushing his chair back and standing.

She bobbed a quick curtsy then studied him a moment. He wondered what those stunning eyes saw. More than the other girl, no doubt, who had looked right past him as if he'd been no more than the blotter on his desk.

"You're Father's secretary?"

He nodded. So, this lovely creature was the offspring of Mr. Shepard.

She put a finger to her chin and tilted her head. "This is the first time he's brought his secretary out to Richmond, at least as far as I can recall." Her cheeks dimpled. "But then, I'm rarely home myself, so I wouldn't know."

He fingered the pencil he still held in his hand, trying to maintain a poise he was far from feeling. "I imagine your father wanted to have this project finished as quickly as possible. It demands much time and attention right now."

She cast a glance over the papers on his desk. "All

Father's projects seem to require much time and attention." Was that irony in one so young? Her lashes, the same deep coppery tone as her hair, formed deep curves against the delicate, pale skin.

He frowned at her statement. "One doesn't rise to the importance of Mr. Shepard without a lot of time and effort."

Her eyes came up to study him. "You admire him."

"There is much to be admired." He lifted his chin a trifle defensively.

She ran a slim forefinger along the edge of the beat-up desk as she walked around it. He found he could breathe slightly easier when she'd moved a few feet away from him. "Most people do, don't they?" She glanced back at him, her finger still on the desk. "Admire him, I mean?"

"I imagine they do."

She nodded. "Is he a nice employer to you?"

He raised his eyebrows at her direct question, unaccustomed to someone asking him about his situation. "I have only been in his employ a fortnight, and it is not my place to comment on your father's treatment of his employees."

"Of course not. You were very cool to Victor."

Her statement threw him, until he realized she was referring to the young gentleman just in the room. "A playmate of yours?"

"I've known them both since childhood."

"Does that make them your friends?"

She tilted her head and a slow smile spread across her face. "I…don't know. I'd never really thought about it."

As if the mention of them summoned them, he heard their voices once again from the end of the corridor.

"Now, I say, Alice, we've searched this place from top to bottom—"

She sighed and took a step toward the door. "I'd better leave you to your work before they barge in on you again. I do apologize for interrupting your work, Mr. Tennent. I'm sure it's important."

He shook his head, trying to dispel the wave of disappointment he felt at her departure. "No need to apologize." He looked down at his column of figures, reassuming a business-like tone. "Good day to you, Miss Shepard."

"It was a pleasure to make your acquaintance, Mr. Tennent."

She sounded like a society lady, the kind of women he only saw from a distance in London. Hearing Victor's voice closer, she flashed him a smile then spun on her heel and left the room, once again the young schoolgirl.

Victor and Lucy pounced on her as soon as they saw her. "Where in the world were you?"

Alice laughed, the sound coming out breathless and excited. "You sillies, I was behind you all the time." She'd moved far enough from the office door that they wouldn't suspect where she'd come from.

Victor turned away from her and marched in the direction he'd come from. "I say, this game is silly. I, for one, am too old to be playing at hide-and-seek."

Alice stifled a laugh. He only thought it was silly because he hadn't found her. "All right, what do you suggest we do?"

At the moment all she wanted to do was be alone somewhere and ponder the encounter she'd had with Papa's new secretary. *Miss Shepard.* The way he'd said it sounded so grown-up and ladylike. Everyone else called her Miss Alice. She would not be Miss Shepard for another year-and-a-half at her coming out.

In those few moments of conversation, she'd felt taken seriously by an adult. A young gentleman, at that. Her heartbeat quickened at the intensity of his gaze.

She went over his features in her mind. Dark, short-cropped hair over a high forehead, a thin face, a high-bridged nose. But most arresting were his deep-set eyes, their irises almost black, the eyebrows straight and dark above them before arching outward.

"Let's go riding." Victor's voice, always peremptory when he wanted something, brought her thoughts to a halt.

"It's too hot to go riding." Lucy sounded peevish.

She took the girl by the arm. "Come along, we can take a walk in the grove. It'll be cool in the shade."

Two weeks of holidays stretched out before her. How she'd hoped that she'd be able to see Father. But he was always off to London and she was forced to entertain unwanted guests. There'd be no peace now until she returned to school.

Alice stood on the grassy tennis court, her attention fixed on Victor, her racket held firmly in her hand. "Come on, put some spirit into your serve."

Just as she knew they would, her words brought a frown to his face. The next second, he slammed the rubber ball across the net.

But she was ready. The ball sailed out of her reach. With a laugh, she sprang towards it and then hit it dead-on with her racket. It went flying back, forcing Victor to sprint to connect with it. "I say, you're not playing the game as it should be played."

She laughed again. "I'm playing it the way I saw it played at Wimbledon last spring!"

"This is not a competition!"

When she sent it back again, she aimed it at his partner, Lucy. The girl didn't move from her position, merely raised her arm halfway in a vain attempt to reach the ball.

Alice blew her bangs off her forehead in frustration. "Lucy, it went right to you!"

Lucy made a face at her and let Victor fetch the ball. "You're not playing fairly, Alice. You know you mustn't make me reach for it."

What a bore it was to play with these three. She glanced over at her own partner, a neighbor's son, also home for the holidays. He was looking away from the court, leaning on his racket. Oh, to be paired with someone who showed a little spirit!

She lunged to the right, almost missing the ball Victor served back to her. Despite his indolence in the drawing room, once she taunted him, he was roused to make some effort. *Thunk!* Her racket connected with the ball and it went whizzing back to him.

A tall figure coming around the corner of the high yew hedge caught her attention.

She recognized the new secretary immediately. She hadn't seen him at all again yesterday, and wondered if he was forced to take his meals with the servants or all by himself in his little office off Father's library.

In the time it took for the ball to return over the net, Alice made up her mind. She knocked the ball at the wrong angle, so that it missed the net altogether and bounced sidelong into the shorter trimmed hedge on her side of the court.

"Alice! What are you doing?" Victor's voice was filled with disgust. With a shrug and shamefaced smile his way, she skipped toward the hedge. She stooped to retrieve the ball where it had landed in the soil beneath the hedge and stood in time to meet the young secretary coming along the path.

"Hello, Mr. Tennent."

He looked different in the bright sun. Hatless, his short ebony curls gleamed. His face was slim, the cheekbones rather prominent, but his eyes were as dark and intense as the day before.

They widened slightly as if surprised that she'd remembered his name. "Hello, Miss Shepard."

She thought of him confined to that tiny office. "Would you like to join in the match?" With his tall, lean build, he would probably prove a swift player.

His gaze flickered over the court then returned to her. "No, thank you." His tone sounded more formal than yesterday.

"We're having ever so much fun."

He looked away from her. "I have no time for sports."

She fingered the edge of her racket, refusing to give up so easily. "I should think playing a hard game of tennis would help you in your work."

A slight crease formed between his dark brows. "I fail to see how swinging at a ball on a grassy lawn would aid me in figuring the financial assets of a company."

"Exercising your body will keep your mind sharp."

Amusement began to dislodge the severity of his expression. She leaned forward, pressing home her point. "It's been scientifically proven. You are breathing more deeply of oxygen, for one thing. More than in that airless cubbyhole my father has you closeted in."

Before he could say anything, Victor shouted from the court, "Are you going to join the game or remain talking to a clerk all day?" Laughter from the others drifted over to them.

She turned back to the court, ashamed of her friends in that moment. She remembered the secretary's question of the day before. These "friends" were mere acquaintances, offspring of her parents' friends, forced on her during the holidays to keep her company.

Mr. Tennent's face remained expressionless. "If you'll excuse me—"

"Wait." She stopped, casting about for another way to lengthen their exchange, not quite sure why. "Why don't you join me for a game tomorrow—" her mind ran on, thinking of possibilities "—before breakfast, before you begin working."

He looked away from her. "I know nothing of the game." The words came out stiffly as if forced out of him.

She laughed, relieved. For a moment she'd thought perhaps it was her company he didn't want. "That's all right. I can teach you."

His eyes widened slightly before resuming their formality. "I have no time for games. Good morning." Before she could draw breath to argue, he hurried off.

She looked at his receding back, frowning at the rebuff.

"Come on, Alice, or you shall have to forfeit the game."

With a sigh of frustration, she hurried back to her place, prepared to meet Victor's serve.

Lucy gave a disbelieving laugh across the court. "Goodness, Alice, are you so bored you're forced to seek out your father's employees?"

"Why shouldn't I be nice to Father's employees? Maybe he'll prove a better tennis player than all of you!" More determined than ever to get the serious young man out on the tennis court, she whacked the ball that came flying toward her.

* * *

Nick shook his head over the report. The mining company had already had one shaft collapse in the last year. Another was hardly producing. If he were a partner, he'd recommend to Mr. Shepard that he sell his shares of the company.

He gathered up the papers and prepared to go to the larger office adjoining his "airless cubbyhole," as the young Miss Shepard had put it. He paused, considering once again the girl's invitation to a game of tennis. To lessons, no less! He told himself once again, as he had all the rest of the afternoon, that it was nonsense. No matter that no one of her class had ever bothered to notice someone as lowly as a clerk, let alone issue such a friendly invitation....

The girl was no more than fifteen if she was a day. She was his employer's daughter. He had no business daydreaming of her, lovely creature or not.

He stopped at Mr. Shepard's door, hearing a female voice. Nick paused, his hand on the knob, his breath held.

"But Papa, why can't you go rowing with us? The day is glorious and we shall have such a grand time on the water."

"You know I must return to town tomorrow, and I have work this afternoon. Now, you have your friends here you must amuse." Shepard's voice was firm.

"You're forever working. It's a holiday."

Something in the plaintive feminine tones caught at Nick's heart, and he eased open the door a crack.

Miss Shepard stood with her back to him, in a maroon dress with a large bow at the back where the ruffled material was gathered. Its mid-calf length and her long hair worn down with a matching ribbon told him more clearly than anything else that she was still a schoolgirl.

"You'll just have to content yourself with seeing me at

dinner this evening." Mr. Shepard stood and indicated the meeting was over.

"Very well, Father." She turned around, her chest heaving in a sigh.

What kind of a man could ignore such a tender request? The next instant he remembered his own cold refusal of her invitation to play tennis the day before. But that had been different. He was here to work and not to amuse himself. Still, the image of himself as a hard-hearted brute like the girl's father persisted as he waited behind the door.

What he'd seen of his employer thus far—a man who expected a lot and was all business—qualities Nick admired—took on a different perspective when seen from his personal life. Something about the glimpse of Miss Shepard's forlorn face as she dragged her feet toward the exit, elicited a response he'd never thought he'd feel for someone of her pampered station. There were enough people in real want not to waste his sympathy on a spoiled little rich girl.

When the door clicked shut behind her, Nick waited a few more seconds before clearing his throat and entering the library from the side door to his office. His footfalls made no sound on the thick Turkish carpet as he advanced toward the large mahogany desk planted in the middle of the room as if to proclaim its owner firmly in control of the space.

Nick cleared his throat again.

"Yes, what is it?" Mr. Shepard didn't look up, and a trace of impatience underlined the clipped words. He was a man in his fifties, his hair still thick but with threads of gray fading the burnished coppery mane. It occurred to Nick that Shepard must have had his daughter late in life.

"I have the information you requested on Rafferty, Limited."

Shepard adjusted the spectacles on the bridge of his nose and thrust out his hand. "Well, bring it here."

Nick handed him the sheaf of papers, hoping his employer would notice the careful analysis he'd made of the mining company. But with a wave of his hand, Shepard dismissed Nick. Nick's years clerking at a bank had inured him to being treated in such a manner. Clerks were usually ignored until someone needed something pressing and then barked at to produce it immediately.

But he'd looked forward to just a hint that Mr. Shepard had noticed all his extra effort.

Nick returned to his office, unable to help comparing his own footsteps with those of the girl who'd been just as summarily dismissed.

This was a mistake. Nick knew it, yet found he could do nothing to change his course of action.

Setting his alarm clock for an hour earlier than usual, he rose with a sense of foreboding that he was about to make a fool of himself. After washing and shaving, he stood a moment looking at his sparse wardrobe of black suits appropriate to a clerk. What did one wear to a game of lawn tennis?

Finally, he donned a clean white shirt and waistcoat and one of his two black frock coats, calling himself a number of names as he buttoned up the front. He looked like he should be heading to a counting house instead of outdoors. The young men he'd observed the other day had worn light-colored trousers and loose jackets.

Nick did own a straw boater—more appropriate in the country than the top hats he usually wore.

Setting it on his head, he headed out the door, not

bothering to go by the dining room to see if breakfast had been laid out yet. This household was not one to rise early, he'd observed in his few days' residence.

He walked past the garden beds, deciding he'd see if Miss Shepard was there and return at once if she wasn't. If he saw anyone else, he'd pretend he was out for an early morning stroll. Surely the girl hadn't meant the invitation seriously. He imagined her sleeping form. Of course she didn't remember a casually issued invitation. Yet, she'd remembered his name. That fact still amazed him.

The grass was damp with dew. The toes of his polished shoes were already wet before he'd gone halfway across the lawn.

He recalled Miss Shepard's words about exercise being good for his mental acuity and couldn't help smiling. What did she know about real toil? He'd been up at the crack of dawn since he'd been able to walk, toddling out after his brothers and mother to the mill.

A riot of birdsong hailed him from the great boughs of the trees on the vast property. He realized he'd never been in such a pleasant setting. Childhood was a memory of dismal, gray surroundings and of hunger and barrenness. Since coming to London, he'd lived in a different sort of gray, from sunup to sundown in a treeless environment, going from his dingy room, downing a quick breakfast in the drab dining room crowded with half-a-dozen other young clerks, and rushing to catch the steamer across the gray Thames to the grim city of finance.

He passed the last flowerbed and looked over the hedge at the carefully clipped, emerald green lawn with its chalked lines marking out an oblong.

He stopped short at the sight of Miss Shepard holding

a racket in one hand. Her head was lifted up, a hand shading her eyes from the early morning sun. He followed her line of vision and saw a bird in flight. His gaze returned to her. Her long hair fell down her shoulders like melted caramel to the small of her back. For all the loveliness of her silhouette, something about it conveyed loneliness. His gut tightened as he recalled the sound of longing in her voice toward her father.

She must have seen him out of the corner of her eye because she dropped her hand and ran over to him.

"You came!" She stopped about a foot from him, her smile wide. In that instant, all his doubts evaporated like the dew in the warm morning sun. He didn't doubt the welcome on her face; she was too young to have learned to mask her feelings.

He found himself caught once again by her beauty. She had the most exquisite features, delicate and perfectly formed like a porcelain doll's—pink-tinted cheeks, a perfect little nose, lips a deeper pink than her cheeks, her teeth white and even. Her heart-shaped face was framed by those silky locks of hair.

Then he looked down at the damp grass, remembering his ignorance of the game. "Yes."

"Have you really never played tennis before?"

Did she think the average person indulged in tennis? How little she knew of life. His eyes met hers again, expecting to see triumph, but only simple interest was visible in those blue depths. "No."

"Very well, let's get started. I imagine you haven't much time."

"You imagine correctly." What was he doing here? He should be finishing breakfast and going to his desk.

"I brought an extra racket, in case you decided to come." She slanted him a friendly smile as she spoke, leading the way to the edge of the court.

She picked up a racket from a white wrought iron chair and a wire basket full of rubber balls. "You take this side of the net. Stand in the middle since we're playing singles, and I'll go on the other. I shall serve to you and you try to hit the ball back to me. Just follow my motions."

Still amazed that she wanted to teach him, he took the racket from her and gripped it in his hand. It didn't weigh much, its handle made of wood and wrapped in leather at the base.

She hit the ball with an underhanded swing and it came over the high net toward him. He didn't even have to move to reach it. He swung with all his might and with a sense of triumph connected with the ball. Instead of going back over the net where he expected it to, it flew up toward the sky and landed back on his side of the net, skittering away in a series of small bounces.

His face flamed at her laughter.

"You needn't hit it quite so hard to return it across the net," she said in a kind tone. "Also, a lot depends on the angle of your racket when you hit the ball. Let's try again, shall we?" She stooped and grabbed another ball from her basket.

He gripped the racket, determined to hit the ball over the net this time. He controlled his swing, barely tapping the racket against the ball and sent it dribbling into the net.

"That's better," she said, no hint of laughter in her voice. "Let's try another."

She continued sending balls his way. He missed as many as he managed to hit, but she continued encouraging him with every one.

Then he began to catch on and managed to send more balls back to her. Gradually he gained confidence because Miss Shepard was so patient and encouraging. He enjoyed watching her vitality as she ran across the court, so unlike the passive stance of the other women he'd glimpsed on the court at other times in the day. Perhaps it was because she was still a girl. She had not yet assumed the airs of a young lady just come out. Even the perspiration making her face shine appealed to him.

In some ways she reminded him of the girls of his boyhood. In their ragged frocks and bare feet, there was no room for stiffness and formality. They ran and skipped about, unfettered by social constraints or petticoats and high-buttoned shoes.

She continued sending balls his way a while longer. He was beginning to think it a tame sport when a ball went flying over the net so fast it made a whooshing sound as it cut through the air. He had to sprint to connect with it. He just made it and sent it back over.

She laughed as she went running for it. "This is the way I prefer to play!" Again, it came hard at him, and he had to jump to the side to reach it. He missed it.

"I see." He retrieved the ball and returned to his place. He swung hard at it and again, the ball went too high.

"I'm over here, you know!" Laugher bubbled in her voice.

He winced in embarrassment at his overconfidence. Before he could run after the ball, she had gone for it. This time she resumed her gentler game. "I think we need to practice a bit more before you're up to my speed." The words were said to him in a friendly manner but he took them as a challenge, vowing to find a way to master this game.

Beads of sweat rolled down his temples as the sun grew warmer in the sky. At that moment, she picked up the ball and strolled to his side of the court. "You really need proper tennis garments. You must be sweltering in your suit. Why don't you take off your coat?"

He mopped his brow, thinking how unpolished he must look compared to the suave young men she'd played with yesterday. Instead of removing his coat, he snapped open his watch. "I really must go. I need to get to work."

She nodded, though her down-tilted face and puckered lips expressed disappointment. Then she brightened. "Have you breakfasted?"

He shook his head.

"I haven't either. Come, you must be as hungry and thirsty as I am." Before he could refuse, she was walking off the court. "Leave the racket here. I'm sure someone will be out to play later. Hurry, I'm famished!" She waited for him to catch up to her and the two walked back to the house.

Her next words surprised him. "Are you from London?"

He wasn't used to anyone taking a personal interest in him. "No. I grew up in Birmingham."

She tilted her head. "That's funny. You haven't any accent that I can tell."

"That's because my mother was—" He bit his tongue, he'd almost said "a lady." He hesitated. "From Kent."

She smiled. "Not far from here?"

"A bit. She was born in Whitstable."

"Ah, by the sea."

He found her blue eyes fixed on him as if waiting for more information. "She was a governess before she married my father." He looked away. "He was a miner."

"Oh." The single note was filled with wonder. "However did they meet?"

"She was working with a family up there and had left them." Refusing the master's advances, he added mentally. "She had begun a small school for the miner's children."

"And she met your father!" Her eyes gleamed in excitement. "Oh! Love at first sight, I bet it was."

He looked straight ahead of him, amused and irritated at the same time by her romantic schoolgirl notions. "He died when a mine shaft collapsed, leaving my mother to raise four sons. He was a widower, when they met. His two boys were at the school. Then my brother and I came along."

"How sad," she said softly. "My mother died giving birth to me."

He looked sharply at her. Her tone was almost casual. "I'm sorry," he said finally, feeling the inadequacy of the words.

"Oh, it's all right. It happened so long ago. Tell me what happened after your father died."

He took up the thread of his own history, his mind still on her motherless condition. "My mother moved us into town, where she found work in a mill."

Miss Shepard was silent for only a moment. No doubt she'd lost interest by now. "And when did you come to London?"

He smiled at her persistence. No one from her station had ever asked him about his origins. "When I was fifteen, my mother gave me five pounds she had saved and bought me a rail ticket to London. I found work at a bank. I was good with numbers, you see. Numbers and letters. She'd made sure we all received learning."

"And now you've become my father's private secretary?" He nodded.

"That's good. Poor old Simpson is becoming forgetful, I've heard. He's been with Father forever!"

They reached the house and he held the door open for her then followed her into the breakfast room. He still hadn't gotten accustomed to the fact that there were separate rooms for breakfasting and dining—and that most in the household took their breakfast in bed.

He stopped short at the threshold of the breakfast room at the sight of his employer. Mr. Shepard was seated squarely behind *The Times* and Nick debated a few seconds what to do. Retreat? Go forward as if accompanying the man's daughter were the most natural thing in the world?

Before he could decide, Miss Shepard breezed in ahead of him. "Good morning, Father. You've beaten us down to breakfast." She leaned over and kissed him on the cheek.

"What are you doing about so early?" He glanced over his paper, then lowered it further when he caught sight of Nick. Nick greeted him, hesitating at the doorway. The man gave a mere nod in acknowledgment and turned his attention back to his young daughter.

"I was just practicing tennis. Look whom I found." She turned to Nick. "He hasn't breakfasted either, so I brought him along. What will you have, Mr. Tennent?" Before her father could say anything, she moved to the sideboard and began lifting lids. "There's scrambled eggs, kedgeree, bacon…"

Mr. Shepard grunted and turned back to his paper.

Nick followed to the serving dishes and took up a plate. The girl had succeeded in distracting her father from any mention of tennis lessons. He pondered her adroit maneuver as he helped himself to the wide array of food. His own boarding house fare usually consisted of lumpy porridge and a weak cup of tea.

Concentrating on his food, Nick listened to Miss Shepard chattering away to her father. He answered in monosyllables, with an occasional "What's that you say?" thrown in, but he never lowered his paper more than a fraction.

Nick marveled at how Shepard could have produced such a lovely creature—and not realize what a treasure he had. Poor motherless child. He knew she had a much older brother. Nick had seen him a few times at the firm—Mr. Geoffrey Shepard, a pompous man in his late twenties.

Miss Shepard leaned forward, setting down her knife and fork. "Did you hear me, Papa?"

"What's that you say?"

"I said we are planning an excursion to Richmond Park. Can you not come?"

"I return to London this afternoon. Take Miss Bellows with you."

Nick knew he referred to a companion of sorts he'd briefly met in the servants' quarters. His gaze rested in sympathy on Miss Shepard's crestfallen features. He turned with a start to find Mr. Shepard focused on him, his gray-blue eyes sharp and piercing. "I'll need those figures on Henderson, Ltd. before I go."

"Yes, sir." Nick drained the last of his tea and stood. "I'll get to it right away."

Miss Shepard smiled at him. "So long, Mr. Tennent. Perhaps I shall see you tomorrow?" Her eyes told him she was referring to the tennis court.

"Perhaps. Good morning, Miss Shepard." With a bow, he left the room.

Of course, he couldn't join her again tomorrow. It was sheer folly…

Chapter Two

Awake since the sky had begun to lighten, Alice let out a massive sigh of relief when she saw Mr. Tennent walking across the lawn toward the court.

Not until that moment did she realize how disappointed she would have been if he hadn't shown up. She'd prayed hard last night that he wouldn't be discouraged after only one lesson.

She fingered the head of her racket as she watched his long stride. His serious air made Victor and the other boys of her acquaintance seem just that—boys! Biting her lip, she glanced down at her calf-length plaid skirt and sailor top. How she wished she were one year older and wore ankle-length dresses like a lady. Did Mr. Tennent see her as just a schoolgirl? She cringed, remembering the silly game of hide-and-seek she'd been playing the day she'd burst in on him.

She smiled as he approached her. "Good morning."

He nodded, his dark eyes meeting hers, their formality lessening as he gave her a slight smile. "Good morning, Miss Shepard."

She tilted her head. "Ready to have another go?"

"If you've the patience and fortitude."

Her smile widened in relief. She handed him the extra racket. "You did very well for your first time. Come, I'll serve first."

"Very well." He shed his coat this time and laid it carefully on a wrought iron chair by the side of the court.

She began gently, giving him a chance to review what she'd taught him the day before. They played for about twenty minutes before taking a break.

"I brought some water for us," she said, leading him to the yew hedge where she had stashed two stone flasks. "It should still be cold."

"Thank you." He took the one she handed him then waited until she had uncapped hers and brought it to her lips before following suit. "How did I do today? Any improvement?" he asked, lowering the flask.

"Oh, a vast amount. You're a natural athlete."

He made a sound of disbelief.

"You don't believe me? It's the truth. I can tell. You're nothing like most of the boys on the court who try and act as if they knew something." She studied his face, hoping she was convincing him not to give up, but the steady way he regarded her was hard to read.

Mr. Tennent wiped his brow with his handkerchief, pushing back his dark curls.

Hoping to draw out more about his fascinating past, she said, "Tell me more about your mother."

He looked away from her, and she bit her lip, afraid she had offended him. Her governess had always said she was too direct.

But he answered with no sign of displeasure. "She

had to take us into the mill with her when we were young, and put us to work as soon as we could wind a thread around a bobbin."

"She must have been a brave woman to raise four boys all alone." His tale had haunted her last night. It had sounded so unbearably romantic.

He pocketed his handkerchief. He was standing in his vest and shirtsleeves. Even in his typical clerk's attire, he stood out. There was something distinguished about him. "No matter how tired she was," he continued in a quiet tone, "she always gave us a lesson after dinner in the evenings before we went to bed. She had saved a few school-books and one or two storybooks from her teaching days. Those and the Bible formed our only amusement at home."

She pictured the cozy scene, a mother with her four boys surrounding her on a settee, or with her arms around them on a wide bed flanked by soft pillows. "It must have been nice to have a mother read to you at night."

"Didn't anyone ever read to you at bedtime?"

She blushed beneath his close scrutiny. "My nurse told me stories when I was very young, and then Miss Duffy, my governess, read to me when I was a little older."

"I'm sorry you didn't have a mother to read to you at bedtime," he said softly.

His tone was so gentle it was as if he had known how lonely her childhood had been. Afraid he'd pity her, she set down her water bottle and picked up her racket. "Come on, let's get back to our game before you have to work."

He followed her out to the court. This time, she hit the ball a little harder and enjoyed watching him run to meet it. She, too, was forced to run across the court when he returned it equally forcefully. Laughing from sheer joy at the physical exertion, she swung at the ball and watched it clear the net.

By the time they finished their lesson, they were both red in the face, but never had she had more fun on the court.

"What about tomorrow morning?" she asked him, hoping she didn't sound too eager.

"It depends on your father. I might be called back to London."

Her shoulders slumped in disappointment. "Of course." Trust Father to ruin her fun. "Do you think he'll bring you back out again?"

"I have no way of knowing."

"Well, if you should come back, I challenge you to a match."

He nodded slowly, his deep set eyes looking into hers. "You're on."

As soon as he had a free moment back in London, Nick inquired of one of the clerks in the firm and found out where he could get tennis lessons. It meant money he could ill afford, and having to go across town to Regent's Park, but he was determined the next time he faced Alice Shepard across the court, he would no longer be a clumsy novice.

He hadn't been able to get the young girl out of his mind since he'd returned to the city, no matter how many times he'd told himself he was being silly to keep thinking about her.

But her smiling face wouldn't leave his thoughts despite the effort he put into studying his employer's files and tallying columns of numbers.

He'd never been in love. No young woman had yet caused him to veer from his single-minded focus on the path to success.

The feelings Miss Shepard elicited in him were a puzzle to him, not least because he didn't know how to classify them. She was too young for it to be love, he felt. But if it wasn't love, it certainly was a sort of obsession, which he'd have to eradicate sooner or later. He could ill spare time for such dangerous complications.

In the meantime, however, at a safe distance in London, he preferred to postpone the moment and content himself with daydreaming about her as he rode the early morning ferry to work, as he walked the distance to the office, as he made the return journey in the evening.

And every evening, after work and a light supper, he stood across the net from his new instructor, imagining Miss Shepard in his place. He'd spent part of his last salary on a lightweight pair of twill trousers and a linen jacket, vowing to look as dapper as any young gentleman when they next met.

Back and forth went the ball, the instructor calling out advice as he sent it across the net to Nick. Nick grew to enjoy the thrill of competition. He found it as thrilling as predicting the direction of the price of a company's stock.

He remembered Miss Shepard's words. *You're a natural athlete.* Did it mean she'd actually looked past his shabby frock coat and seen something more than just her father's secretary? He'd never thought of himself as athletic, even though until coming to London, he'd spent any spare moment outside when he wasn't working in the noisy, dusty environment of the mill. But that was playing in the street with boys his age, with no sports equipment. A ball was a rotten cabbage, a cricket bat a broken chair leg. But even those had been few and far between as any piece of wood was quickly consumed in the stove, and extra food was rarely to be found.

Nick had no idea when and if he'd be going back to the Shepards' country house, but he'd be prepared just in case, even if it cost him a fortnight's wages.

He wanted to match Miss Shepard's skill and show her he was a worthy opponent.

Each morning he joined the hundreds of anonymous young men clad in black frock coats and top hats hurrying down Fleet Street to their offices. He pulled open the brass-handled door, glancing a moment at the understated plaque to the right: Shepard & Steward, Ltd., Investments.

Some day it would read Shepard, Steward, Tennent, & Partners.

He hurried down the corridor to his office, nodding his head to the various clerks he passed. "'Morning, Harold. 'Morning, Stanley." Rushed syllables as everyone hurried to his place in the maze of corridors and cubicles.

He entered the quieter sanctuary upstairs in the rear, the executive offices of the full partners. His own desk, situated in a small corner of an office he shared with the senior secretary, was neat, the way he'd left it the evening before.

Nick sat down and opened the file he'd been studying the previous day, glad for the momentary solitude. Mr. Shepard would expect a report by noon on the assets of the small factory, which manufactured iron fastenings.

"Shepard wants you."

He looked up to find Mr. Simpson, the other secretary, walking to his own desk, the larger of the two in the room. The old man guarded his boss from all he considered intruders, including Nick.

Nick stood now and grabbed up his pad and pencil. "Yes, sir."

The man stood by the doorway, as if to make sure Nick

obeyed the summons. His bristly gray eyebrows drew together in their customary frown as Nick passed him with a curt nod.

Dark walnut wainscoting covered the walls of Mr. Shepard's private office. Oil landscapes in heavy wooden frames lined the space above. Some day he would have an office like this one.

Shepard stood at a window overlooking the busy street below, his hands clasped loosely behind them. He turned only slightly at the soft sound of the door closing.

"Ah, Tennent, have a seat. I need you to take a letter."

"Yes, sir." Nick crossed the deep blue Turkish carpet and sat in the leather armchair facing the wide desk.

Mr. Shepard twirled his reading glasses in his hands. "This is to the Denbigh Coke Company, Denbighshire, Wales.

"Gentlemen— After a careful review of your firm, it is with regret that we inform you that we must decline the opportunity to offer you the venture capital you requested to expand your colliery. Although your firm's net profits for the preceding year showed…"

Nick's pencil hurried across the paper, his mind unable to suppress the satisfaction at Shepard's decision. It mirrored the one Nick would have made in his place.

Mr. Shepard's peremptory tone interrupted his thoughts. "Read it back to me."

"Yes, sir." He began at the top.

"Very good. I'll sign it as soon as you have it ready. Make sure it goes in today's post."

Nick stood.

"I will be heading back out to Richmond this weekend. I have various projects that need catching up on. I trust you will be free to accompany me?"

Unable to help a spurt of excitement at the announcement, Nick's fingers tightened on his pencil. It was quickly doused as he realized his employer would keep him too busy to allow him any free time for recreation. "Yes, sir."

"Very good."

Nick reached the door.

"Bring enough to stay a week."

Nick turned slowly. A week in Richmond? His heart started to thump. "Yes, sir."

An entire week in the same house as Miss Shepard. This time he couldn't contain his excitement. He even began to whistle as he made his way back down the dark corridor.

Alice returned from church at noon on Sunday.

She stopped short in the doorway, her hands flying to her cheeks as at the sight of the tall young man emerging from her father's library. "Mr. Tennent!"

To her further surprise, he smiled, looking as glad to see her as she felt to see him.

"When did you arrive?"

"Early this morning," he said. "Your father was going to come Friday evening but was delayed with other engagements."

She moistened her lip, trying to appear collected. "I— I've just come from church."

"I see."

An awkward silence ensued. Then her eyes widened in sudden horror. "Have you been working?"

He colored. "I was just going to read up on some documents."

"On the Sabbath?" She couldn't help the shock in her voice.

He looked away as if ashamed. "Yes."

She frowned. "Father doesn't forbid you from attending services, does he?"

"No, of course not. I...I've already been to services."

"You have? I didn't see you."

"That's because I attended chapel."

"Chapel?" Her eyes widened in further shock as she understood his meaning. "You're Methodist?"

His dark eyes seemed to hold a touch of defiance. "My mother was Church of England, but she attended chapel with my father."

"Oh!" She wondered at the thought of a lady leaving her church for the lowly Methodist chapel for the sake of her husband. She thought of something. "Our cook, Mrs. Clayworth, attends chapel."

"Does she?"

She bit her lip, afraid she'd offended him. Did he think she equated him with their cook? Actually, she'd always been curious about those attending this other sort of church. All she'd ever heard of Methodists was disdainful. The only one she knew, the cook, was firmly decided in her faith. "Maybe I can go with you some time?"

He drew back a fraction as if surprised. "Perhaps." There was no encouragement in the reserved tone.

She shifted on her feet, wondering if he was still interested in playing tennis. Then she remembered she had a prior commitment. "A party of us is going riding this afternoon. Would you like to join us?"

He fingered a corner of the sheaf of papers he held in his hands. "I—I was just looking over some correspondence your father has given me." He cleared his throat. "He's away this afternoon."

She smiled in relief. "Perfect. Join us at the stables after lunch. We're riding to Richmond Park. It's awfully nice there. There's a wonderful view of the Thames from the top." When he didn't say anything, she suddenly understood his hesitation. "Oh, if it's about proper clothing, you can borrow a habit of my brother's. He's a little stockier than you, but he has outfits in his wardrobe from when he was younger. I'll ask the butler to take something out for you." When he continued to hesitate, she tilted her head. "What is it?"

Again came the defiant lift of his chin. "I've never ridden before."

"Never?"

A faint smile tinged his lips. "Perhaps I've been atop a donkey once or twice when I was a boy."

"Well, it's not so very different. You can have Maud. She's a gentle mount."

He glanced away. "I'd only slow your party down."

"Nonsense. It's not as if we're racing. It's to be a leisurely ride to Richmond Park and back. You'll have a grand time, you'll see, Mr. Tennent. I'll meet you at the stables at three. You mustn't work all day."

Before he could refuse her, she hurried down the corridor, calling behind her, "I'll see you at three!"

She'd go down to the stables and make sure a groom had Maud saddled and waiting.

Father would certainly not approve of a Methodist in their riding party. That was worse than Low Church! For once, Alice was thankful her father was away.

A grand time, indeed. Nick frowned at the pale horse beneath him. With a groom's help he'd managed to mount the beast—nag, he amended, glancing down as he remembered young Victor's derisive snort when he'd seen the horse being led out—without disgracing himself.

Miss Shepard walked up to Nick's mare and patted her neck. "Hello, there, Maud. Aren't you glad you're not being left behind today?" She smiled up at Nick. "She was my first horse after I'd graduated from a pony. Father bought her for me. She's a trustworthy soul."

At the wistful note Nick forgot his discomfort of being atop a horse. He attempted a smile but before he could say anything, he stiffened as the groom bent down to adjust his stirrups. Nick held his tall boots tightly against the horse's flanks. At least the animal seemed as gentle as Miss Shepard promised. It hadn't moved since being brought out of the stables.

"Good for the glue factory," Victor muttered with a snide look in Nick's direction, before moving off to his own mount. Nick was tempted to box the young fellow's ears, but the eager look on Miss Shepard's face stopped him.

But how was he was to maintain his balance once the creature started moving? There was no pommel on the saddle, just a smooth leather seat. Nick's knuckles were white on the reins.

Thankfully, the horse was relatively small in stature. Not like the great beast that Victor rode. The young gentleman certainly looked elegant seated atop the deep brown horse, holding the reins and riding crop loosely, looking as if he and mount had been born for each other.

Miss Shepard stood back from his horse and looked Nick up and down. "You need to sit farther back in the saddle and loosen your hold a bit. Remember, it's not about gripping the saddle, but about balancing on your horse. She'll carry you."

Before he knew what she was about, she moved down to his boots and took hold of one of his ankles, causing him to jerk back in surprise. "Easy there," she murmured. "Keep your feet bent slightly out, not gripping the horse's flank. That's right." She adjusted the position of his foot to illustrate her point. "Yes, like so."

She gave him a few more pointers, all the while touching his legs and boots to demonstrate. Unfortunately, with each movement, he grew more tense, his breathing more erratic.

She looked up at him, her blue eyes earnest, and took his hand in hers. He realized how unaware she must be of what her touch was doing to him. It only proved how young she was. "Now, hold your hands about that far apart, not closer. Don't let the reins touch the horse's neck." She ran her hands up his arm, adjusting its angle. The more she spoke, the more afraid he became of moving lest he lose the correct position; the mare would undoubtedly know and take advantage.

As if reading his thoughts, Miss Shepard smiled up at him. "You'll get the feel of it after a while."

Victor maneuvered his horse alongside them. "Are we going or not?"

"Just a minute." Miss Shepard's usually polite tone held a trace of asperity.

"If I'd known you were going to give a riding lesson, I would have opted out of this excursion."

"Well, you may still do so."

With a sneer, Victor wheeled his horse about, causing the mare under Nick to shift. Nick couldn't help splaying his hands on the saddle beneath him, ruining all Miss Shepard's careful positioning.

Instead of scolding him, she immediately went to the

mare's bridle. "There, Maud, Mr. Tennent meant nothing by that. You must be patient a moment longer." She didn't even turn when Victor spoke to the other young lady in a loud voice.

"Come along, Lucy. They can catch up when he finally figures out how to get his horse to move." With a snide laugh, he urged his horse forward, Lucy following behind.

Nick gritted his teeth. How he'd love the chance to show Victor a thing or two. "Perhaps this is not the right time for me to go riding."

"Nonsense, Mr. Tennant. Victor just likes to show off. You mustn't mind him. Now, let's see, where were we?"

"How to get her to move."

Miss Shepard smiled. "Right, just a very gentle contact with the horse's mouth." She explained some more and showed him how to bring the mare to a halt. Not until he had done so a few times was she satisfied.

"Very good."

Before he could take any satisfaction in this small success, Miss Shepard went to her own mount, a beautiful bay mare. A groom was immediately at her side but she gave him no chance to assist her. She placed a foot in the stirrup and swung herself up in one deft move. He watched her graceful figure in a blue riding habit. She seemed perfectly at ease on her horse.

At least he needn't be ashamed of his own appearance. The riding habit he'd borrowed—a tweed jacket, tan-colored jodhpurs, and tall boots—fit as if made for him. Even the snobby Victor had given him a keen look.

Miss Shepard turned her horse about. "Ready?"

He nodded. She conveyed the message to her horse, and with a second's hesitation, Nick gave his own horse the command. The other riders were nowhere to be seen as they clip-clopped out of the stable yard.

Thankfully, his horse followed the other as they walked down the long, tree-lined drive that led away from the house.

Miss Shepard turned briefly to him. "We're going to go away from the river and head uphill. The way is easy, only a gentle rise."

Soon, they spotted the other riders farther up ahead. Nick was too busy concentrating on staying on his horse to attempt any further conversation as they rode down the lane. Before he knew it, they'd left the village behind and were among tree-studded meadows.

The tension in him began to ease as he realized his mare would keep her steady, sedate pace, and he allowed himself to enjoy the countryside. For as far as he could remember, he'd lived in the city, between its stone and brick, dirty, choking heat in summer and thick, sulfurous fog in winter.

The ride proceeded smoothly from there. Miss Shepard stayed at his side, instructing him now and again as to the proper handling of the horse.

"She pretty much knows what to do on her own. You are just her guide, to nudge her gently now and again."

Victor rode back to them at a trot, and tried to engage Miss Shepard in conversation, but when she only answered his mocking comments in monosyllables, he rode off again, muttering about having slowed down the whole group.

Soon they could see the Thames far below them, edged in lush green foliage, small wooded islands visible here and there along its snaking course.

They continued climbing along terraced walkways. "We'll go into the park through Sheen Gate," she said. "I'm sure that's the route Victor took." A short while later they entered Richmond Park and spotted Victor and Lucy ahead. Miss Shepard quickened her horse's pace a little, and Nick gave his own reins a slight tug to raise the horse's head, as indicated by Miss Shepard, and tightened his knees the least bit. The horse obeyed and followed after the other one at an increased gait.

His initial fear of falling wearing off, Nick relished the faster pace. They soon caught up to the other riders.

Miss Shepard guided her horse abreast of Victor's. "Let's stop at Bishop's Pond and rest a moment."

"Had enough already?" His words were directed to Miss Shepard but he swung his gaze back toward Nick.

"No, but neither are we in any rush." Without waiting for Victor's answer, she slowed again until she was just ahead of Nick. She twisted in her saddle to him. "It's a pretty spot."

They arrived at the willow-edged pond and dismounted. Nick had another moment of uncertainty, wondering if his horse would stand still while he got down. He held the reins in one hand and swung one leg over the back of the animal. With a breath of relief, he found himself with his two feet firmly planted on solid ground.

Miss Shepard walked her horse toward him. "Let's lead them to the pond. I'm sure they're thirsty." She petted Maud's withers. "Aren't you, dearie, after that long ride in the sun?"

The others had already left their horses at the water's edge and were walking about the shaded glen.

Miss Shepard showed him how to remove the horse's bit before letting them drink.

She knelt beside the water's edge and removed her gloves. Taking a handkerchief out of her jacket pocket, she plunged it in the water. Squeezing out the excess water, she used it to wipe her forehead and cheeks. "Ah, that feels refreshing." She grinned up at him, her rosy cheeks damp.

Without thinking, he pulled out his dry handkerchief and handed it to her, finding that around her he merely reacted instead of deliberating before an action. He envied her impulsive behavior, though she was young, not yet out of the schoolroom. His eyes traveled over her, her contours already those of a woman.

"Oh, thank you." She took the handkerchief from him and wiped her face dry before jumping back to her feet. Re-folding his handkerchief, she gave it back to him. He took it without a word. Bending down to the water, he wet it and did what she had done, squeezing it out and using it to mop his own damp forehead. The water felt cold and helped to ease the heat he felt in his face, heat that was due to more than the sun.

She took the wet handkerchief from him. "Here, we'll spread our hankies out on this rock and they'll be dry by the time we leave. Come, I want to show you my favorite spot."

"What about the others?" He gestured to Lucy and Victor. Lucy sat on a boulder, fanning herself with her hat. Victor was throwing stones into the pond, causing a plopping sound with each one.

Miss Shepard shrugged. "He's trying to scare the frogs."

He also seemed to be ignoring Miss Shepard, for which Nick was thankful.

"Come on!" Miss Shepard urged. "We shan't be long."

They walked along the pond's edge and bent down under some willows trailing their long fronds into the water. It was about ten degrees cooler in the shade.

"Isn't it like a cave here?" The shadow and sunlight speckled her face, and he felt as if they could have been under the water, in another world.

He stared at her. Words seemed to get trapped in his throat. What was happening to him that he couldn't form a coherent sentence?

She squatted down by the water's edge again, this time resting her folded hands and chin on her knees. "How do you like working for my father?"

He stood beside her, observing the shadowy light on the crown of her hair. She'd tossed her hat on the ground beside her. Her hair was twisted in a loose knot at the nape of her neck, making her look older than—

"How old are you?" he asked sharply.

She jutted her fine chin out a notch. "I shall be seventeen next month."

"Sixteen then." His heart plummeted at the discovery of how young she truly was.

"Almost seventeen."

He couldn't help smiling at her insistence.

"How old are *you?*"

Her direct question startled him. "Twenty-three." His lips twitched. "Last March. Eons older than you."

She closed one eye and tilted her head upwards. "Six years, that's not so much. But you do seem old."

He drew his brows together at her appraisal. "How so?"

"You're so very serious." She nodded toward the other end of the pond. "Take Victor. He's not so much younger than you. He's nineteen, but he seems like a boy compared to you."

"I've had to grow up a lot faster than Victor."

"Were you always so serious?"

He mulled over the question. "I've never thought about whether or not I was serious."

"You can't always have been serious." There was a glint in her dark blue eyes.

"Perhaps I was born serious."

She laughed. "You *do* have a sense of humor."

"Alice!" Victor's annoyed shout came through the trees.

With a loud sigh, she stood and shook out her pleated riding skirt. "I suppose we should walk the horses."

"Yes." He picked up her hat and handed it to her.

"Thank you." Her quick smile was grateful and friendly.

She probably had no idea what it did to him, making all his years of rigid self-control slip away.

She was still a child, he reminded himself as he held the feathery willow strands aside for her to walk through.

Victor stalked toward them, his hands in his pockets, his features sulky. "Are you ready yet? There's nothing here."

Lucy came up behind him. "Where shall we go?"

"Let's ride up to Oliver's Mount so we can get a good vista of the river." Without waiting for an assent, Miss Shepard headed for the horses, which stood quietly grazing on a sunny patch of grass.

Victor hung back and gave Nick a look. "I say, old fellow, you were a sport to take that sway-backed old nag." His lips turned upward at one corner. "You looked quite a sight on her. Your legs were practically dragging on the ground." His voice lowered. "You know, Alice likes to put first-timers on old Maud. Sort of her secret joke, you know. But I think you've passed the test." He winked. "Why don't you turn the tables on her and try my mount? Show her what stuff you're made of. She's quite a horsewoman, as you've seen. She'd admire you to no end if she saw you on a real horse." With a last wink, he walked away from Nick and joined Lucy, leaning down to help her mount.

Nick considered the youth's offer. He was tempted to accept. How much different could the other horse be? He'd seemed to behave well during their ride over.

Shaking his head, he scolded himself for being a silly fool. He was too old to fall for some masculine gauntlet thrown down before him to impress a young girl.

With a sigh, Nick gathered up Maud's reins. Just as he was about to put his foot into the stirrup, Victor led his horse up. "Well, what'd you say, old boy, have a go?" His gray eyes held an unmistakable challenge.

Ignoring the voice of reason, Nick exchanged reins with him, telling himself if he maintained a sedate pace, everything would be all right. Victor had been right about one thing, he had made a ridiculous picture on that mare, as he now observed Victor sitting atop her.

"What are you doing?" Alice drew alongside of him on her horse.

Victor smiled disarmingly. "Oh, nothing to turn a hair about. I just offered the fellow a decent mount."

Nick wondered if the boy even knew his name.

He managed to get himself astride by himself, although this horse was considerably higher. He drew a deep breath as the horse snorted and shook his head.

Miss Shepard's eyebrows were drawn together in a frown. "Are you sure you're ready to ride Duke?"

He managed to pat the horse's neck to show his ease, but that only caused the horse to paw the ground as if sensing Nick's own nervousness.

Before Miss Shepard had a chance to voice any more objections, Victor started to move away from the pond.

Duke immediately began following the other horse, and Nick had no choice but to concentrate on maintaining his balance. Victor got Maud to go at a much faster clip.

"Victor, slow down." Miss Shepard's admonition was in vain. Duke kept a good clip, determined to follow the lead horse. Nick tried to slow the horse, but that only seemed to make the horse more determined.

They reached a wide open field. Victor slowed and waited for Nick's mount to catch up to him. "How does a real horse feel beneath you?" His smile held something nasty in it.

"Fine." Nick sat erect, trying to remember all Miss Shepard's directives. The horse shifted restively beneath him.

"Well, let's try for a little canter, shall we?" Without waiting for Nick's response, he gave a smart swat with his riding crop to Duke's rump.

The horse responded to the whip with lightning speed. If he hadn't already been gripping hard, Nick would have flown off. Instead, everything became a blur as he flattened himself against the horse and squeezed his thighs against its sides.

He heard Miss Shepard's alarmed shout. "Victor, what are you doing? Mr. Tennent, just keep your balance—" The rest of her words were lost in the wind.

How in all that was holy was he supposed to stop a galloping horse?

His lips stiff with fear, his throat paralyzed, Nick hung on. The ground flew by in a dizzying mass of green, every sound drowned out by the thundering hooves against the earth. If the horse tripped on a tussock, Nick would be done for.

Why had he accepted the stupid challenge? To prove himself to some naïve young girl?

He had no more time for rational thought. All he could do was pray that he'd keep his seat. He grabbed a hunk of mane with each hand, his knees the only thing keeping him atop the beast's great heaving body.

A hedgerow faced them. Would the horse clear it? As he braced for the jump, the horse suddenly veered to the side.

"Drop your stirrups!" He heard Miss Shepard's scream and just in the nick of time, he let his boots slip from the irons. A split second later, he felt his hands wrenched from the mane, his body thrust from the saddle and he was sailing through the air, headlong across the hedge.

Chapter Three

Alice reined in her horse and stared in horror as Mr. Tennent went flying over the hedgerow and landed with a thud against the earth.

The next second she was off her horse, running to him. "Lucy, my horse," she shouted over her shoulder, "Victor, go after Duke!"

She tore through the holly bushes, unmindful of their sharp leaves and knelt by Mr. Tennent. He'd landed on his side and now with a groan rolled over onto his back, one arm clutching his ribcage.

"Are you all right, Mr. Tennent? Where does it hurt?" She smoothed back the hair from his forehead. The far side of his face was scraped along the cheekbone.

He began to sit up, his face contorted. She pushed him gently down again. "Lie still."

"It's my shoulder and side." His voice was laced with pain.

She glanced up as Victor's shadow loomed over them. He didn't have his horse.

"Where's Duke?"

"Long gone." He kicked the ground in disgust, hardly sparing Mr. Tennent a glance. "He'll come back as soon as he's run off his high spirits."

She glared at him. "How could you give him Duke to ride?" With a shake of her head, she turned away from Victor, pressing her lips together to keep from saying more. He'd hear about his irresponsible behavior later, she promised herself. "We need to get Mr. Tennent back. He's hurt." She leaned over him and drew in her breath at his ashen face. "Do you think, if we helped you mount, you could ride back atop Maud? We'll take her reins. It's just too far for you to walk if you've broken something."

"Yes…all right." With a grimace, he began to sit up, still clutching his arm. Quickly, she put her arm around his shoulders to help him. "Victor, get on his other side. Let's see if you can stand, Mr. Tennent."

Lucy stood behind the hedge, holding two of the horses, her face frightened. "Is he all right?"

Alice made a quick decision. "Lucy, ride back and have them summon Dr. Baird. Quickly!"

The girl did as she was told and hurried off.

Alice turned back to Victor. "I'll have Mr. Tennent ride in back of me. Help him mount once I'm in the saddle."

"But Alice—"

Without waiting for Victor to finish his sentence, she led her horse through a break in the hedgerow and brought him to stand near the two men. At least Victor had helped Mr. Tennent up. Alice swung up onto her horse then looked down at Victor. "All right, see if he can mount behind me."

Victor bent down and cradled his hands for a foothold for the other man. With a sharp intake of breath, Mr. Tennent attempted to lift himself onto the back of her saddle. Alice twisted around to see if she could help pull him up, but he was managing to swing his leg over the horse's rump. His stifled groans made her wince, but finally he settled on behind her.

"Just hold on to me with your good arm." Without asking his leave, she grasped it from behind her and brought it around her waist. "I'll get us home as quickly as possible without jostling you more than necessary, I promise. Are you all right, sir?"

"I'll make it."

Without a word to Victor, Alice picked her way around the hedgerow and back down the path.

Mr. Tennent said nothing more on the ride home, but she could hear his intake of breath each time his body was jarred. *It's all my fault,* she thought, not knowing which was worse, taking a first-time rider on such an ambitious jaunt or not stopping Victor. Obviously he'd challenged poor Mr. Tennent to mount the gelding.

"We're almost there, Mr. Tennent," she said, trying to keep her voice cheery. "See, there's the rooftop already visible over the treetops." At last they were going up the long drive. A couple of stable hands were waiting for them as soon as she pulled the horse to a stop in front of a house. At least Lucy had alerted them.

"Help him down gently. He may have broken something."

"Yes, miss." John, an able-bodied stable hand raised his arms to help Mr. Tennent down. "Have no worry, we'll get you down. What happened?"

"He took a spill and landed on his side. One arm is injured."

Once on the ground, Mr. Tennent remained hunched over, cradling his arm.

Alice swung down from her horse and handed the reins to the other groom. She turned immediately to Mr. Tennent and gasped at the sight of his pale face. "John, help him inside. I hope the doctor has been summoned."

"Yes, miss. Miss Lucy told us to have him fetched."

"Good. Come, Mr. Tennent, let's get you where you can lie down." She walked on his other side, a hand on his elbow.

The servants stood gawking when they entered the house, lifting up a murmur as Alice led him to the nearest sofa. A maid brought a throw and the housekeeper piled pillows behind Mr. Tennent. Although he thanked the servants and didn't complain, she could see he was in great pain.

As if sensing her distress, he looked up at her, one corner of his lips lifting. "Don't worry, I'll be fine."

She drew near, kneeling beside the sofa. "Oh, Mr. Tennent, I'm so sorry this had to happen."

He shook his head briefly and reached out his good hand to her. "Don't upset yourself. It wasn't your fault," he said.

Finally Dr. Baird arrived. The elderly doctor set down his bag and looked Mr. Tennent up and down through his spectacles. "Well, young man, what have you been up to?"

"Falling off horses," he said through a grimace, as he began to swing his legs off the sofa.

"There now, hold still before you do yourself more harm." The doctor helped him sit up and motioned to one of the servants. "Get his coat off." Mr. Tennent flinched as the arm of his coat was gently slipped off. Alice bit her lip, cringing with each jar and jostle of his shoulder.

The doctor took Mr. Tennent's chin in his hand and tilted it upward. "Scraped yourself good there, I see. Bring me some soap and water and be quick about it," he told a servant, then proceeded to poke and prod Mr. Tennent's shoulder. "Humph. Hurt, does it? And there?"

After a few more hmms and humphs, he straightened and peered over his spectacles. "Good news. It looks like your shoulder isn't dislocated. Just a fractured clavicle." At the question in the other man's eyes, he cleared his throat. "Your collarbone is broken. You'll have to bear up a bit longer while I set it. Now, where else does it hurt?"

Mr. Tennent indicated his side with his hand.

He had the servant remove his vest then palpated some more through his shirt. "Your ribs don't appear broken, but I'll have to do a more thorough examination." He turned to the others in the room. "Why don't you leave us alone, so the young gentleman doesn't feel he might disgrace himself before the ladies." He turned to the housekeeper. "Mrs. Thorpe, a glass of water. I'll give him something for the pain afterwards."

The woman nodded her head. "Yes, sir."

Alice left the room reluctantly.

After what seemed like ages, she was allowed back into the side parlor. Mr. Tennent, his shirt draped over his shoulders, had a sling around one arm and a wide layer of white bandaging across a good part of his chest. A square white gauze covered part of one cheek. He gave her a crooked smile.

She sat down beside him on the sofa. "Oh, Mr. Tennent, how is it? Are your ribs broken, too? Is it very painful?"

"A few bruised ribs, but I'll live."

"I'm so terribly sorry to have brought this about."

He frowned at her. "You have nothing to be sorry about. You didn't do anything but help me. I was the one who behaved foolishly," he said, turning away in disgust.

"Oh, no! It was I who should have stopped Victor."

"It was stupid to take his offer."

"Mr. Tennent, did you happen to notice what startled the horse so? The next thing we knew Duke was off at a gallop. Did something spook him?"

He eyed her a moment. "You didn't see anything?"

She shook her head. "No, Lucy and I were in front of you. Tell me—"

Before she could finish her thought, she noticed Mr. Tennent looking past her.

"What's going on here?"

She jumped at the sound of her father's voice. He strode across the room and planted himself in front of Mr. Tennent, who stood immediately.

Alice joined him. "Oh, Papa, poor Mr. Tennent has had an accident. He was thrown by Duke."

Her father looked his secretary up and down.

Alice touched his good arm. "You must sit down, Mr. Tennent. You've had an awful accident."

Her father motioned for him to take his seat. The younger man hesitated but at her father's impatient gesture, he finally complied.

"Mr. Tennent hadn't been riding before, and Victor challenged him to ride Duke—"

Her father's heavy brows drew together. "What the dickens did you mean going riding if you've never sat a horse?"

Alice interposed herself between her father and his employee. "Father! Didn't you hear me? It's my fault. I invited him to come along with us. It's Sunday, after all, and I knew he wasn't working. I had him ride Maud. You know Maud is the gentlest creature alive, but Victor played a very mean trick on Mr. Tennent—"

"Quiet, Alice, and let Mr. Tennent explain himself. I'm sure he doesn't want to hide behind a schoolgirl's skirts."

She stopped, feeling herself color with shame. A schoolgirl's skirts! He made it sound as if Mr. Tennent was some sort of coward and that she was—why, not even a young lady but a little girl!

Flushed with embarrassment, she moved away without a word. Surely, her father wouldn't hold her defense of Mr. Tennent against the poor man. She chanced a glance at him and bit her lip at the set look on his face. Once again, he stood. His face was awfully pale, and she was afraid he might pass out. "Papa, Dr. Baird said—"

Her father flicked his hand once again. "Leave us, Alice."

There was no use arguing with her father when he took that tone. With an audible sigh, she stepped back from the two men. Giving Mr. Tennent a last look of sympathy, she dragged her feet to the door, hoping she'd catch something of their conversation, but neither man said anything.

"Close the door, Alice."

"Yes, sir." Once she'd exited the room and closed the door softly behind her, she put her ear to the door. At first, there was only silence, then came the low sounds of masculine voices, but she could distinguish nothing.

At least there were no shouts on her father's side, but she knew from experience that her father never raised his voice. His low tones could be as scathing as another man's roar.

Nick waited, squaring his shoulders and trying not to wince at the pain the movement caused him. Would he lose his job over his own stupidity?

The older man gazed at him a moment, an unreadable expression in his eyes.

"I brought you here to work, not to take a medical convalescence." The dry words, expressing no anger, were all the more quelling for their subtle sarcasm.

"I assure you, Mr. Shepard, this will in no way hinder my job. I can still work." He moved his hand to prove his point. Unfortunately, he couldn't keep back the spasm at the sudden jolt of pain that shot through his collarbone.

Mr. Shepard grunted, clearly not impressed with his stoicism. "Well, take your rest today and we'll see about tomorrow. If you're not fit to do any work, I'll have to send for another clerk."

Before Nick could think of a suitable reply, Mr. Shepard wheeled about and headed for the door.

As soon as he was alone, Nick collapsed back onto the settee, letting his head fall onto his good hand. What had he done? Risked the best position of his life to go gallivanting about on a horse? A silent, bitter laugh escaped his lips.

A soft clearing of throat caused him to start up again, sending another stab of pain along his collarbone. Miss Shepard stood just inside the doorway. She looked so pathetically sorry, he wished he could comfort her. She'd been wonderful, taking charge and bringing him home.

He straightened despite the pain in his ribs. "It's all right."

She ventured farther into the room until she stood by the settee once again. "Was Father very hard on you?"

He managed a smile. "No. He told me to rest today."

Relief flooded her pretty face. "Oh, yes, you should. Why don't I help you up to your room?"

She was still thinking of his comfort. He hadn't felt so taken care of since he'd been a toddler. "That's all right, I'll manage."

"At least let me ring for a servant to help you up the stairs. You're on the top floor, aren't you?"

He didn't relish the thought of all those flights of stairs to the attic. Nor the stifling heat once he got up there. "Very well."

She hurried to the bell pull. Instead of leaving him alone, she pulled up a chair and waited with him. With her hands folded in her lap, her normally rosy cheeks pale, she looked like a young schoolgirl called before the schoolmistress. He contrasted it to her self-possession right after his fall. She'd even assumed all responsibility before her father.

"I should have listened to you," he said with a forced smile.

"It's all right. I bet Victor made it sound like you'd be a coward if you didn't mount Duke."

He shook his head in self-contempt. "But I'm old enough to know better than to accept a schoolboy's challenge."

She tossed back her bangs. "Oh, I know how Victor is."

He remembered her hand stroking his forehead, her small hand grasping his and bringing his arm around her waist.

"I hope this unfortunate experience won't put you off horseback riding forever."

Her remark was so ludicrous under the circumstances, he had to laugh, then winced at the pain in his side. "Let us hope not."

"Oh, I'm sorry to make you laugh."

He shook away her apology.

"What I meant was that, someday, when all this is behind you, I hope you'll get back on a horse again. That's the only way to overcome any bad memories of a fall. When I was first thrown—"

"*You* were thrown?"

"Oh, yes, everyone is thrown at least once, especially when first learning."

Before she could continue, a young male servant entered the room. She stood. "Oh, Davy, please help Mr. Tennent up to his room and have something cool brought up to him to drink. Help him in any way he needs."

"Yes, miss." The young servant took Nick by his good arm and smiled. "Just tell me, sir, whatever it is you want."

The two made their way slowly up the stairs. All Nick wanted to do was collapse on his bed. The region around his collarbone and his whole right side pained him terribly, despite the powder the doctor had given him. He'd been partially truthful to Mr. Shepard about his ability to continue working. He flexed his fingers now, ignoring the pain the movement caused up in his collarbone. At least his fingers weren't broken, too. He prayed that by tomorrow the pain would have diminished enough for him to be able to write.

He tried to forget the doctor's words about avoiding using that hand and arm. "The bone will take about twelve weeks to heal. The pain will diminish gradually. Don't use your hand if it gives you any pain. Little by little you'll be able to do things again. If it hurts, desist activity."

Twelve weeks. The words were like a death knell. Would Mr. Shepard be that patient with him? Would he still have a job after his bones had knit back together?

When she didn't see Mr. Tennent at breakfast, Alice went to look for him, wondering how he had fared the night.

She spotted the servant coming down the stairs. "There you are, Davy. Did you go up to Mr. Tennent yet?"

The servant stopped halfway down. "Yes, Miss Alice. I brought him up a breakfast tray."

She smiled in relief. "Oh, thank you for remembering him. How was he?"

"He looked better than yesterday, but he's in a heap of pain." He shook his head. "Nasty thing, broken bones. I know, when I dislocated my shoulder once, it hurt something awful and took weeks to mend."

She drew in her breath, feeling Mr. Tennent's pain afresh. "Did yours heal completely?"

He swiveled one arm around and grinned. "Yes, miss, right as can be. But it laid me up some weeks, believe me."

"Well, thank you for being so attentive to Mr. Tennent."

"Think nothing of it." He frowned. "He insisted on getting up and dressed." He added hastily, "I helped him, o' course. I'll check on him again around lunchtime."

"Very well, thank you, Davy."

Alice turned toward the library, knowing she would have to insist Father send Victor away immediately. He hadn't shown the least remorse, even going so far as to claim it was Mr. Tennent's fault for not being competent with a horse.

Unfortunately, Father hadn't wanted to discuss the matter further with her last evening at dinner. Well, he'd have to listen to her this morning, she decided, as she turned and headed in the direction of his office.

Alice left her father's office feeling worse than ever. He'd told her she had behaved irresponsibly, taking a man who knew nothing of horses riding up to the park. He hadn't even agreed that Victor should be sent away.

Feeling at loose ends, she reached Mr. Tennent's small office. Maybe she could tidy it up for him while he was laid up.

His door was ajar. She pushed it open and gasped. "Mr. Tennent, what in the world are you doing in here?"

Her father's secretary glanced up from the papers spread out before him on the desk. "Good morning, Miss Shepard. I'm doing precisely what it appears I'm doing."

The words held no reproach, but were uttered as a simple statement of fact. She was glad to see Davy had placed a fresh gauze bandage over his cheekbone. The white sling around his arm and neck contrasted sharply with his black coat and accentuated the paleness of his face.

She frowned, noticing how he was attempting to write with his left hand. If he hadn't looked so pitiable, she would have found the sight amusing. Not waiting for permission, she entered the cramped office and planted herself in front of his cluttered desk. "It looks to me as if you are *trying* to work."

He set down his pencil. "Your conclusion is correct."

"You suffered a bad fall yesterday and broke a bone and bruised some ribs. You are supposed to be resting. Surely, Father doesn't expect you to be writing!"

He ran his left hand through his short sable curls. "See here, Miss Shepard, I truly appreciate your concern." The trace of impatience in his voice softened. "Thank you for sending Davy up to me yesterday and again this morning. However, as much as I like being waited on hand and foot, the reality of my situation is that your father is paying me to carry out certain functions within a given time and if I prove incapable of doing so, I cannot fault him for finding a replacement."

He took a deep breath as if gearing up for what he was going to say next, and she couldn't help catching the grimace the gesture caused him. "This is the best job I've had in my career. If I lose the opportunity given to me, I may not get another. I do not plan to end my life as a clerk."

She walked around the desk until she was standing close to him, his words both touching and intriguing her. "How do you plan to end your life, Mr. Tennent?" she asked softly.

He lifted his chin a notch. "Owning a company of my own like your father, so I can make a difference in the world."

Make a difference in the world. No one had ever spoken to her like this before. As if what one accomplished mattered in the world.

"What kind of difference would you make in the world, Mr. Tennent?" she asked softly.

Instead of waving away her question as if she were too young or too ignorant to understand, he seemed to ponder it. He rolled his pencil in his good hand. The lamplight gleamed against the rich color of his hair.

"I would use my wealth to help those in need. Build schools, provide good housing, clean water, hospitals…" He glanced up at her. "Do you know what it's like to have a gnawing pain in your belly because you have nothing to eat?"

She shook her head, mute.

"Do you know what it's like not to have a dwelling to come home to at night after a long day's work? There are many people who do, Miss Shepard." He drew in a breath, then stopped, the pain evident. "That is why I want to become a very wealthy man, so I can do my bit to help alleviate the want of others."

The words thrilled her to the marrow. Suddenly, she felt as if she understood her own undefined yearnings and dissatisfaction. To have such a noble purpose in life!

"I hope you realize your dream, Mr. Tennent."

A few seconds passed between them in silence. Then he gave a short laugh. "I may be farther away from it than ever if I don't get this work done."

The two of them surveyed the papers on his desk.

Before he had a chance to stop her, she took the pencil from his loosened hold and the paper he'd been writing on. "Very well, Mr. Tennent, you dictate and I shall be your fingers."

She glanced around, spotted a chair, and dragged it over.

"I—you can't very well—this involves mathematics—"

She stuck out her chin. "Mr. Tennent, I am not ignorant of mathematics. In a year, I shall finish my schooling and I'll have you know I get outstanding marks in mathematics. Now, what were you calculating when I walked in?"

With a resigned sigh, he turned back to his papers. "Very well, but only because it seems I have very little choice at the moment. Just stop any time you are tired of amusing yourself."

Did he think she was simply seeking to entertain herself? She would just have to show him.

An hour later, after making steady progress, she sat back with a satisfied sigh. "I say, what you've taught me about stocks and shares is a lot more useful than what they teach us at Miss Higgins's Academy. I never knew Father was involved in so many enterprises."

Mr. Tennent adjusted his weight on the wooden chair, carefully cradling his injured arm.

"Does it hurt you much today?"

He touched the area just under his collarbone. "Some. It's still a bit swollen here."

She looked down. "I tried to convince Father to send Victor away, but he refused."

"You didn't have to do that." He sounded displeased.

"I explained how Victor tricked you into mounting Duke." She moistened her lips together, recalling the most unpleasant part of the interview. "He also knows the responsibility I bear. He agrees I was foolish and impetuous as always…" Her voice trailed off. By now she ought to be accustomed to her father's dry tone, which never failed to erode her confidence when pointing out her faults to her.

"You were in no way to blame." His tone gentled. "It was gracious of you to invite me for an outing. You cautioned me about riding your friend's horse. It was silly pride on my part, so I deserve what I got."

She reached out and touched his hand. "He's not *my* friend—not anymore. As a skilled horseman, Victor was the most responsible. He should have known better. You could have been killed."

His glance went to her hand and she felt herself coloring. Quickly, she removed it and sat with her hands clasped in her lap.

"He is, isn't he?"

She frowned. "He's what?"

"A skilled horseman."

She made a face. "Oh, that. Well, yes, naturally."

"Naturally." He mimicked the word. "I suppose he has been riding since he was five."

She giggled. "Oh, probably since he was four."

His dark eyes lit with humor. "His parents probably sat him atop a horse before he could walk."

"Oh, no, before he began to crawl!"

They both ended up laughing.

"Alice, what are you doing here?" Her father stood in the doorway to the library.

She jumped up from her chair. "I am acting as—" she gave a little bow "—Mr. Tennent's secretary."

Her father pursed his lips, his eyes going from her to Mr. Tennent and back again, making her feel as if she'd done something wrong. "That is not amusing."

"Of course it isn't. Mr. Tennent is injured, and I feel partially responsible. As such, it is only right that I assist him while his injury heals."

"Mr. Shepard—" Mr. Tennent stood rigid, and her heart went out to him, having to work for her father.

Her father advanced into the small room, cutting him off. "So, you are unable to write?"

"I—" He cleared his throat and began again. "In a few days, perhaps—"

Did Father inspire such fear in all his employees? "Dr. Baird gave clear instructions that Mr. Tennent is to do nothing to put undue pressure on his collarbone for a few weeks. He mustn't bend his arm in a way that will aggravate the bone."

Her father had turned his attention back to her halfway through her speech. "In that case, I shall have to summon Mr. Simpson."

She gave a disbelieving laugh at the mention of Father's old secretary. "Mr. Simpson is getting forgetful, you said so yourself. We are making splendid progress." She took up the papers she'd completed and handed them to him.

He took them without a word and examined them.

Mr. Tennent cleared his throat. "Mr. Shepard, I assure you, in a few days, I'm sure I can manage on my own."

Her father handed the papers back to his secretary. "Very well. In the meantime I have to return to London. I shall determine things upon my return." He turned to her. "I don't want you making a nuisance of yourself here."

"I shan't be a nuisance."

"Nevertheless, I prefer you not spend your time here, Alice."

She pressed her lips together, knowing it was useless to argue with her father and knowing just as certainly that this was one command she was going to disobey.

Chapter Four

The next few days were like a little bit of heaven to Nick. Despite the pain in his collarbone and ribs, coupled with the inconvenience of wearing a sling, he had never enjoyed such a time in his life. He felt as if he was living an interlude where all the best things were combined: work he enjoyed with a helper he was coming to admire more and more each day, carried out in the most agreeable surroundings he'd ever known in his life.

Her father's prohibition notwithstanding, Miss Shepard appeared in Nick's little office every morning promptly at half-past eight and didn't move from her chair until he gave in and let her help him with any writing he needed done.

He realized now, looking at her bent head, that working had never been so lighthearted. For despite making progress on the reports he had to write, the hours seemed to fly by and many moments were spent in laughter as Miss Shepard found something amusing in what they were doing or reading.

He eased the kinks out of his neck then stopped short

at the shot of pain to his collarbone. Dr. Baird had not ex-aggerated when he'd warned Nick it would take some weeks before he was fully healed.

"Are you all right?"

He looked over to find Miss Shepard's eyes on him. "Yes, I'm all right." He'd also never had anyone as solici-tous as she, seeming to anticipate his every need and be aware of every twinge of discomfort he experienced.

She laid her pencil and pad on her lap. "You should take a rest. You've been bent over this desk since early morning."

There was still a lot to do before her father returned. Mr. Shepard hadn't said how long he'd be away, yet Nick expected him at any moment. "You're the one who should take a break. You are on holiday. Why don't you go outside and play a game of tennis. You haven't played since I had my fall, have you?" His tone came out sharper than he'd intended, but he thought once again about Mr. Shepard and what he'd say if he came back and found his daughter holed up in this office.

She shrugged. "No. But I prefer being in here helping you. Besides, there is no one to play with."

"What about Victor?" He'd seen the boy hang about the corridor the first few days, looking daggers at him at the sight of Alice sitting beside him.

Her eyes lit up in hilarity. "He finally packed his bags and had the pony cart hitched up to take him to the train station this morning."

"Where is your young lady friend?"

"Lucy? Oh, she had to go home, too. Her family was going hiking in Scotland." Her voice sounded wistful, and he realized once again how lonely this wealthy girl's life was. The only mother figure she seemed to have was a middle-aged companion who preferred spending time with the housekeeper.

Nick stood. "Well, it's time we both had a break. It's almost lunchtime anyway." Usually he'd had a tray brought to the office but he decided to do something differently today.

Miss Shepard stood immediately, a smile breaking out on her face. Nick steeled himself against that smile, reminding himself his life had no relation to hers. She clasped her hands in front of her. "What shall we do?"

He hadn't got as far as thinking of that part. "What would you like to do?"

She tilted her head a fraction and thought a moment, a slim finger against her chin. Then she looked at him, a sparkle in her eyes. "Have you ever played chess?"

He smiled in relief. Finally, there was something he did know how to do. "Yes."

If she was surprised, she didn't show it. She turned to leave the room. "Well, come along then."

She led him to a wide veranda with latticed railing in the back of the house. "It's too nice a day to be inside." She sat on the floor and brought out a polished wooden box and a folded game board from a shelf under the low table and began to set out the ivory pieces.

He remained standing, watching her array the carved chessmen in rows at either side of the checked board. "My mother taught me to play chess."

"My governess taught me. She said it was a good game of strategy…and patience." She smiled as she added the last.

"Were you in need of those qualities?"

She shrugged. "All I knew then was that if I learned how to play chess, perhaps I could play with Father. But he had little inclination for games that last so long."

Before he could comment on that statement, she waved him to the low couch facing the board. "Have a seat, Mr. Tennent." She gave him a sly smile under her tawny brows. "This should be an easy win for someone good at mathematics. I shall even let you be white, since you are the guest."

He sat down across from her and soon they were immersed in the game and even forgot about lunch.

He found he enjoyed pitting his skill against hers. Just as with tennis, she didn't make things easy for him, and he appreciated that. Whenever she captured one of his pieces, she'd give him a small smile of triumph.

They played in silence for quite some time, when Miss Shepard raised her eyes to him. "Mr. Tennent?" There was no amusement in them now. "What was your house like growing up?"

Surprised at her question, he answered flatly, "Small and dingy with the smell of boiled cabbage. It was always damp. And cold in the winter. My brothers and I would huddle together under a blanket."

She leaned her chin on her fist. "Were you the youngest?"

He shook his head. "The second to youngest."

To his bemusement, she continued questioning him about his family, and he found himself telling her about his brothers—from Jim, working in the mill, and Thomas the postal clerk, to young Alfie, with his dream of opening his own shop.

"So, you are the only bachelor among them?"

"Yes," he said in a guarded tone.

She tilted her head a fraction, a gesture that never failed to enchant him. "Why haven't you married? You are certainly old enough."

He shrugged. "Up to now, I haven't had either the desire

or the opportunity, I suppose. And although I am certainly old enough, I'm not *that* old."

She frowned. "But all your other brothers found the time."

"I have put all my energy into my work." To help his brothers continue their education and support his mother. "It takes money to set up a household."

"Does it take so much money to support a wife?"

"It certainly takes money to raise children."

"Do all your brothers have children?"

"The oldest two do."

She smiled. "So you are an uncle at least."

"Yes."

"Are they all still in Birmingham?"

"Yes."

"And your mother?"

He nodded.

"Do you see them often?"

He looked down. "No."

"That's a pity." She sighed.

"A clerk has few holidays."

She sighed again.

He focused once more on the board between them.

"I'm almost a woman now."

He raised startled eyes to her. Where had that thought come from?

Her violet eyes stared guilelessly into his. He kept his voice neutral, for fear of what she might read in it. "You have a few years yet."

With another sigh, she lowered her gaze to the chess pieces.

Nick followed suit, determined to keep his thoughts on the game. He waited for her to move, his heartbeat thudding between his ears. What had she meant by that remark? He mustn't forget himself around her, he cautioned himself, as he found himself doing countless times each day in her company.

"Checkmate." Amusement laced her tone.

His glance jerked up. "What?" He followed her slim fingers, which held the queen she'd just moved. "How is that possible?"

"See?" She gestured over the board. "If you move your king here, my knight will knock him off. If you move your king in the only other square, my other knight will get him."

He studied the only two possible moves available to his king, his brow knit. How had she done that?

She sat back with a satisfied sigh. "Maybe if someone had been paying closer attention to his game, he wouldn't have left himself open for attack."

He looked across to her laughing eyes. "Maybe if someone felt more comfortable with her skills, she wouldn't have to rely on distracting me with idle talk to win the game."

"I won fairly and squarely. If you allow yourself to be so easily distracted, I can't be held responsible for your loss. Now, if you'll excuse me, my queen shall take your king to her castle and lock him in her tower." She lifted both his king and her queen off the board in one swoop.

Without thinking, he seized her hand in midair. "My king will call out his legions of knights to rescue him—"

She giggled, pulling her hand away but he held it fast. "If you want your king back, you shall have to pay the ransom," she said with a thrust of her chin, her laughing blue eyes glinting with challenge.

He tightened his hold on her hand imperceptibly. "And what do you demand for the release of my king?"

"A kiss."

Her gaze held his as securely as his hand held hers. Somewhere he heard a bird twitter on the lawn and far-off footsteps in the corridor, but he was helpless to look away.

Like a spectator in a drama, he watched himself inch forward until her face was inches from his, and he breathed in the sweet flowery scent of her downy skin. Shutting off the warnings in his head, he closed the gap between them, touching his lips to hers.

He leaned his elbows against the table, ignoring the pain the movement caused. Miss Shepard pressed her lips inexpertly against his.

"Sweet Alice," he breathed against her, taking a gulp of air before sealing her lips once again with his. This time they parted beneath his.

He didn't know how much time had elapsed—a few seconds or an eternity—when the clearing of a masculine throat penetrated the fog of his mind. Miss Shepard and he broke apart simultaneously.

"Father!" She jumped up from the floor, her hand going to her mouth.

Nick bumped his arm against the table and stifled the cry of pain as he struggled to his feet.

He stood up as Mr. Shepard advanced into the room.

His employer's dark gaze traveled from one to the other. He gestured to Nick. "I didn't realize I was paying you a salary to amuse yourself with my daughter."

Heat flooded Nick's face, and he swallowed, unable to defend his conduct in any way.

"Father, Mr. Shepard isn't—"

Mr. Shepard flicked his fingers in her direction. "Alice, leave us, please."

"But Father—"

"Alice." His tone was that hard, unyielding one Nick recognized from the office.

"Yes, Father." She lowered her head and walked back into the house.

Mr. Shepard waited a few moments until they no longer heard his daughter's footsteps. "I want you out of here. Now. You can collect any outstanding wages at the office."

The worst had come to pass. Nick stared at him. "But—you don't—" He cleared his throat, hating the tremor his voice betrayed.

The man eyed him as if he were a lower form of life. "I don't want to hear any explanations from a man who presumes to rob my daughter of her innocence. Understood?"

He nodded.

Shepard turned away and began walking out the way he'd come. At the entrance he paused. "You can request the pony cart to take you to the station. Do not make any attempt to see my daughter or to address her in any way." His heavy eyebrows bristled at him. "Is that understood?"

Nick swallowed. "Yes, sir."

In the echo of the closing door, Nick looked down at the toppled chess pieces. Slowly, he began picking them up with his left hand and setting them back into their box. He replaced the lid, his heart thudding all the while.

Numbness invaded his thoughts as well as his heart.

He had no idea where he would go or what he would do.

His future was finished.

He returned to London on the afternoon train as soon as he'd packed his small bag. He'd been forced to ask for Davy's help and had to fight the sense of shame that he was being run off the property. Davy chatted away as if nothing out of the ordinary had occurred. He probably assumed it was natural for Nick to return to London after his week of convalescing.

A part of Nick kept hoping for one last glimpse of Miss Shepard before he left the house but she was nowhere to be seen. She'd probably been sent to her room. How were young ladies of her class punished for stealing a kiss from an unsuitable young man?

He leaned against the high-backed seat in the train, his growling stomach reminding him it had been several hours since breakfast. He gazed out at the landscape, his mind going over Mr. Shepard's words. He had no justification for what he'd done. How to explain to a man that he'd found his young daughter irresistible, that in all the years of his youth, he'd never done such a thing, until he'd met her—a girl on the brink of womanhood, more special, more beautiful, like no other girl he'd ever met?

On arriving in the city, he stopped that same afternoon at the office and collected his wages. He stared down at the measly pile of coins. They were his only protection from the streets until he was well enough to seek another job.

Suddenly, a spurt of rage replaced the numbness. After all these years, he would not return to the pool of anonymous clerks from which he'd used every ounce of toil and ingenuity to rise above. Because of one moment of foolishness, would he be condemned to the ranks of slavery the rest of his life?

Pure, blind rage filled his veins and brought a pounding to his temples. He clenched his hands, ignoring the pain that shot through his collar. He thought of his oldest brother, breathing in the dust-laden air in the cotton mill, of Tom, who was trying to support his young brood on the hundred pounds he made a year as a shipping clerk, of Alfie, who dreamed of owning his own shop one day.

How was he going to help each one get ahead? His mother counted on him. When she'd given him all she had to come to London, she'd told him, "The Lord has blessed you with a fine mind, Nicholas. It's up to you to use it and make your way in the world to help your brothers."

And now none of that would materialize. All because of one moment of insanity with a young girl way above his reach.

He banged the door of Shepard & Steward behind him, ignoring the call of one of the clerks. He didn't stop until he reached the street. Then he kept walking, thrusting himself through the crowded sidewalk.

"See there, watch where you're going!" A red-faced hansom cab driver waved his whip at him.

Nick stopped just in the nick of time at the edge of the curb.

He didn't know where he was going, he only knew he had to walk somewhere—anywhere—until this knot of rage loosened from his windpipe. It was strangling him.

He continued walking, unmindful of how many blocks he'd gone. His collarbone ached with the swinging movement of his arm. His ribs throbbed with each stride.

He was in no shape to seek another job now. Not until the sling was off. But he would not return to clerking in a bank. Soon, his wages would run out. He'd have to find something before then.

His steps slowed as he reached the river and stood gazing outward.

He pictured Miss Shepard's face, the way she'd met his kiss with innocent ardor. He shook the image away. She was only a girl. Best to forget the sentiments she'd awakened in him.

But he couldn't prevent the bitterness that threatened to swallow him up at the notion that she could never be his. He was tired of Britain and the ceiling it imposed over his head. No matter how much he worked, he'd never be good enough to set his sights on anyone like Miss Shepard. It was vain to think that some day, if he earned enough money, he could ever win the approval of her father.

He tried to pray, knowing the Lord advocated humility and forgiveness. But he felt no inclination now to humble himself and accept the consequences of his rash act.

Was it so wrong to fall in love with a girl like Miss Shepard?

And for a few moments he allowed himself to dream of what it would have been like to be able to work to attain her. He could have risen in her father's firm to the position of a junior partner. And then he would have dared to offer for her. He would have worked hard for her. He wouldn't have begrudged her anything.

But it was never to be. He'd never find a comparable position as he'd had at Shepard and Steward, not now, when Shepard would likely give him a bad reference or none at all.

It was time for a drastic change in his life.

He looked at the ships downriver and he felt the answer. Was the Lord telling him to leave England? Did his future lie across the ocean where so many had gone before him to make their fortunes?

The idea took hold. He'd take his last wages and book passage to America.

He'd work as hard as it took. By the grace of God, he'd make it and then—

Then he'd return and claim Miss Alice Shepard's heart.

Confined to her room for the rest of the day, Alice spent the time on her knees, alternately pleading for leniency for Mr. Tennent and reveling in the memory of her first kiss.

What had come over her to ask him to kiss her? Her cheeks heated at her brazenness. But she was not sorry she'd done it. She remembered the look in his dark eyes: shock and then wonder and then he'd leaned toward her and she'd been astounded to know that he felt the same as she did.

Oh, the second his lips had touched hers, she'd felt herself falling off a precipice, a delightful precipice from where there was no return.

Why had Father walked in at that moment? He'd ruined everything. She hadn't been able to hear anything through the door and had had to run up to her room, afraid he'd see her in the corridor when he left the veranda.

She looked in vain out her window, but it faced the back of the house, and she had no idea what could have happened to Mr. Tennent.

Nicholas. She whispered the name to herself, liking the sound of such a fine name, watching the glass cloud up under her lips. *Nicholas Tennent. Alice Shepard Tennent. Mrs. Nicholas Tennent.* Her heart thrilled at each variation.

Her father would have to allow them to marry now, since he'd caught them kissing. No matter that she wasn't quite seventeen. She was willing to wait however long Father required. Surely, by the time she was eighteen she would be old enough to be Nicholas's wife. She'd prove how able she was!

* * *

At dinner, her father summoned her downstairs to his office.

"I've sent Tennent away," he said with no preamble.

"Away? Where, Father?"

"It doesn't matter." His tone was its usual even one, with no emotion, simply matter-of-fact as if he were discussing his latest business acquisition.

She took a step forward on the thick carpet. "But Father, I love him. You can't just send him away."

"You have behaved disgracefully today. I cannot have my only daughter carrying on with every man in my employ as if she were some hoyden."

"Father! I was not carrying on! I love Mr. Tennent and am going to marry him!"

He looked her up and down. "Has Tennent actually had the temerity to propose to you?"

She tossed her head. "You didn't exactly give him the opportunity."

"You'd better get any notions of marriage out of your head. There will be no proposal. Tennent has left my employ. It's clear you cannot be trusted to carry on like a well-behaved young lady under your own roof, so I will have you spend your future holidays with your Uncle Sylvester and Aunt Hermione." He raked a hand through his hair and gave a weary sigh. "I should have done so long ago…since your mother died."

She fell back. Her father sounded as if he were giving up on her for good. What had she done so wrong, but fall in love?

In the coming days, no matter how much she cried and pleaded with him, her father remained unmoved. As she watched her trunk being packed, she waited for rescue from Mr. Tennent. Somehow, he must be able to get word to her, so she could tell him that she was being sent away.

She had no idea how to reach him, and her father had Miss Bellows, her companion, watch her like a hawk now.

She spent the final days of her holiday far from home with her strict aunt and uncle and their unpleasant offspring. They treated her like a person in disgrace.

Of her father she heard nothing. By the time she returned to school, her tears had dried up. Life held no joy and each day was a drudgery to be gotten through.

The hope she had of hearing from Mr. Tennant grew slimmer and slimmer over the year until it finally disappeared altogether, leaving only a hollowness in her heart.

Chapter Five

July 1890

Nick allowed his valet to put the final touches to his cravat and turned from the glass. "Thank you, Williams." He turned to the room's other occupant. "Well, will I pass muster?"

"The picture of a young millionaire." Lord Asquith, a good-looking gentleman in his mid-thirties, lounged against the settee in Nick's hotel suite.

Nick raised an eyebrow. "Young?"

The baron rose with an easy grace, his evening suit looking as natural on him as if he'd been born in it. "Of course. What are you? Thirty-five, thiry-six?"

He grimaced. "Thirty-eight last March." Where had the last decade of his life gone?

"Just as I said, young, rich, powerful, just returned from America, and—" he lifted an eyebrow significantly "—unattached. The society mamas will latch on to you like a swarm of hungry locusts. Come along, I know just the place to take you this evening."

Nick picked up his white kid gloves from the table. "What did you have in mind? I hope nothing like last night when I was subjected to about as much boredom as a man should be required to endure for an evening."

Asquith chuckled. "Oh, no, nothing like. I do apologize. I know Lady Petersham is insufferably stuffy, but she has connections. If she accepts you into her circle, then everyone will follow suit."

"Who said I wanted to be accepted?" Nick closed the door to the hotel suite at the Savoy and the two headed down the corridor.

Asquith just shook his head as if the question were not even worth an argument. Upon his arrival back in England, Nick had been introduced to Asquith by a business associate. The young baron had taken a liking to Nick and decided he needed to be "introduced" to London society.

They rode down the lift to the spacious marble lobby of the newly opened hotel. At the front doors, the porter bowed and held one open. "Do you require a cab this evening, sirs?"

Asquith gave a brief nod.

While they waited under the porte-cochère, Nick glanced down the busy street. Gaslights cast their glow over the dark sheen of cabs and private carriages. Pedestrians hurried down the Strand. It was a city as choked with traffic as when he'd left it fifteen years ago.

"As I was saying, you'll have a very different experience this evening at Mrs. Alice Lennox's gala."

Alice. Nick cast a quick glance at Asquith, but then gave a mental shake. The name was common enough.

The truth was he'd been thinking of the person the name conjured up ever since he'd decided to return to London.

It had been too many years, he'd told himself every time he thought of her. Too late to do anything about something that never really had a chance to begin.

Nick hardly heard Asquith's words as he pictured the lively face of a girl he'd known for such a brief time, but whose equal he hadn't met since.

"…a most elegant woman, charming, beautiful and eminently worthy. I tell you, her virtues are innumerable."

Nick pulled his thoughts back with an effort. "Who can find a virtuous woman? For her price is far above rubies…"

Asquith quirked an eyebrow at him. "What's that you say?"

"It's something my mother would oft quote me."

"Well, your mother would doubtless approve of Mrs. Lennox. A modern day saint, if there ever was one."

Nick slapped his gloves against the palm of his hand. "I have yet to find one who couldn't be bought off with a fine pair of rubies."

"You are a cynic when it comes to women."

"Merely a realist." He'd discovered that to his misfortune once he'd achieved financial success, and time had not proved him wrong as his wealth grew.

"Ah, but you haven't met Mrs. Lennox."

A hansom cab pulled up at the curb and the two got in.

Nick glanced at Asquith as the porter closed the folding doors in front of their legs. "Where are we headed?"

Asquith opened the trap door behind them and spoke to the driver. "Clarendon's." Then he settled back in the snug seat and rested his hands atop the ivory head of his walking stick. "You know the hotel on Albemarle, don't you?

"I know *of* it, though I've never been in it."

"Now, where were we?"

"A paragon among women," Nick replied dryly.

"Ah yes, Mrs. Lennox. You said yourself you were looking to make a donation to a worthy charity. Well, Mrs. Lennox is your answer."

Nick glanced sidelong at Asquith, his curiosity aroused. "How's that?"

"She runs a housing charity."

Housing was an area of definite interest to him. "Tell me more."

"She is forever fighting with the building companies for decent housing for the working classes. Tonight she is hosting a ball for the charity, as a matter of fact. It has a long name to it. The Society for the Betterment of the something or other." Asquith tapped his fingers against his walking stick. "It'll add to your stature if you donate to a cause such as hers. She's loved by society and working man alike, not to mention the fact that she's a goddess among women."

Nick pictured some imposing matron as cold and quelling as a London fog. Certainly not the girl he'd dreamed of for too many years before relinquishing the cause as a hopeless youthful fantasy. God had blessed him immeasurably in his business pursuits. It was enough.

They were driving through the most fashionable streets of the West End. He peered through the hansom window at the streetlamps and quaint facades of the men's clubs along St. James's.

"Have you joined any clubs yet?"

He looked at the young lord in surprise, not having considered such a prospect. "As I recall, those require membership by invitation."

Asquith shrugged. "I can put your name up at a few of

mine. Filled with doddering old bores for the most part. Still, you'll want to join one or two. They're quiet places where you can read the papers and get a hot meal when you tire of hotel fare."

Nick shook his head, glancing back out at the passing street, unable to accustom himself to his new stature in London. When he'd left, he hadn't enough in his pocket to buy provisions for his sea journey, and now he was negotiating to buy entire companies.

They entered a quiet tree-lined square before being stalled amidst several coaches. "We can get out here or we'll be sitting in our cab all night. Mrs. Lennox's balls are renowned. Come on."

Nick followed Asquith out of the cab. On the next block, a crowd congregated under the portico of the large hotel. Ladies in long dark silk capes and upswept hair ascended the red-carpeted steps on the arms of gentlemen in black evening attire. Music wafted from the open doorways into the street.

Asquith nodded to several people on his way in but didn't stop for anyone. "The invitation says it's in the grand ballroom." Nick followed him up the curving marble staircase at the rear of the lobby.

The strains of music grew louder as they approached the room on the floor above. Asquith presented his invitation to a doorman and they entered the long ballroom studded with marble columns and crowned by crystal chandeliers.

They stood a moment at the edge of the sea of well-dressed people. Although he'd attended several society events in San Francisco, Nick had never grown used to them. London society was a different kettle of fish altogether. He'd never learned the subtleties of family names and histories. His gaze traveled over old and young faces. All looked as if they were part of an exclusive club to which only they knew the language.

His senses were assaulted by perfumes and pomades overlaid with cigarette smoke. The chandelier light glinted off the jewels in women's hair and around their throats.

With a tap at his elbow, Asquith began to weave through the crowd. Nick followed in his wake, his suit brushing against a palette of colorful gowns, taffetas and crepes, lace ruffles and wide puffed sleeves.

He had little chance to observe anyone in detail as Asquith strolled from group to group as if greeting guests in his own drawing room. "Good evening, Lord Dellamere… Good evening Mrs. Stanton… Yes, a lovely evening… I saw him at the club earlier…"

Amidst his casual exchanges, he turned to Nick. "Come on, let's find the bar."

The marble-topped bar in an adjoining room was three-deep in black-coated gentlemen and wreathed in smoke.

"Just a soda water for me, thanks."

Lord Asquith gave him a second look before nodding. "Very well."

Nick took the time to let his gaze wander back through the wide doors into the ballroom. Not one familiar face, but he hadn't expected to see any acquaintance. He'd certainly not moved in these circles when he'd left.

"Here you go, soda water."

He took the thick tumbler from Asquith. "Thanks." He'd never cared for spirits much. His mother had been a strict teetotaler and during all those years of fighting to succeed, he'd considered it just another dangerous habit and needless expense when every penny counted.

Now that he could afford to be liberal, he had no taste for the stuff.

Asquith lifted his champagne coupe in a salute. "Welcome back to the beau monde." They sipped their respective drinks in silence.

An orchestra was playing a waltz and the ballroom filled with dancing couples. The thrum of voices swirled around him like a swollen river, its noise undulating in volume but never lowering enough to make the words distinguishable from one another.

"Where do so many people come from?" Nick mused.

"I told you Mrs. Lennox's galas are coveted events."

Asquith surveyed the room over the rim of his glass. "Quite a good turn-out. The Society's coffers should be filled. Ah, there she is." With the stem of his glass he indicated a cluster of people coming through the ballroom doors. "The queen of the event. Surrounded as usual by her court."

Nick focused on the group of well-dressed ladies and gentlemen. They did indeed appear to be surrounding one individual but he couldn't see her through the mass.

Asquith took him gently by the elbow and urged him forward. "Time for introductions."

Nick had to fight the urge to hang back. Would this grand lady look down her nose at him, seeing beyond the evening clothes to the former clerk, the son of a miner?

With a greeting here and a pleasantry there, Asquith made his way to his target. Before reaching it, the group abruptly parted, and Nick saw her.

Standing about ten feet from her, he came face-to-face with the girl of his dreams.

The years fell away, and he was back in Richmond, a

twenty-three-year-old clerk with nothing to recommend him but his ambition, and Miss Alice Shepard was exacting a kiss from him.

He stared at her, hardly believing the reality. She hadn't changed. As beautiful as on that long ago summer, and yet completely transformed. For the woman in the emerald green evening gown that hugged her small waist before flaring out at her hips in a fall of cascading lace was no longer a sixteen-year-old schoolgirl but an exquisitely fashionable lady as foreign to him as he must appear to her.

He'd both dreaded and longed for this moment. Torn between the desire to go in search of her once he returned and a greater fear that he'd wake to the grim reality of finding her another's, he'd been paralyzed into inaction.

At that instant her eyes met his.

Like a dream, he read the question in her eyes give way to uncertainty. He knew the instant she recognized him.

She left the company around her and directed her footsteps toward him. Would she indeed remember him? He swallowed, finding his throat tight. His heart drummed in his chest and his breathing became erratic.

Nicholas Tennent. Alice could scarcely believe her eyes. Was her memory playing tricks on her? Surely the distinguished gentleman looking so intently at her was not the same man she'd given her childish heart to so long ago?

She didn't have to search her memory for his name. How many times had she repeated it to herself and written it down in her diary, making long scrolls under his name and hers in her schoolgirl script?

Nicholas Tennent. The name evoked pain and longing.

For a second she thought she would faint. All the old wounds of anguish and abandonment threatened to erupt.

No. She clamped down on those old emotions. She had come a long way from the girl she'd been. The wounds were long since healed over and the scars practically faded.

The thoughts and questions tumbled through her mind in chaotic jumble. What was Nicholas Tennent doing here after all these years? Where had he been all this time? Surely not in London? Wouldn't they have run into each other at some point?

Leaving her companions in mid-conversation, she began walking toward him. She no longer recollected how long it had been since her heartbreak. Her glance skimmed over his features. His hair was as dark as she remembered, combed away from his high forehead, his bearing straight, still slim but his shoulders broader.

Did he remember her at all? He must, the way he was looking at her. His dark eyes hadn't moved from her face.

They reached each other and she held out her hands, hesitating only an instant before she spoke. "Mr. Tennent, is it truly you?"

"Miss Shepard." He bowed, taking both her hands in his.

"Mrs. Lennox, now. She is the lady I have been telling you about." Lord Asquith's amused drawl came from the side.

Alice drew her gaze with difficulty away from Mr. Tennent's bowed head to see Asquith swirling his champagne glass around. "Telling him about…?"

"The newly arrived Nicholas Tennent, who has come all the way across the Atlantic to attend one of your galas."

Her eyes turned back to Mr. Tennent unable to absorb what Asquith was telling her. "America?"

"Yes." His dark scrutiny was unnerving. "You are Mrs. Lennox now?"

She nodded.

Lord Asquith drew her attention away again. "May I infer from this that you two are old acquaintances?"

Mr. Tennent answered before she had a chance to collect her thoughts. "I worked for her father for a short time."

Indeed her thoughts felt scattered in a thousand different directions. All her years of social poise slipped away at the keen way Mr. Tennent was regarding her. Her hands still felt the pressure of his hands on hers although he'd let them go immediately.

Lord Asquith rocked back on his heels. "You worked for old Shepard? When was this?"

"A long time ago."

"I must hear more." He turned to her. "Come, Alice, if the man is going to be close-lipped, you must give me the particulars."

Before she could think how to answer, Mr. Tennent turned to her. "Would you care to dance?"

"I beg your pardon?" She couldn't seem to stop staring at him. In the few seconds in his company, she felt like the girl she used to be.

"I merely asked you for this waltz." His voice, by contrast, sounded smooth and composed.

When had he undergone such a transformation? Realizing he was awaiting her reply, she nodded, hardly knowing what she was saying. "All right."

He handed Asquith his glass and offered her his arm. As he led her toward the ballroom, he leaned closer to her. "I thought it the best way to escape Lord Asquith's curiosity."

"Oh, I see." His proximity was making her dizzy. It

was just the shock, she told herself, like seeing someone one had thought long dead.

Only years of training enabled her to follow the waltz that was just commencing. She kept her eyes fixed on Mr. Tennent's even as her thoughts wondered where he had learned to dance so effortlessly. Had he known when she'd met him? She remembered how he hadn't ever ridden, or played tennis. Long suppressed memories tumbled into her head, sitting beside him at the desk, working and laughing over any silly thing that struck her, all ending the day of that fateful kiss.

"What are you thinking? You seem far away."

"I was thinking about Richmond."

His dark eyes looked into hers as if he, too, were remembering that day. But then he answered and she only detected amusement in his tone. "You doubtless remember an awkward young clerk. As I recall you said I was too serious."

It seems he didn't recall their kiss at all. Taking her cue from him, she put aside the memory and strove for a light, cordial tone. "I remember the serious, but I don't recall awkward. My memory is of a young man of great intelligence and ambition with a very strong sense of purpose."

He looked slightly taken aback with her description and she found herself blushing. "I didn't think you'd remember me at all," he said quietly.

She frowned in puzzlement. "Why shouldn't I remember you?" She wanted to add that she'd never forgotten him, but realized how foolish that would sound.

"It's been a long time."

Slowly, she nodded. His face had matured. Gone was the thin, pale, slightly long visage. In its place was a darker, more rugged complexion, as if he'd spent much time in the outdoors. "I'm surprised you remember me at all," she said with a laugh that sounded nervous to her ears. "An awkward young girl, pestering you as you tried to carry out your secretarial duties."

Amusement crinkled the corners of his eyes. "Let me assure you my memory is of a beautiful young girl poised on the verge of womanhood."

She could feel the warmth steal into her cheeks and felt shaken by her reaction. It couldn't be, not after so many years. She'd been married and known real love.

As if reading her thoughts, he said, "There have been a few changes since that time. You are married."

She looked away. "*Was*. My husband…passed away four years ago." Dear, sweet Julian. How she still missed him.

"I'm sorry," was all he said, his tone betraying little.

Her gaze traveled back to his face and she found him still watching her. "There's something different about you."

She caught a hint of humor in his eyes. "Perhaps the cut of my suit? Savile Row's finest."

She remembered the dark, stiff suits he wore on the tennis court and almost laughed. Then she shook her head, hardly giving his black cutaway coat and snowy white shirt a glance except to note how handsomely he filled them out. "No, it's not that." She tilted her head a fraction. "There's a self-assurance I don't remember."

"The suit—and enough money in the bank to buy out half the people in this room." His glance went beyond her and skimmed the ballroom.

The words gave her pause. They had a harsh ring to them. "Have you achieved your dream?"

His gaze returned to hers. "You remember?"

She nodded her head. "Of course I do."

The music came to an end and the two stood there as other couples walked by them. With an inquiring lift of an eyebrow, he took her arm and led her to the edge of the dance floor.

"Things didn't quite turn out the way I expected," he said.

She wasn't sure what he was referring to but suddenly she needed to know. "What happened the day Father found us?"

If she'd thought he'd forgotten their kiss, she'd been mistaken. He stared at her. "You don't know?"

"No. Father never told me anything but that he'd sent you away."

"I was sacked immediately—deservedly so."

She drew in her breath. "I didn't know. The only thing I knew for certain was that you'd disappeared. I'm sorry you lost your job over me."

"Don't be. As it turns out, it was the best thing that could have ever happened to me."

The abrupt tone cut her to the quick. What had been her banishment had meant freedom for him.

"You've prospered in America."

"I left London determined to seek my fortune across the Atlantic."

"And have you?"

He shrugged. "America has treated me well."

Something in her felt saddened at the man standing before her. He was no longer the earnest young secretary but a hardened, self-assured businessman. The kind of man she'd vowed never to give her heart to.

She didn't catch what he was saying. "I'm sorry?"

"I said, was your father very angry with you that day?"

She looked down at her clasped hands. "As it happens, he sent me away, too."

"He sent you away?"

At his sharp tone, she lifted her head. "Yes, to some relatives in Scotland. I spent the holidays with them from then on."

"I didn't know." He cleared his throat, the first sign of hesitation since she'd been in his company. "Did they treat you well?"

"They were tolerable." She smiled, not wanting to dwell on the unpleasant things of the past. "Father concluded he could do no more with his wayward daughter. They kept an eagle eye on me for the next year or so, until he finally allowed me to come back to London when I finished school."

He was staring at her. "I'm truly sorry. I should have behaved more honorably."

She felt herself redden again. "You did nothing wrong."

After a moment, he said, "You were married."

"Yes. I met my husband shortly after I returned to London. We were married after my twenty-first birthday." Without her father's approval, she added silently. "Julian—my husband— was ill when we met but he recovered for a while. But then the consumption recurred. But he left me with a great gift."

Before he could ask her anything about that, she said in a determinedly bright tone. "So, you've been in America. Is that the reason I haven't seen you in a London ballroom until tonight?"

He nodded slowly, as if still puzzling over what she had told him.

"How long have you been away from England?"

"Since I last saw you."

"But that's been—"

"Fifteen years."

"Has it really been that long?" she whispered, not sure which stunned her more, the fact of how much time had passed, or that he remembered.

He nodded, his dark eyes studying her.

They were interrupted by one of the trustees of the housing charity. "Mrs. Lennox, may I have a word with you?"

Alice looked at Mr. Tennent, torn between wanting to continue speaking with him and wondering if it were not better to let the past remain where it was. "I'm sorry, Mr. Tennent. If you will excuse me?"

He bowed over her hand. "Thank you for the dance, Miss—Mrs. Lennox."

She smiled. "The pleasure was mine." Against her better judgment, she asked, "Are you in London for long?"

"That depends."

His gaze held hers, and she found herself saying, "If you are free tomorrow, I will be home in the afternoon."

He nodded. "What time?"

"Two o'clock? Number fifteen, Park Lane."

"I'll be there."

Nick watched Miss Shepard—Mrs. Lennox, he reminded himself—finding it difficult to reconcile his image of a carefree girl with this elegant lady. Soon, she was surrounded with other guests, and if he thought he'd have another opportunity to approach her, he saw it was a vain wish. Better to wait until the morrow when he could find out more about what had happened to her since that fateful day of their kiss.

A widow. What kind of man had she married?

A thousand questions swirled in through his mind.

Seeing Lord Asquith heading his way, and reluctant to answer even the most general interrogation about his acquaintance with Miss Shepa—Mrs. Lennox, Nick turned and weaved through the crowded room until able to exit without being seen.

Although the evening was young, he headed back to his hotel suite. His mind was too full of memories and questions to be able to concentrate on anything else. Not even work would distract him tonight.

Chapter Six

Nick arrived promptly the next day at Mrs. Lennox's address. He paid his cab fare and proceeded through the black wrought-iron gates up the walkway to the colonnaded façade of the Park Lane mansion. Similar imposing structures lined the wide, tree-lined avenue. Once, he'd aspired to such a London address. Now, he glanced indifferently at them, his thoughts fixed on the coming visit.

He'd found it hard to sleep when he'd arrived back from the gala. For so many years he'd worked toward this moment until as the months turned into years and his goal nowhere in sight, he'd realized what a pipe dream it was and gradually he'd abandoned it.

And now, he'd seen her again, when he was the man he'd dreamed of becoming and she was free.

The moment had found him unprepared.

Why hadn't he come back sooner? The question had plagued him all night, and he'd not been able to come up with a satisfactory answer.

He adjusted his silk tie and rang the bell, feeling as nervous as a boy on his first courtship.

He thought again of what she'd told him of her being sent away. Shepard had proved more hard-hearted than he could have ever imagined. If he'd known she'd be sent away, would he have left like that? But what could he have done? A penniless clerk with no job prospects would make a poor knight to a sixteen-year-old damsel in distress.

No. He'd had to make his fortune to be worthy of courting Miss Shepard. And that had taken him many more years than he'd foreseen.

But was he fifteen years too late?

He smoothed his hair back and gave his tie one final adjustment just as a maid opened the door.

As soon as Nick gave his name, the servant stood to one side. "Yes, Mrs. Lennox told me to expect you. Come this way, please."

He was led to a drawing room at the rear of the house where no street noises penetrated. "I will inform madam that you are here."

"Thank you." Left alone, Nick glanced about the well-appointed room. Oil landscapes filled the walls in gilt frames, dark velvet couches graced two sides of the room. Everything exuded refined taste. He walked over Oriental carpets to peer through the long windows facing the back. Precisely clipped yew hedges formed geometrical shapes within the walls of the wide garden. Bright flowers bobbed their heads within the green borders.

A slight noise behind him caused him to turn away from the view and look back into the room.

He saw no one. His eyes traveled slowly over the furnishings, the book spines on a floor-to-ceiling shelf, a piano at one end of the room, a set of nested tables, a chintz-covered armchair and a carved trunk before backtracking.

He heard it again, a low sniffle. He walked toward a desk, glad for the thick carpet which muffled his footsteps.

He peered under the desk.

A young boy, his large dark eyes looking up at him through a mop of dark bangs, sat crouched within the small space meant for a person's legs. He clutched a furry stuffed animal to his breast.

Nick smiled tentatively. "Hello."

The boy didn't reply to the soft greeting. Could he be Mrs. Lennox's son? The thought jolted him.

Of course. It would be natural for her to have children. Nick straightened and took a step back. "I'm not sure how comfortable it is down there. I know when I was a lad, I liked to find odd nooks and crannies. You can pretend to be in a cave, hiding away from a band of pirates, or perhaps you're in your tent, bivouacked with your troops, planning tomorrow's battle."

The boy continued staring at him.

Nick leaned against the back of a couch, and put his hands in his trouser pockets, pretending to be at ease. "What is your friend's name?"

The child looked from Nick to the stuffed animal in his hands. It appeared to be a rabbit from the long floppy ears hanging off the sides of its head. But at Nick's scrutiny, the boy took the animal and hid it behind his back.

Before Nick could think how to reassure him that he was not going to take the thing away from him, Mrs. Lennox entered the room.

"Good afternoon, Mr. Tennent. I'm so glad you could come today. I was almost doubting that it was really you at the gala yesterday evening." She advanced toward him with a welcoming smile.

She seemed more relaxed than she had last evening. But just as beautiful. She wore a high-necked blue gown with long sleeves which were gathered at the shoulders. Her hair was done up but in the sunlight filtering through the sheer curtains, he detected once again the coppery highlights he remembered so well.

He took her hand in his, feeling its soft warmth. Reluctantly, he let it go. "I know exactly what you mean." To fill the silence, he looked back towards the desk.

She followed his gaze. Immediately seeing the boy, she bent down and held out her hand. "Austen, my dear, what are you doing down there? Have you said hello to Mr. Tennent? He is an old friend of Mama's."

So, it *was* her son. He drew in a breath, still having difficulty reconciling the young girl he'd known with the mother of a boy already in short pants and sailor collar.

The little boy took his mother's hand and slowly let her lead him out of his hiding place. When he stood, Nick saw that he was older than he'd supposed. Perhaps six or seven instead of four or five.

Mrs. Lennox turned to Nick with a smile. "Let me present you to my son, Austen Lennox. Say, 'how do you do, Mr. Tennent.'"

The little boy held out his free hand, his large brown eyes gazing up at him through black lashes. Nick took the small hand in his, closing his hand around it. As soon as the handshake was over, the little hand disappeared into the pocket of the boy's short pants.

She turned to Nick again. "It's such a lovely day, would you like to sit out on the terrace?"

He agreed and followed her to a brick terrace overlooking the garden he had seen from the window. Mrs. Lennox ordered coffee to be brought out to them.

Austen stood behind his mother's skirts, and she bent over him, her hand on his head. Her hands were exactly as he remembered them, pale and slim. She wore only a thin gold band on her ring finger. "Would you like to stay with Mama and Mr. Tennent, or would you like to go up to Nanny Grove?"

"Nanny Grove," he whispered. She straightened and smiled at Nick. "Austen is going up to his room and wants to bid you goodbye." With a little nudge from her, he stepped forward and held out his hand.

Nick felt a pang, transported back to his own childhood for an instant. He used to be afraid of large strangers at that age. He stooped down before the boy and took his hand with a smile. The thin little wrist stuck out from his navy blue shirt. "It was nice to have met you, Austen. I hope we'll see each other again."

The boy only nodded. Nick released his hand and took a step away from him, imagining his height might intimidate the boy.

"I'll be up to see you soon and we'll go to the park later, all right?" his mother whispered, bending over Austen again.

Nick moved off to stand at the edge of the brick terrace, unsure what to say. It wasn't often he was unsure of himself these days.

How to begin with a woman he had only briefly known so many years ago? A woman who had impressed him to the extent that no other lady had succeeded in displacing her memory?

This elegant lady was no longer the vivacious girl he

remembered. Would the two of them have anything to talk about? This Alice Lennox seemed remote, with none of the young Miss Shepard's impulsiveness or enthusiasm. Yet something in her slim straight shoulders affected him in a way that made him feel as vulnerable as he hadn't since he'd left his native shores for America so long ago.

Had that young girl's spirit been irrevocably suppressed? Was there any hope of resurrecting it? What had come to take its place?

He turned around when he heard Austen's departure. The two watched him for a moment.

With a sigh, Mrs. Lennox motioned to a cushioned wicker settee. "Please, have a seat, Mr. Tennent."

He took the place beside her as a maid set down the coffee tray. Mrs. Lennox poured dark Turkish coffee from the long-handled copper pot into two tiny porcelain cups. He took the one offered him. "Thank you." He waited until she had sat back and had taken a sip from her cup before he spoke. "Your boy is quiet."

She colored and looked away, as if the remark were aimed at herself. "Yes, Austen is rather bashful. He…well, he was only three when he lost his father, and I don't know how much it has affected his behavior." She ran her finger along the rim of her cup.

Nick was suddenly transported back to the afternoon he'd first met her in his tiny office. She'd walked along the edge of his desk, running her slim finger along its edge. Little had he realized then how the young girl would turn his life upside down.

He blinked away the sudden image. "I beg your pardon, what did you say?"

"I was saying that Austen was a happy baby, but it seems

he has become more timid with each passing year. He's also a bit frail. Like his father. I worry about him. I know I shouldn't. I trust in God's mercy." She sighed.

"I don't know too much about children," he said, seeking of a way to reassure her, "but I imagine a lot of children are naturally shy at his age. How old is he?"

She smiled and he felt he'd said the right thing. "He's seven."

He cleared his throat. "How is your father?"

"He passed away last year. I moved back here to be with him four years ago when I was widowed. This was Father's London home."

The news stunned him. He'd always thought of Shepard as being in London the day he returned successful. "I'm sorry."

She sighed. "But I still have my brother. Do you remember him?"

"Yes, I met him a few times."

"He runs Father's firm now."

He nodded, hard pressed to imagine the man he remembered running anything. Perhaps he'd matured.

An awkward silence followed. "You never married again?"

"Oh, no." She looked as shocked as if he'd asked her if she'd committed a crime.

"Most women do. You've been widowed how long?"

"Four years. But I loved my husband."

He felt a twinge of envy for the man who had inspired that kind of love and loyalty.

"Besides, I have Austen. And my work."

The wicker creaked as he sat back against the settee, feeling he'd offended her with his blunt remark. "Your work?"

She smiled sheepishly. "Actually, you were the one to inspire me in this direction."

He paused in the act of sipping his coffee. "Me? How so?"

"You were the first one to ever cause me to question my privileged station in life. You challenged me to look around me at how other people lived."

His lip curled up at the corner. "I was a rather priggish, unyielding sort back then, as I recall."

She smiled. "Not at all." She looked past him, sobering. "Later, when I met my husband, he helped me see even more how we must help our fellow man."

Nick's pleasure at having inspired her in any way evaporated as he listened to her wax on about her husband's role in her life. He'd taken her off to live in a small vicarage and given away anything they had to the needy in their parish. To hear her tell it, Julian Lennox had been a saint among men.

After several moments of listening to an extended eulogy about the poor curate's selfless life among his parishioners, Nick concluded the man had been a weak individual who had caused Miss Shepard to be cut off from her parents' wealth.

Mrs. Lennox took a sip of her coffee, her eyes sad. "I think it broke his health eventually, but he wouldn't have been happy any other way. Since Julian's passing," she went on, "I returned to London and with a few other dedicated women have formed a society to help those working families who have no decent place to live. When I was widowed, I realized my own plight. With few resources, I would have been hard-pressed to find a wholesome place for Austen and myself."

He frowned. "With few resources? But your father?"

She looked down at her half-empty cup in her lap. "My father disinherited me when I married Julian."

Nick's frown deepened. "And yet you returned to him?"

"Yes. He was willing to accept his grandson, and I had few options.

"Since my father passed on, my brother, Geoff, allows me the use of this house." She sat up and smoothed her skirt. "But that's more about me than I meant to bore you with. What brought you to London after so many years?"

"My mother's funeral."

He heard her soft intake of breath and he met her gaze, which was full of sympathy. "I'm so sorry."

He stared down at the dregs of his coffee and without planning to, found himself saying, "I always meant to come back sooner." Her own story of nursing her consumptive husband only made him feel the inadequacy of the monetary assistance he'd rendered his mother.

"Was she ill very long?" she asked gently.

"No, not with the last illness." Why hadn't he come back sooner, he'd asked himself continually since the day he'd received the cable of her death.

"She had been sick often?"

"Off and on through the years." He gave a humorless laugh. "Poverty and lack are what ultimately killed her."

"Again, I'm so sorry."

He set his cup down on the table. "She worked long and hard over a lifetime until she was worn out. I helped her once I began earning wages, but I always meant to come back earlier. Alas, I was too late."

"I'm sure she knew your heart."

Their eyes met and he read genuine sorrow in hers. "Your loss was worse."

Her eyelashes flickered down. "I miss Julian. It was very difficult at first, but at least I know where he is. He had the assurance of the resurrection and of his Savior's love. He died peacefully at the vicarage, with those he loved around him."

They sat quietly some minutes. Nick thought about how blessed the departed man had been with such a woman's love. He'd known no such love in all his years abroad. Ever, really.

She offered him more coffee and he gave a brief nod.

"I also came to London for business."

"I see." She stirred her cup and set the tiny spoon down on the saucer. "Tell me all about America," she said, sitting up straighter. "Is it as big as one hears? Why did you decide to emigrate? Oh, I know, you probably had heard that fortunes are made over there practically overnight, but it seems so brave to set out by yourself. I want to hear all about it."

As her questions tumbled forth, Nick recognized the young girl of fifteen years ago. He wasn't sure if she was just making an effort to distract him from his grief, or if she was genuinely interested, but he decided to indulge her.

He took a sip of coffee. "After I left your father's firm, I didn't even wait until I was fully healed but booked passage aboard a steamer bound for New York harbor." Shaking his head, he continued. "I traveled steerage, a way I would never recommend to anyone."

"Was it very bad?"

"Overcrowded conditions in the airless hold of a ship, through calm waters and stormy. What was most disagreeable, I think, was the lack of fresh air. The food wasn't the worst I've eaten, and the company comprised all kinds of people, mainly families hoping for a new start, or men going on ahead and hoping to send for their families as soon as they'd saved for their passage."

She leaned forward, her chin in her hand, fascinated with his description.

"The trip lasted ten days, and whenever the skies were clear, I took my blanket up on the deck and slept under the stars."

"Oh, I should love to do that! You weren't afraid of rolling off the side?"

He smiled at her little understanding of a steamship. "I found a nice little sheltered spot under a smokestack. Anyway, it was my first and last experience traveling steerage. I'm happy to say this time around I was able to travel first class."

"And what did you do once you arrived in New York? Did you know anyone?"

"Not a soul." He could laugh about it now. Arriving with no money in his pocket and no acquaintances had been a different matter. "I went along with some of the single men I'd traveled with. There was a sort of network of immigrants. These men knew of others who'd gone before them; some had family members. I found a room in a boarding house, full of Irishmen, Scotsmen, Russians, Swedes and Norwegians and soon found work on a construction site."

Her eyes widened. "A construction site? Not as a secretary?"

"No. I had only my old bank references—" He stopped, realizing too late where that might lead. "Anyway, I didn't want to start over as a clerk, I'd spent too many years toiling in that department. So, I used my meager muscles this time instead of my brains."

She looked down. "My father didn't give you a reference when you left his employ?"

He shrugged. "He found me kissing his daughter, as you may recall. He was in his rights to send me packing with nothing."

They looked at each other steadily. "It was my fault you were dismissed."

"No." The word came swift and sharp. He rubbed a hand across his jaw, looking away from her at last. Did she regret it? "If not for his dismissal, I would never have gone to America and found the opportunities I did there."

"How did you go from a laborer to the owner of your own firm?"

Again, he smiled. "It didn't happen overnight. I spent some months at construction work, until deciding to head west. I heard from many that California was the place to be if one wanted to get ahead. I hopped a freight car from New York and was on my way."

"Oh, what an adventure! I wish Austen could hear you. How long did that trip take?"

"Quite a long while because I didn't go directly to California. I stopped several times in between, picked up a little work here and there—harvesting fruit in orchards, working as a farmhand for a bit on the great farms in the Middle West, ending up on a ranch in the West for a while." He smiled ruefully. "I was determined to get over my fear of horses after that fall."

She laughed. "I'm so glad! I was afraid you'd never want to get on another horse again."

"I not only did, but learned to ride a Western saddle. Even learned to lasso a steer."

"A real cowboy." She shook her head. "Austen would love to hear your stories," she repeated.

Did this mean she wanted to see him again? "Perhaps I can share them with him."

But she only nodded and said, "Perhaps."

Nick continued telling her the highlights of his adventures, playing up the amusing incidents and downplaying the months and years of deprivations and hardships before he'd had his first break.

She sighed as if satisfied with a well-told tale. "So you ended up in San Francisco."

"Yes, I found work in a dry goods store, unpacking cases, stocking shelves. Soon, I was working as a clerk, keeping track of inventory." His lips curled upward. "So, after all that time, I ended up doing what I had tried to avoid."

"What was that?"

"I'd vowed never to go back to clerking."

"Ah, but this time, it seems it was not in vain."

"No. It still took a few years, but gradually I worked my way up until I was manager of the store, and when the owner decided to branch out, he put me in charge of another store. Soon, I was overseeing a whole district. I saved every penny until I was able to invest my money. I borrowed some and went into a partnership with another fellow and we bought our own store.

"After a few years, having paid off the debt and making a profit, I began to buy other things—railroad stock, tea from China, government bonds…"

She drew in her breath. "You've been to the Far East?"

"I've made a few crossings."

"Goodness. My own life seems very dull in comparison."

He looked downward. "I've learned something about

such a life. If one doesn't have someone to share one's success with, it is a lonely journey."

"You never married?"

He shook his head slowly, once again debating how much to tell her. "I had little time when I was working toward success until recently." He shrugged, his tone taking on a cynical edge. "I quickly discovered that when one has money, it's very easy to attract a woman's attention. Unfortunately, one cannot easily trust the authenticity of any avowals of love and fidelity given to a wealthy man."

He drained the last of his coffee and set the cup down, knowing he should go. "I am grateful for all I have been given. That is one of the reasons I wanted to see you again. Lord Asquith had already been telling me about your charity, and I wanted to look into it. Besides opening a branch of my firm here in London, I've returned to England because I wanted to donate something to a worthy cause."

"Oh, that's wonderful, Mr. Tennent." Her face took on an animation he remembered. "Would you like to visit our charity and see something of the work we do?"

He nodded. Any reason for seeing her again would be a good one. "Yes, very much so." He paused for only a second before saying, "Would tomorrow morning be too soon for you?"

She blinked as if surprised, but then agreed.

They discussed a time then he stood. He'd also learned not to overstay his welcome. "Thank you for the coffee and conversation."

Nick left the Shepard mansion, deciding to walk back to his hotel. He needed the time to sort through all the impressions he'd received in the last hour in Mrs. Lennox's company.

The impression that superseded all the others was that the girl he remembered was still there beneath the elegant society lady. Her eyes had sparkled with enthusiasm at his tales of his adventures in America's West.

As a man of thirty-eight, he found himself as fascinated by this woman as he had been at twenty-three by the girl on the verge of seventeen.

Where would this fascination lead him?

His pace quickened at the anticipation of seeing her as soon as tomorrow. He wasn't a man to spare any effort once he set his course.

Would Alice Lennox see anything in him worthy of her time and attention after all these years? After knowing the love of a truly worthy man like her late husband?

Chapter Seven

The next morning after spending some time with Austen in the nursery, Alice went to the small office of the Housing Society she oversaw. She was deep in budget matters, when her assistant popped her head in. "There's a gentleman here to see you." She handed Alice a card.

Alice took it from her. *Nicholas Tennent. President. Tennent & Co.*

The card was on high quality paper and the letters printed with understated elegance. She set down the card, trying to ignore the sudden flutter of nerves. Since issuing her invitation yesterday, she'd been of two minds about this meeting. "Send him in, please."

Mr. Tennent entered and once again Alice marveled at how distinguished he looked. She couldn't help a sense of proprietary pride that she had known all along that he'd make his mark in the world. She stood and held out her hand. "I'm so glad you could stop by today. I know you must be very busy."

His hand enveloped hers and gave it a quick, firm shake.

His dark eyes appraised her. She had the sense that he missed very little.

"Please, won't you have a seat?"

"Actually, I'd be more interested in seeing your facility and looking at some of the projects you've undertaken."

"Of course." She could see he wasn't a man to waste time. "Come then, I'll give you a quick tour and then perhaps we could look at a group of houses we have constructed in Bethnal Green."

"I look forward to it." The two exited her office and she led him down the corridor. "When did you first move into these quarters?"

"About two years ago. When I first came back to London, I was a bit at sea. Austen, of course, was very young, and I spent most of my time with him. But he had his nurse, and I found I had too much time on my hands. It…made things worse." She didn't like to recall those lonely weeks, feeling so out of place in her parents' old home. She sighed, brushing away the memories. "I had been very active with my husband in his parish, so little by little, I began informing myself of the situation here in London. This is a much bigger place, so at times the situation of the needy can seem overwhelming. That's when I decided to focus on one area where I might be able to help.

"I met a woman—Macey Endicott—who was very involved with the housing question. She is a remarkable woman. I hope you will meet her. She is on the Society's board of trustees. It was she who encouraged me to use my influence in society—" she gave a disbelieving laugh "—whatever little influence I had left, to help raise awareness of the situation."

He raised an eyebrow as if in surprise. "Little influence?

What I saw the night of the gala showed me a lady of great influence."

She shook her head. "Four years ago, I would say I had very little. I had been away from London society for many years."

His eyes remained on her. "But you seem to have overcome that drawback."

"Perhaps. If so, it was due in great part to Miss Endicott. She is quite a champion of women and their rights." She shook her head with a smile. "She is quite respected, being wealthy in her own right, and by virtue of her many publications on such subjects as the reform of women's education and women's suffrage."

Alice watched him as he listened carefully, asking questions from time to time. She showed him the rest of their small quarters. He appeared interested in every detail.

When they stood outside on the curb, he hailed a hansom for them. "I notice there were only women in your office. Is that deliberate?"

She nodded, surprised that he'd noticed. "In a sense. You see, there are very few options for a woman who finds herself either widowed or single with no means of her own. A woman depends wholly on her parents or on a husband to support her, but you'd be surprised at the number of women who have neither alternative.

"I wanted to be able to offer some type of employment for women in this situation. Some of these women have children and it becomes even more challenging for them to find decent care for them. That is why you'll frequently find a child or two playing quietly by his mother's desk."

"My mother would have benefited from women such as you."

A hansom pulled up at Mr. Tennent's summons.

He handed her up into the cab and then came up to sit beside her. There was little room on the seat and her skirt brushed against his trouser legs. She made a show of adjusting her gown in the small space, suddenly conscious of his nearness, and attempted to continue her discourse. "One of my dreams is to offer a facility here under our roof as a nursery. Perhaps rent the floor above us for such a venture." She turned and slid open the hatch in the back and gave the driver instructions.

Mr. Tennent raised an eyebrow. "Shoreditch?"

When she turned from the hatch, she found his face very close to hers. She moved back a fraction then chided herself for her sensitivity. "I wanted to show you some of the housing that has been built over the years for the working classes and compare it with what we've done. The area around Spitalfields and Shoreditch has grown enormously and there is a terrible lack of adequate housing. It's also a railroad terminus which results in very mixed neighborhoods from lower middle class to very lower class."

The cab turned sharply at a corner and she was thrown against Mr. Tennent. Before she could right herself, he reached up a hand to steady her. "Tha—thank you." She adjusted her hat to conceal her confusion. What was wrong with her?

"It's quite all right." She could feel his glance on her but his words revealed nothing out of the ordinary. "Would it cost so much?"

She'd lost the thread of their conversation. "To what?"

"To fix up a room for your female employees' children."

"Oh. Yes, it would. That would mean fewer funds available for our building projects. Presently, almost all donations we receive are used to help people with their housing. That need is most pressing of all." She shifted into her corner seat in preparation for another turn. "Tell me how it is in America. Are there such frightful conditions among the working classes?"

He described the cities he had seen. She listened, studying his three-quarter profile, finding herself remembering how drawn she'd been to him so many years ago. The strong lines had matured into the face of a very striking gentleman. His jaw was cleanly shaven. He hadn't really changed much over the years, but there was a cragginess to the lean contours of his face. The slight diffidence she remembered was gone but in its place was a subtle irony. It reminded her of her father, and she recoiled from the thought.

"Overcrowding exists in many workmen's neighborhoods but there is much industry and mobility." He glanced beyond her at the passing streets. "London has certainly grown since I was last here. Not that it wasn't a busy place then."

"Yes, it has seen unprecedented growth. No other city comes close, even your New York City."

"New York is a remarkable city."

"I should like to see it some day."

His dark eyes turned to her. "Perhaps you will."

Why did she feel there was more to his words than his light tone implied? She shook aside her fanciful notion. "I doubt it…at least not any time in the near future."

"You sound so very certain."

She folded her gloved hands on her lap. "I have my work here.   nd Austen is young still."

"When you were a girl, you struck me as someone who would seek the kind of adventure found in travel."

Her smile was bittersweet. "Yes, I was full of dreams."

"Haven't any of them been fulfilled?"

Was it whimsy or gravity she read in his tone—or irony? "Not in the way I had foreseen," she answered carefully.

"What *had* you foreseen?"

How could she answer that? That she'd foreseen a future with him? "A place to belong," she finally said, looking past him. So many years of yearning for what she'd never found in her home.

When he said nothing, she risked a glance at him. A furrow had formed between his brows. "Didn't you find that?"

"Oh, yes. But not where I had imagined." She took a deep breath. "It took a very humble, patient man to show me that it was only to be found in the Lord, that He loved me no matter how unlovable I might consider myself."

Before she could discover if he had understood what she meant, they arrived at their destination. Mr. Tennent descended the cab and turned to give her his hand. She stepped onto the broken pavement, still feeling the firmness of his hand after he'd let go and turned to the driver.

He paid the man and instructed him to wait for them then turned to survey the neighborhood. In the distance they could hear the rumble of trains.

They walked along a street lined with small shops. "We're not far from the Great Eastern Goods Station."

"This area looks fairly prosperous." He sniffed the air, which had a yeasty smell to it.

"There's a large brewery a few blocks to the east of us." She led him down Commercial Street. "There are quite some shops and warehouses along here due to the railroad station." As they continued farther, the storefronts and buildings became more varied. "You'll see how things begin to deteriorate the more distant from the station."

She turned down a narrow side street. Here, the buildings were clearly more dingy, many in a state of disrepair. Children of all ages ran and played in the streets, despite the traffic of wagons and drays. The scent of brewer's yeast grew stronger.

She indicated a row of two-story brick buildings. "The London Building Society put up this row of dwellings, but already the tenants have complained of countless problems. Partitions separating the individual dwellings are less than a full brick length, which leads to noise traveling through, not to mention the more serious problem of water leakage. Shoddy bricks are used, hollow ones which are cheaper, of course, but also ones that crumble easily over time."

She stopped in front of one dwelling, where rubbish was piled in the front. "No foundation has been laid, or worse, the existing gravel is hauled away and sold, and rubbish is used to fill the holes. You can imagine what happens over time."

"The building begins to sink."

"Yes. Many of these buildings were put up ten or twenty years ago when there was such a clamor for housing, and speculators bought up the land and quickly put up dwellings. It's only now that the problems are manifesting." She pointed to a roofline. "See how it sags? Too few scantlings in the rafters."

He smiled. "You seem as knowledgeable as a builder."

"I've learned over time. Our Society has put up some buildings in the last few years, and I wanted to be sure they would be sturdy and well-ventilated. We'll go there next, so you can compare the difference."

They turned a corner and the area became grimmer. Here, the houses were much older, their brick exteriors dilapidated. Several idlers lounged on the broken front stoops. Windows were boarded up. Piles of refuse filled the narrow, muddy street. Mr. Tennent stopped at the sight of a group of dirty-faced men standing nearby. "Perhaps we should turn back."

She hesitated. "Yes, I just wanted to show you how quickly the neighborhoods degenerate. Here, you see men who are habitually unemployed. The only activity is drinking." As she took a step back, she noticed one of the men eyeing her.

Before she could take another step back, he sauntered over to her. "Wot are the toff doin' in our neighborhood, I'd like to know?" He spat, just missing their feet by inches. His grimy shirt was pulled half out of his trousers and his vest was missing buttons. He carried a half-empty gin bottle in one hand.

Mr. Tennent took her lightly by the elbow and began to back away.

The man was quicker than he looked. He circled around them. "My, aren't we the fancies."

In a few seconds they found themselves surrounded by a group of ill-featured men. The acrid smell of sweat mingled with the pasty smell of yeast.

Mr. Tennent stopped and eyed them. "We didn't mean to intrude on your private turf, gentlemen," he said politely.

The man snapped his suspenders back and guffawed. "*Our* turf." He turned to the others. "How d'ye like that, eh? *Our* turf? That's wot hit is, awright." He swaggered up and took hold of one of Mr. Tennent's lapels. "I like the feel o' this coat. Feels pretty foine to me, hit does."

Alice began to pray silently. She eyed the rest of the men nervously.

Before she could decide what to do, the man flipped out a knife from his belt. Alice jerked back.

He brandished the knife before Mr. Tennent's face. "I think I'll have this coat." He brought the knife up to his jawline.

A soft cry escaped her lips. The sound distracted the man and he turned to her. "Foine lady we 'ave 'ere."

She shrank back and experienced an instant's reassurance as Mr. Tennent's hold on her arm tightened. Her fear returned as she realized how impossibly outnumbered he was.

The man's unshaven jaw came to within inches of hers, his foul breath fanning across her face.

She prayed even more.

Nick judged the distance between himself, the knife, and the malodorous fellow threatening Mrs. Lennox.

He pressed her elbow an instant to reassure her then moved a step. "Leave the lady alone, or aren't you man enough to face me?" he said, infusing his look and tone with scorn.

The man's attention swung immediately back to him, his stubbly cheeks deepening in color and his broken-toothed leer fading. "Why you—" The knife swung out, but Nick was ready for him. In a deft movement, he grabbed the man's bony wrist.

As he'd calculated, his hold wasn't as firm as it had appeared, the alcohol probably giving the man more confidence than warranted. Nick easily pulled his arm up and over, spinning him around and bending him double. The knife and bottle fell to the muddy ground. "Pick up the knife, Alice." Keeping his tone quiet but commanding, he held the man's arm up at a painful angle. Half-starved wretch. Nick had met many like him in his early days on the road.

With a push strong enough to put him out of commission until they left the area but not enough to seriously hurt him, Nick shoved him to the ground and kept a foot between his shoulder blades. He turned to Alice, relieved to find she had done as he'd asked. She held the knife as if it were a snake. He took it from her by the blade then brandished it slowly to the ring of men. "Anyone else care to have a go?"

They all backed away from him a few steps.

"We meant no disrespect entering your neighborhood. This lady runs a charity to build decent housing for men like you and their families."

The men began mumbling denials that they'd meant no harm and bowed to Mrs. Lennox.

One of the men shuffled his feet, not quite meeting Nick's eyes. "Charlie there was just sportin' wif you."

"Well, we'll call it even then." With his free hand, Nick dug into his pocket and fished out some coins, all the while keeping the knife pointed up. "Here, if anyone is in need of a hot meal." Was it a hopeless wish that they wouldn't spend it at the nearest tavern? But he couldn't leave them with nothing. He knew what it was like to be hungry.

They grouped around him eagerly and he made sure that each one got something. With a hand to the brim of his hat, he finally backed away from them, taking Mrs. Lennox firmly by the elbow.

When they arrived on Commercial Street with its busy traffic, he stopped and turned to her, only now allowing the tension to drain from him. "Are you all right?"

She brought a shaky hand to her cheek and gave a jerky laugh. "The question is, are you?"

Amazed that she could think of him, he glanced at the knife he still held upside down by the haft. "Remember, I'm armed now." He looked around him but seeing nowhere to dispose of the knife, he stuck it in his belt, under his coat. "I'll get rid of this when we're far from here."

"Yes, please do." Her voice sounded shaky.

He tipped her chin up with a fingertip, permitting himself to study her face more closely. "Let me take you somewhere for a cup of tea."

Her eyes met his. "No…I'm quite…all right. Let me recover a moment." She took a step back and he let her go immediately, wondering if he had overstepped his bounds. "Do you think the hansom is still waiting for us?"

"Yes, I'm sure of it. Come, if you're up to walking a block further. We should get away from here, at any rate."

"Oh, yes." She immediately began to move. He hurried to catch up with her and put his hand on her elbow once again. She felt fragile beneath his light grip. He thanked God that they'd escaped the ugly situation. If anything had happened to her—

It was only then he recollected he'd called her Alice. Would she remember? Would she be offended?

She turned to him with a rueful smile. "I do apologize for bringing you here. It was not my intention to put your life in danger. You must think us far more uncivilized than Americans if as soon as you arrive you are threatened by a bunch of drunk idlers."

"It wasn't your fault." He frowned at her. "I'm more concerned that you should ever come to parts like this on your own."

"We usually come in groups. And I don't make it a habit of going into the worst neighborhoods, but as you can see, sometimes it's only a matter of turning down one street corner."

His brow knit, thinking of her exposed to such dangers in the course of her work.

"I'm still marveling at how quickly you disabled that man."

He was more amazed at how quickly she'd discounted the risk to herself. "It wasn't so difficult. He was drunk, as well as emaciated by hunger. His grip was actually feeble. Any able man could have disarmed him."

"Still, he had the knife, and he was surrounded by so many."

"I've met more than my share of poor unfortunates consumed by drink and hopelessness. I've learned it's often the ringleader one must disable and the rest prove harmless."

She gave a disbelieving laugh. "Have you been in many such situations before?"

"Some. But the same tactics often hold true in business."

They arrived at the hansom and he helped her up. As they rode away from the area, she turned to him. "You called me Alice back there."

She had noted it. He tried to read her expression. "I'm sorry. I suppose I wasn't thinking clearly at that moment."

"There's nothing to apologize for." She looked down at her lap. "In a way it seems we've known each other for a very long time, although in truth, we've barely had a chance to become acquainted."

He felt a spurt of hope. "Perhaps we shall have an opportunity now."

She smiled, the sweet, angelic, beautiful smile he remembered. "I feel we could be friends again," she said slowly.

She had said "friend." Did that mean there was hope

of nothing more? He cleared his throat, hesitating. "Would you mind very much if I called you Alice…and you called me Nicholas—or Nick?" He waited, hardly realizing he held his breath.

"No." Her voice was whispery soft. "I'd like that."

"Very well…Alice."

The shy look in her eyes made her look seventeen again. "Pleased to renew the friendship, Nicholas."

He liked the sound of his name on her lips, even as he yearned for their friendship to deepen into something more. Had he waited too long? He found it a miracle—a god-send—that she was free after so many years. He didn't even care at the moment that her heart had been given to an idealistic young curate, if only there was the possibility of a future with her.

She was a woman like no other, and he was determined in that moment to make her his own.

"If you still have time, I'd like to show you some of the terrace houses we've built."

He blinked, disconcerted that her train of thought had taken a completely different turn. "I thought after our run-in, we could go someplace for a cup of tea."

She chuckled. "Oh, I'm quite recovered now, thank you. Do you have time for one more visit, this time as far as Bethnal Green?"

She sounded so hopeful he didn't have the heart to turn her down. In truth, he had many pressing things to do at his office that morning, but at the moment, all he wanted was to prolong his time at this woman's side.

"Yes, of course. That is why I came, after all." Not the whole truth, but that could wait. He already felt the years slip away and much territory regained since he'd first met her. At her answering smile, he sat back, content for the moment to steal glances at her soft profile while the hansom bumped along.

Alice. Even her name mouthed in silence was nectar, and he savored the syllables on his tongue.

Alice took Nicholas—even pronouncing the syllables to herself caused a blush to steal over her—to the working class suburb just to the northeast of London. She waved to a line of two-story row houses along one side of a quiet street.

"Our society was responsible for this construction. They are four-room dwellings as you can see, with plenty of windows for ventilation." They walked down the paved sidewalk as she pointed out the features. "We used the latest construction methods, including plenty of running water and toilets—radical fixtures according to many, but why should the poor live with things the rest of us are taking for granted?"

She waited for his reaction, but he said nothing, appearing to study the plain facades.

"You see they are well-kept."

He nodded. "No rubbish in the streets." Children played on the pavement. A few stopped their game to stare at them.

Alice walked up to the door of one dwelling and rang the bell. "Let me see if Mrs. Brown is at home. Then perhaps you can see the inside of one of these."

A red-cheeked woman in her twenties, holding a baby in her arms, answered the door. A smile broke out on her face at the sight of Alice. "Oh, Mrs. Lennox, what a pleasure."

"Hello, Mrs. Brown. I have brought an old friend from America. I wanted to show him some of the houses the Society has built. Would you mind very much showing us your home?"

The woman moved inside. "Oh, not at all, madam. Come right in. Would you like a cup o' tea?"

"No, thank you, we don't want to trouble you."

The woman led them from a small front parlor to the kitchen at the rear of the house, where a toddler sat playing on the floor. She showed them a narrow back garden where a scullery was located. Then they climbed a staircase to the upper floor and ducked their heads into two small bedrooms, one facing the street, one facing the back.

Nicholas turned to Mrs. Brown as they walked back down the stairs. "How many children do you have living here with you?"

"Four, sir." She smiled proudly. "The two oldest be at school now. They'll be along shortly."

He nodded.

Alice smiled and held her hand out to the woman. "Well, thank you ever so much, Mrs. Brown." She tweaked the baby's cheek. "How big she's grown since the last time I saw her."

Mrs. Brown beamed. "Yes, that she 'as."

"How is your husband?"

"Oh, Jerry's ever so well. He found work at the railroad just up the road."

"Well, let me know if you need anything."

Nicholas shook her hand at the door. "Thank you for showing us your home."

"That's quite all right. We be ever so grateful to Mrs. Lennox for 'avin' put such a good roof over our 'eads."

They walked back down the steps. Alice chanced a glance at Nicholas's profile. He appeared deep in thought. So long accustomed to thinking of him as Mr. Tennent, his first name made her feel like a schoolgirl again, as if she were breaking the rules somehow.

"You can see the difference, can you not? Although both neighborhoods hold families earning very low wages, anywhere from eighteen shillings a week to twenty or twenty-one. And that is when they can find work. Mr. Brown, for example, was unemployed when I first met Mrs. Brown."

"How did you meet her?"

"I was working at a mission run by Miss Endicott, the lady I mentioned to you earlier. They offer food and temporary shelter to unemployed people."

He glanced at her. "This woman seems to have had a profound influence on you."

She tilted her head. "In a sense. I believe, more, that she offered me an outlet to make myself useful after I was widowed and had come back to London to live. Julian was my true inspiration."

He said nothing.

"He had a servant's heart. He wasn't afraid to go into any quarter where there was a soul in need." She sighed, feeling the familiar sense of unworthiness whenever she thought of him. "It was probably on such a mission of mercy that he contracted the tuberculosis that eventually killed him."

"You are carrying on his work."

It was a statement not a question, she realized. She pondered it as they made their way down the sidewalk past the row of terrace houses. "In a sense. Being his helpmate opened my eyes to the futility of my father's way of life."

He raised his eyebrows in question.

"Living to make a profit."

"You find that futile?"

"It's all Father ever cared about." She smiled sadly. "He

suffered a heart attack a year ago and his work was over. There was nothing of it he could take with him. Julian's life, on the other hand, had a sense of eternal purpose."

"But your work would not go forward without the help of those whose purpose is to make a profit."

She pursed her lips. "I suppose you are right. But I'm glad I am not of their ranks."

He helped her back into the hansom and once he'd seated himself beside her, asked, "Where to now?"

Afraid she'd taken up too much of his time already, she laughed. "I imagine you have had enough of London neighborhoods. You can drop me off at the Society. Thank you for coming with me this morning." Once again his rescue filled her heart with relief and admiration. He had certainly come a long way from the secretary whom she'd taught tennis and horseback riding. The tables had somehow been reversed, and it was she who now felt in his debt.

"It was my pleasure. It was most informative. I was serious about making a donation. That's one of the reasons I've come back to London."

She looked down at her clasped hands, remembering his bravery. "You were very kind to those men back there. It was generous of you to give them something." She felt a deep sense of relief that he was not, after all, cut from the same mold as her father.

"It doesn't mean I believe in simply giving a handout. It's not the answer."

She nodded thoughtfully. "It depends on the individual case. In this case, it was generous of you, all the same."

When they reached her building, he accompanied her to the door. "Are you sure I can't take you somewhere for a cup of tea?"

She held out her hand with a smile. "Thank you, but no.

There are things I need to do, and I've taken too much of your time already. I truly am grateful that you came with me today. Perhaps you can visit us again some time."

"I should like that, Alice." The words were spoken quietly, but the way he was looking at her made her think he meant more than merely a visit to the charity.

She inclined her head a fraction, wondering whether to leave the invitation open-ended or make it specific.

"You used to do that."

She smiled. "What?"

"Tilt your head like that. Like a wood nymph deciding if it wants to flicker its golden wings and flitter away."

She laughed, delighting in the fanciful imagery. "I never suspected you of being poetic."

"I'm not. It is only you who brings me to any flights of fancy."

Now, the look was unmistakable. She glanced away and tried to keep her tone light. "I'm surprised you remember such a detail about me."

"I remember a lot of things."

"Do you still play tennis?" she asked to change the course of the conversation.

"I do."

Her eyes widened.

"You find that surprising?"

"I suppose I imagined you too busy with your business to leave you any time for trivial pursuits."

"I have been. But I found the time to continue with the game. Don't forget, you were the one to challenge me to look beyond the world of finance." He grinned, erasing the years between them. "I wanted to be able to hold my own with you on the tennis court and on the chess board." He looked sheepish. "Did you know I even paid for extra tennis lessons when I returned to London?"

Her eyes widened. "You did? And I never knew…" She laughed aloud, feeling lighthearted all of a sudden.

He joined in her laughter.

Then she said on the spur of the moment, "Would you like to come back out to Richmond on a weekend? We could have a match. Or, a re-match, should I say?" Her smile faded. "I'm sorry. Perhaps that place holds unpleasant memories for you."

"Not at all. Why should it?"

"Because of your riding accident…and my father."

"No, I have no bad memories of Richmond." His voice was quiet, his gaze warm.

"I'm glad. Let me know when you'd like to come out."

"Would this weekend be too soon?"

It was too soon. Once again, apprehension filled her. Things were moving too quickly. But she found herself saying, "Not at all. The weather is too hot to stay in London anyway. We can take the train out. I like to get out of the city for Austen's sake."

"You said he was frail."

She looked away and nodded.

"Very well. This weekend then."

"We can ride out Friday evening if you'd like," she told him. "I generally take the five o'clock train out of Victoria. I shall invite Miss Endicott as well. I'd love for you to meet her."

"Very well. I'll meet you at the station." Once again, the look in his brown eyes said more. But she chose to ignore it as the fancy of a sixteen-year-old girl who no longer existed.

Chapter Eight

Nick walked back to his office with a buoyant step. He'd had a remarkably good morning in the company of Alice.

His steps slowed, remembering their brush with danger in that rundown quarter. He didn't like to think of her involved in such hazardous work. He wondered over this new friend of hers—Miss Endicott—who seemed to hold such influence over her.

These questions revolving in his mind, he arrived at his new London headquarters. He'd arranged to have it purchased through his London agent before he'd even stepped foot back on his native soil. The imposing gray granite office building was a suitable testimony to his years of toil. It overlooked the Bank of England and the Stock Exchange in the heart of the financial district. His gaze traveled farther down Threadneedle Street. Only a few blocks away was the office of Shepard and Steward, where he'd been forced to leave so dishonorably fifteen years earlier.

A pity, he could no longer show Mr. Shepard what he'd lost in dismissing him. His ire rose anew at the thought of her father disinheriting Alice. How could a man with so special a daughter be so cold-hearted? And what of her brother? Hadn't he defended his sister's share of the business?

He turned slowly, glancing to the east, remembering again the encounter with the derelict man. Beyond the wealth represented by this financial district lay neighborhoods filled with men who'd been broken by adversity. Had the Lord sent him back to his homeland to do something with his wealth to help these men and women? Together with Alice to mitigate the circumstances of their lives?

Not one given to romantic notions, he believed in the blessings that came to those who worked hard. Nevertheless, he recognized his good fortune was also due to God's grace. Having achieved far above what he'd set out to, he wanted to put his money to good use in education and decent housing for those who were laboring the way his mother had.

His office's shiny brass plate winked at him: Tennent & Company, Ltd. He entered the building and let the door shut behind him, muting the traffic sounds and sunshine.

"Good afternoon, Mr. Tennent." Clerks greeted him as he walked past them and headed for the lift to his private office at the top.

His secretary, a young man who reminded him of himself so long ago, jumped up from his desk as soon as Nick entered the outer office. "Good afternoon, Mr. Tennent." He handed him a stack of papers. "I have the letters for you to sign. Mr. Paige stopped by and desires to make an appointment about the impending purchase of Bailey and Company."

Nick took the stack and began glancing through it. "Yes, arrange something for Thursday morning or afternoon. I may be leaving early on Friday."

"Yes, sir. Another appointment?"

"What?" He glanced up. "No, just leaving early for the weekend."

The clerk stared at him.

"What's the matter?"

"Oh, nothing, sir. I—just—you've never left early before. You're usually here later than most of us."

"Well, that is about to change." He carried the letters to his desk and picked up a fountain pen and began to sign the letters. He handed them back to the young man. "I want you to do something for me."

"Yes, sir." His secretary waited, the letters in his hand.

"I want you to find out everything you can about the firm Shepard & Steward, Ltd. Investments. I believe that is still the name of it. At least the name of Shepard will appear in it as the principal partner. Understood?"

The younger man gave a quick nod. "Very good, sir. I'll get on that right away."

"Assets, liabilities, the members of their board, you know the things I expect."

"Yes, sir."

"Dig deep. I want to know what they've invested in over the years."

The young man grinned, enjoying the painstaking work of investigation as much as seeing the accumulation of profits. Nick had chosen well.

When the secretary had closed the door softly behind him, Nick sat down at his desk chair and swiveled it around to stare through the slatted window blinds. The afternoon sun cast several buildings including the Bank of England in shadow. Beyond it rose the dome of St. Paul's Cathedral.

Nick's thoughts strayed from the sight to the things

Alice had told him—or not told him—but which he'd observed in the few hours he'd been in her company.

He stroked a finger against his lips. The dangerous encounter today had had one benefit. It had allowed him to take a step closer to Alice—she'd accepted his friendship. Yet, for all her gratitude, he sensed a reserve in her that went deeper than that natural to a lady toward a gentleman of scant acquaintance. Her strange words came back to him, stunning him as much now as they had when she'd uttered them. "No matter how unlovable I might feel." How could such a beautiful, accomplished woman with every material advantage feel unlovable? He would have given her his whole heart if he could have. Instead, a poor young clergyman had been the one privileged to show her love.

Dear God, why? He didn't miss the irony. He'd left, thinking himself too poor to offer Alice anything; yet, she'd chosen a man probably more destitute…almost as if rejecting everything her father's world stood for.

Alice had forsaken all wealth to follow her heart. Nick had never known that kind of love, except for his mother's to his father.

Would Alice hold his wealth against him now?

By early Friday evening, however, Nick reclined in a tub of steaming water and smiled to himself, like a man replete after a full banquet. Perhaps he oughtn't to have felt this way, but he couldn't help himself.

He'd enjoyed the train ride from London in the company of Alice and her son. Any trepidation he'd had over the militant Miss Endicott had quickly dissolved upon meeting the lady. She'd proved an elegant, charming woman in her fifties who was clearly fond of Alice.

After some debate over suitable gifts, Nick had brought Austen a boy's adventure book and Miss Endicott a box of chocolates. Undecided between a bouquet of flowers or a luxurious box of chocolate bonbons for Alice, he'd finally settled on a book for her as well.

"It's the latest Sherlock Holmes tale," he said as she removed the brown paper wrapping in the train compartment.

"The Sign of the Four." She read the title on the cover and smiled at him across the seat. "Thank you. I enjoyed the first Holmes mystery and I'm sure I shall this one, too."

Austen sat close to his mother in the corner of the compartment during the ride, clutching his raggedy stuffed rabbit closely to his side.

As soon as they arrived at the Richmond house— looking little changed from fifteen years ago—they had separated to their rooms until dinnertime. Nick was shown to a spacious bedroom on the first floor. The masculine-furnished room with its four-poster mahogany bed was quite a contrast from his cramped, hot room under the eaves during his first stay in the house.

Now, soaking in the hot, scented water of the tub, he devised a strategy to follow over the coming two days the way he did when approaching the purchase of a company.

During the train ride, he'd questioned Alice some more about her years away from London. She'd spoken little about the time immediately following his departure, but had been quite effusive about her years at the parsonage. In retrospect, Nick decided he had one sole advantage over the late curate. Nick was alive. No lifeless memory could compete in the long run with a living, breathing person.

His spirits lifted as he thought of the coming weekend.

He emerged from the tub and donned the evening clothes laid out by his valet.

He adjusted the gold cuff links in his starched white shirt as his valet tied his black bow tie. After helping him on with the jacket, the man gave his lapels a final smoothing down then stood back, giving Nick a full-length view of himself in the cheval glass.

Nick eyed himself critically. The black swallowtail coat and matching waistcoat fitted him well. His white shirt collar stood up stiffly around his neck. Would he pass muster before Alice? She who had grown up among the well-dressed?

Thanking his valet and giving him the evening off, Nick made his way downstairs. No one else was about as yet, so he wandered onto the terrace.

The evening air was a few degrees cooler than the heat of London. Nick glanced about him. The low table and comfortable sofa were still out here, in the same place they'd been when he and Alice had played that fateful game of chess. He could still remember the feel of her soft lips against his.

He sighed and went to lean his elbows on the wood balustrade. The tinkle of a fountain in the garden made a pleasant sound.

His thoughts drifted back to Alice. How would she view him now? Would she accept him fully into her circle? She had turned into the beautiful woman he'd envisioned. A wonderful mother as well. Unlike many women of her class who relegated their offspring to their nanny, she had seemed to enjoy her child's company.

He debated how soon he could express his feelings to Alice. Would she be ready to accept his suit? Would she ever be over her husband?

He had learned over the years to be patient, to bide his time. He knew how to keep his eyes on a company for many a year until the time came to approach the owner and make an offer that couldn't be refused. He also knew there were times when one had to be more aggressive and make a preemptive strike, buying out a company that in future could be unwelcome competition.

However, neither way seemed clear with Alice Lennox.

"May I join you out here, or do you prefer a few moments of solitude?"

Nick turned at the soft tones of Miss Endicott. Not Alice.

Hiding his disappointment, he gestured to the older lady. It wouldn't do to alienate Alice's friend and mentor. "Not at all. Please do."

Miss Endicott was a tall, slim woman, fashionably dressed in a soft gray evening dress. Her still-dark hair was coiled at the nape of her neck.

She stopped at the latticed balustrade and looked out at the quiet evening. "Refreshing after London, isn't it?"

"Yes."

They stood a few moments listening to the tinkle of cascading water and the chirp of crickets around them.

"Whenever I'm here, I wonder why I continue to live in London." A trace of humor underlay her quiet words.

"Why do you?"

"That is where my present interests lie."

He glanced sidelong at her. "You've influenced Mrs. Lennox in the direction of her interests as well."

"The Housing Society, you mean?" She considered. "Yes, perhaps to an extent, but she was already helping the needy long before. When she came back to London, after she was widowed, I suppose I thought it would help her to overcome her grief."

Had Alice been so grief-stricken at the loss of her husband? "Did you ever meet her husband?"

"No. I didn't know Alice until she returned to London four years ago." She looked down at her hands resting on the balustrade as if debating. "Alice seemed quite lost after Julian passed away, even though they both knew his death was imminent. He'd been ill off and on almost from the day she met him. But I think she kept denying it, even when he knew very well he wouldn't last long."

She gave a deep sigh before continuing. "When I first met her, she seemed a little like a child who doesn't understand why she's found herself alone again."

He looked sharply at her. "Again?"

Miss Endicott pursed her lips, musing. "I sometimes think of Alice as a little girl looking for a loved one…who's never quite been there for her."

Nick thought of Alice's lack of a mother and absent father. "She never found it at home."

There was understanding in her eyes. "No."

But hadn't she found it with Lennox? The thought was a bitter pill.

They remained silent a few more minutes. Then the older woman looked at him. "You know, you're the first gentleman Alice has invited out here to Richmond."

"Am I?" The calm words belied the impact of her words. He cleared his throat. "Was Julian—I mean, Mr. Lennox—never here?"

She gave a small laugh. "Oh, no. Mr. Shepard did not approve of an impoverished curate for his only daughter." She leaned her back against the balustrade and eyed him. "You must be very special."

He made a noncommittal sound, feeling once again that he had no advantage over the penniless cleric.

"It takes a great deal of drive to have succeeded in owning your own firm when you started out as a clerk."

He shrugged, unable to deny her appraisal or willing to accept any undue merit for his success. From what she'd said already, his wealth would be viewed as a liability in Alice's eyes. "A lot of work and the good sense to know when to take the opportunities God has given me are all the credit I can claim."

She nodded her head. "No false modesty. I like that."

"I have never learned the complexity of what passes for conversation in polite circles."

She laughed. "Nor have I. I like a person who knows his own mind and isn't afraid to speak it." She paused. "It almost makes me hazard to ask you what your intentions are toward Alice."

The two stared at one another in the gathering dusk.

He considered. If anyone's blessing were necessary, he calculated it would be this woman's. Before giving himself time to draw back, he gambled on forthrightness. "Alice is the only woman who has ever meant anything to me. I want to marry her."

She blinked. "I see. You don't mince words."

"You said you appreciated directness." He looked away from her and toward the fountain. "The fact that I know what I want doesn't mean I don't acknowledge certain— hurdles."

"Julian."

The name reverberated in Nick's mind like a thousand ripples pushing him away from his goal. "Mrs. Lennox seems to have loved her late husband very much."

"Yes."

He glanced sidelong at Miss Endicott. The tone wasn't wholly affirming.

"There is love, and there is—" Again, she hesitated.

"Worship?"

She turned her eyes on him, as if assessing him. "I didn't know Alice then. I can only conclude from what I've heard from her that she feels a deep gratitude to him."

The words arrested his attention. "What do you mean, exactly?"

"I gather from Alice herself—the little she speaks of her past before Julian—that she was very unhappy growing up. And then her father sent her away. I don't know the reason, but it seems almost as if she was banished." She shook her head, "At a time when most girls are planning their coming out."

Nick's hold on the balustrade had tightened at the mention of her exile. Would this be one more thing to come between Alice and himself?

"Alice was very young and impressionable when she met Julian. And lonely. She had never really known a father's love. When she met Julian, I don't know how much was love and how much was a desire to be loved." She gazed onto the gardens as if looking into the past. "Whereas her father was a man consumed by his drive for money, Julian had no interest in material gain, not for himself at least, only to help those in need." She sighed. "Julian was about as far as she could go from her father's world."

Her words confirmed what Nick had already feared.

She turned back to him, her voice becoming brisk. "I don't know how much Alice has told you about me. I believe in the rights of women."

He smiled slightly. "Alice mentioned a few things…"

"I just say this in order to tell you that I've done my utmost since her widowhood to encourage Alice to be her own person. She never really had a chance to explore who she was since she left home. That is one reason I've persuaded her to take charge of this charitable work. It gives her something of her own."

"I see." The picture Miss Endicott painted for him gave him much to think about. Her next words surprised him even more.

"I would hate to see her give that up in a second marriage."

He met her look squarely. "I have no interest in clipping her wings."

She nodded. "Only a person strong enough in his own identity can allow another the freedom to fulfill hers. Just don't go too fast with her, that's what I suppose I meant to say when I came out here."

Before he could think of how to reply, they both heard a sound at the opened French doors.

Alice stood silhouetted against the lamplight within. He drew in his breath at how lovely she looked. She had changed out of her travel outfit into a deep blue evening gown. Nick allowed his gaze to travel over her slim figure. Her hair was drawn up high atop her head, with soft wisps framing her nape and temples.

"Am I interrupting something?"

Miss Endicott chuckled. "Not at all. Come and join us, my dear."

She took a few steps onto the terrace. "Dinner will be served in a little bit." She turned to Nick with a smile. "I've left Austen with Nanny Grove. Thanks to you, his head is filled with thoughts of pirates and mutiny on the high seas and buried treasure. I hope they don't keep him awake too long."

Miss Endicott moved toward the door.

Alice reached out an arm. "Oh, please don't leave on my account, Macey."

"I'm going to fetch my shawl. I'll peek in on Austen." She glanced at Nick with a friendly look. "It was lovely chatting with you."

He bowed. "The pleasure was mutual."

After Macey left, Alice turned to Nick, feeling unaccountably shy. It was almost as if it was the first time she'd really been alone with him since the evening they'd met. Maybe it was the fact of the semi-darkness or that they were both dressed in evening clothes. There was enchantment in the twilight air.

His handsome elegance took her breath away. She turned away abruptly, determined to bring her thoughts under control. "It was so nice that you could come today, Nicholas." It still felt oddly intimate to be pronouncing his Christian name aloud.

"Thank you for inviting me."

Casting about for something to say, she motioned to the gardens. "Shall we walk a bit before dinner is announced? I can show you some of the grounds, though—" she gave a jerky laugh "—not much has changed since you were last here."

He fell into step beside her. "I had little chance to see the grounds when I came with your father."

She wondered what his memory of those few days was, but didn't ask, afraid to resurrect her own feelings of that time. "There is one new thing. Father decided a few years back to dig a pond. He wanted to stock it with fish, but I think only the goldfish survived. Would you like to see it?"

"Lead the way."

Their footsteps crunched over the small pebbles of the path. Soon they reached the willow-lined pond and Alice led him off the path onto the grassy perimeter of the pond. "I remember the summer Father hired a crew of workers to dig the pond and landscape the area around it." She sighed. "A pity he hardly enjoyed it once it was stocked with fish."

The plop of a frog from the edge into the water broke the stillness. They stopped as if by mutual consent. Nick turned to her. "Do you still have the tennis court?"

She smiled at him, relieved at the safe topic. "Oh, yes. I hope you are ready for that rematch."

His white teeth flashed in the gathering dusk. "Name the time and place."

"Tomorrow mid-morning?"

"I'll be ready." He stood so close she caught a whiff of his cologne, a sharp, fresh scent.

She took a step back. "Shall we return?"

"If you'd like."

She walked by him. He stood perfectly still until she had passed him, then followed silently in her wake.

She was relieved he didn't do anything to detain her. She compared his gentlemanly conduct with that of many of the gentlemen of her acquaintance, who were only too eager to "befriend" a lonely widow. She had grown adept at foiling all advances.

The thought of someone taking Julian's place had always filled her with repugnance. No one could be what he had been to her. Why then did she feel like the girl of sixteen drawn to her father's employee, an intense young man so wholly unlike Julian?

Nick walked outside again in the early morning before breakfast. He'd had trouble falling asleep the evening before, his thoughts troubled over Miss Endicott's words for a long time. He found it hard to reconcile the picture she painted of Alice with the poised and self-assured woman he'd seen thus far. What tormented him the most was what Miss Endicott had said about Alice's banishment. Had she had to pay an unreasonably high price for their innocent kiss?

Had he left her all alone to face her father's wrath?

Nick wanted to ask her what had happened when he'd left, but had already sensed a constraint in her since the evening they'd met again.

Without consciously thinking about it, he strolled along the same path Alice had led him the evening before and found himself back at the pond.

The early morning rays shot through the feathery willow fronds. Ripples in the dark surface attested to the presence of fish. He approached the edge of the water.

A sudden voice halted him.

"Now, you mustn't be afraid. Only babies are afraid."

Nick peered through the low branches of the willow tree to see Austen squatted by the edge of the pond. He had his stuffed animal in one hand and a toy sailboat in the other. He placed the boat into the water and then set the floppy rabbit atop it.

The animal wouldn't stay on and the boy fumbled to get it balanced on the narrow surface. "That's all right, Moppet, I've got you. No, you can't get off yet. Just a few minutes."

He let go and pushed the boat away from him. "There you go, Moppet, I told you you'd be all right. It's not so frightening anymore, is it?"

At that moment, the boat dipped a fraction to leeward and the rabbit plopped into the water. The boy gasped and reached his arm out. "Hold on, Moppet, I'll come for you."

But the rabbit drifted away, a few inches beyond Austen's reach.

Nick ducked under the willow boughs and reached his side. With a glance around, he spotted a broken stick. "Not to worry, we'll fish him out." He maneuvered the animal, which was beginning to sink, alongside the edge of the pond.

Austen immediately scooped up the soggy creature.

"A few hours in the sunshine and he'll be none the worse for wear," Nick said in reply to the boy's troubled look.

"Th—thank you," he whispered.

"Nothing to thank me for." Nick kept his tone casual, afraid the boy would run off. "Watch you don't let Moppet drip on you. Would you like me to carry him for you?"

The boy shook his head but heeded Nick's warning and held the animal farther out from his body.

Nick hunted around for a way to keep the conversation going. He was curious about Alice's son. "It's early to be out. Were you thinking of pirate ships this morning?"

Austen nodded.

Nick indicated the sailboat. "That would make a good pirate ship if you hoisted a skull and crossbones flag on it." He took the string up from the ground before the boat drifted off. As the boy watched him, he paid out more line until the boat was in the middle of the pond. "There's not enough of a breeze here, it's too sheltered by the trees.

What we could do after breakfast, perhaps, is take her down by the river. Would you like that?"

The boy nodded, more vigorously this time.

"How about some breakfast first then?"

Austen stood up. Nick brought the sailboat back into shore and lifted it out of the water. "Come along then. You put Moppet out to dry on the terrace and maybe he'll be ready to go with us after breakfast."

Austen skipped ahead of him. Nick watched the light blue sailor suit disappear around a bend and felt a pang. He could have had a son like that. Where had the years gone? All he'd known was work. He'd allowed little to sidetrack him from his goal. Well, he'd reached his goal and found it wasn't enough.

Macey served herself to some sausage from the sideboard and set down the silver tongs. "I like your gentleman."

Alice looked up from the array of breakfast dishes. "I beg your pardon?"

Her friend filled her plate with eggs and broiled tomatoes before replying. "I said I approve of your Mr. Tennent. He strikes me as a man who knows what he wants."

Alice felt an immediate dislike of Macey's description. It made Nick sound too much like her father. "Mr. Tennent isn't mine. I'm sure he'd be the first to tell you that. We met very briefly years ago, and I was so glad to see him again, to see that he'd achieved what he'd set out to do. I always felt badly that Father had been such a difficult employer."

Macey chuckled. "Excuse me, my dear, I didn't mean to imply that you had any but friendly interest in Mr. Tennent."

Even as Alice searched the older lady's expression for irony, she continued. "I was very impressed with him. I had a nice conversation with him before dinner, and of course, during. It was a very pleasant evening all in all." Macey shook her head. "It is hard to picture him from his humble origins."

"Yes, I'm still overwhelmed by what he has become. He told me once that his mother was a governess, so I'm sure she gave him a good foundation in learning and manners."

"Ah, that would explain it." Her friend seated herself at the table. "May I pour you a cup of tea?"

"Yes, please." Alice finished serving herself and joined Macey. "He wasn't with Father's firm very long." She looked down, fingering her knife. She'd never told the other woman about her friendship with Nicholas. "Father wasn't very fair to him when he had a riding accident." At the look of inquiry on the other woman's face, she nodded toward the window. "It happened right here at Richmond. It was really my fault." She proceeded to recount the horse-back riding incident to her.

"Goodness, my dear, it certainly wasn't your fault. You behaved very responsibly. Victor should have been horse-whipped for instigating such a thing."

"I agree." She shook her head bitterly. "Father wouldn't even send him away. Instead, he ended up firing Mr. Tennent when he couldn't perform his work." That wasn't the whole truth but she couldn't talk about the rest. It was too private and too painful a memory.

Macey set down her fork and knife and pondered. "The last time I saw Victor, he was at the Goodwins' house party right before the Derby. He was showing off his new wife as if she'd been one of the fillies."

"Yes, he's married now and has two children. He's been my solicitor since Julian passed away. Geoffrey recommended him to me, though my insignificant affairs are hardly worth his trouble."

Alice stirred her tea then blinked at the sight of Nicholas and Austen entering the room together, her son actually smiling up at the man. It gave her a pang. Julian should have been walking into breakfast with his son. She strove to keep her tone cheerful for Austen's sake. "Good morning, you two. Where have you been?"

"Mr. Tennent is going to take me to the river to help me sail my boat after breakfast." With those words, Austen walked over to the sideboard and began surveying the food, as if he'd said the most normal thing in the world.

With a quick look at Nicholas, Alice rose and handed her son a plate. "Is that so?"

Nicholas came over to them and picked up a plate of his own. "I met Austen at the pond this morning. Unfortunately, there was no breeze for him to sail his boat."

She drew her brows together. "Austen, dear, I've told you you mustn't go to the pond by yourself."

Austen hung his head. "I forgot, Mama."

Not wanting to scold him in front of others, she spooned some eggs onto his plate. "Well, I'm glad Mr. Tennent found you." She turned to Nicholas, grateful that he'd been there. "Thank you for taking care of my son. He doesn't realize how dangerous a large body of water can be."

"Doesn't he know how to swim?" he said in an offhand tone as he helped himself to the array of food.

She felt a prickle of defensiveness at the question. "No, he's only seven." She lifted her chin a notch. "I never learned myself."

"I'm amazed. You were so accomplished at all sorts of sports."

"I spent all my time away at school and there was no appropriate place. The river's current here is too swift."

"Of course. I didn't learn until I was an adult." Nicholas turned to Austen and winked. "Would you like to learn to swim? There's nothing more fun than swimming, not even sailing."

Austen stared up at Nicholas and slowly nodded his head. Alice noted how similar their shade of deep brown hair was and she felt a catch in her throat. Neither Julian's nor her hair color was as deep a brown. Austen had inherited his paternal grandmother's dark, rich sable shade.

"Good. This is the right time of year." He continued serving himself. "I remember how sumptuous your breakfast fare seemed to me the last time I came out here."

The words distracted her from the notion of how Nicholas proposed to teach Austen to swim. "Did it really?"

"Oh, yes, I'd never seen anything like it."

Macey offered Nicholas tea or coffee.

"Coffee, thank you. A custom I got used to in America."

Alice listened to them chatting, still surprised at how well her friend and Nicholas were getting along. She encouraged Austen to eat. At the moment he seemed too interested in listening to Nicholas. It was the first time she'd seen him interested in anyone besides herself and his nanny. She wondered how this man had succeeded in enthralling both her son and friend in such a short time. Macey was very particular in her acquaintances, shunning most of Alice's set, and Austen…Alice frowned, not liking to dwell on her son's shyness, which seemed extreme at times.

As they were finishing up their breakfast, Nicholas turned to her. "Do you think we could postpone our tennis match until after our sailing expedition?"

She smiled with an effort, realizing it was good for Austen to have a male friend. "Of course. Where are you two planning to go?"

"To the river. We can go to the boat landing."

Alice forced herself to relax. She knew she tended to be overly protective of Austen but he was all she had left. "There's a strong current at the river. Are you sure that's a good idea?"

"Oh, don't worry, I'll keep a close eye on Austen."

She felt torn. "It's just that I know how little boys are. You need to watch them all the time."

"Why don't you come along with us, then?"

She smiled gratefully. He seemed to understand. "Yes, I should like that."

"I promised Austen we'd go right after breakfast. Is that all right?"

"Yes. Why don't we meet at the front of the house in ten minutes?"

Nick handed the line to Austen. "Hold on tight, if you let her go, she might end up all the way in London."

The little boy looked at him with alarm and Nick couldn't stop from reaching out and ruffling his dark hair. With the exception of the darker shade, it was as straight and silky as his mother's.

"Don't worry, if that should happen, we'd send out a search party." He winked across Austen's head to Alice, who stood beside her son. She was looking particularly fetching in her wide hat with a gauzy yellow ribbon fluttering in the light breeze. She wore a light muslin dress in a matching shade of yellow and held a frilly parasol in one hand. "I assume you have some sort of launch here we can use on the river."

She motioned to the pair of flat-bottom boats tied up at the side of the landing. "Yes, these punts are ours."

"You see there? No cause to worry." He steadied Austen's hand on the line. "All right, bring her in a little. See that boat coming downstream? We don't want her to run into it."

A party of summer residents was rowing toward them, their laughter floating over the water.

Alice's hand came onto her son's shoulder. "I see the steamer coming. You must move back."

Nick turned in the direction she was indicating. The large steamship bringing passengers from London was churning the water far downstream. "It's coming on the other side. I think we'll be all right here."

"I don't know, it creates quite a wake as it passes," Alice murmured, worry in her tone.

"We'll move back then." Nick squatted down and helped Austen bring in his boat.

The noise of the paddlewheel grew. When the steamship passed by them, Nick waved and Austen followed suit. The young boy laughed when the passengers crowded along the deck waved back. Nick turned to him in surprise. It was the first time the boy had behaved so spontaneously.

"They don't know us! Why are they waving?"

"People like to wave at strangers when they pass them from a train or ship. Haven't you ever waved at people from a train window?"

He shook his head.

"Well, then next time you can do it."

When the steamer had passed and the water became quiet again, Austen let his sailboat back down into the water.

"Watch it, Austen," his mother cautioned as he bent far over the landing. "Don't lean so far out."

"It's all right, I've got him." Nick was crouched beside the boy.

Alice smiled at him ruefully. "I'm sorry. I just worry."

"It's natural, I suppose," Nick said.

"Do you think Moppet will be dry when we get back?"

Nick squeezed Austen's shoulder gently. "I don't know. He may need all afternoon after the dunking he took."

"Do you think we could put him on the boat next time?"

"I think we could tie him on. That way he'll be sure to stay on. He might get a little damp from the spray, but he can always dry off again in the sun."

Austen nodded and continued his focus on his sailboat.

Nick found himself enjoying the time as much as the boy. It had been eons since he'd played. He remembered sailing a boat fashioned out of old newspapers. Austen's was an expensive wooden boat, detailed down to the view inside the cabin of the pilot's seat. But the experience was the same, he realized. Pretending to be commanding a sailboat over the seas.

He glanced up at Alice, who was watching them. As their eyes met, he smiled. She returned the smile but then quickly glanced back at her son.

Nick reminded himself to go slowly with her. Like a butterfly ready to take flight, she seemed as unreachable as she had fifteen years ago.

Chapter Nine

Nick cut quite a dashing figure on the court. No longer the shabbily-garbed secretary, now he looked equally at home on the court in his light-colored flannels and white shirt as on the dance floor in his evening clothes.

Alice gripped her tennis racket in two hands, ready to sprint to either side of the lawn. The ball flew over the net, and she ran backward to the end of the court and reached it just in time to send it back. It forced Nicholas to sprint toward the net in time to volley it back.

The game had begun gently but soon heated up. Alice marveled at what a competent—and competitive—player Nicholas had become since his first lesson so many years ago. She was hard pressed to keep up with his powerful serve and was already panting with the effort of running back and forth across the grassy court in her long skirt.

Again the ball sped across the net, in a low, powerful thrust. She returned it with a backhand swing and watched in satisfaction at the nice low arc she'd achieved. Nick's racket connected with it and it bounced back. Alice rushed across the court.

She swung her racket, but wasn't in time to hit the ball. Nick's friendly voice came across the court. "Good try."

She shrugged and smiled. "I'm not defeated yet." She picked up the rubber ball and returned to the far end of the court. Swinging her arm overhand, she called out, "Thirty-forty," and sent the ball across the court.

It was a good serve. She watched as the ball skimmed just over the net to the other side of the court. Nicholas slammed it back across and once again Alice dashed to the net to volley it back.

Back and forth it went until she missed it again.

"Game," he called out.

She wiped her forehead with a hanky from her skirt pocket and approached the net. The two shook hands. "You've come a long way since that first game."

His grip was firm and warm and he returned her smile. "That first teacher of mine was very patient. I never forgot her words of advice."

She wrinkled her brow. "What words were those?"

"That exercising my body would aid my mind."

She laughed, surprised and gratified that he should remember the words of a schoolgirl. "Well, I am glad I told you something useful at any rate."

His smile faded. "You told me a lot of things I remember."

She felt her face flush and patted her handkerchief over her cheeks. "Would you like something cool to drink?"

"Yes, I could use something refreshing."

They walked off the court and took seats on the wrought-iron chairs under the shade of a tree. His white shirt was unbuttoned at the collar, exposing his tanned throat, and his sleeves rolled up. He looked more at ease than she'd ever seen him, like a man comfortable with himself. She poured them each a glass of cold lemonade which had been brought out to them.

He patted his own forehead with a handkerchief. His dark hair was damp against the edges of his skin. "Thank you," he said taking the glass she gave him.

She took a sip from her glass and gave a nervous sounding laugh. "I must say that you gentlemen have the advantage over us ladies in playing the game. You can run all you want over the court and not fear stumbling. We, on the other hand, have the encumbrance of our skirts."

"It's amazing you can run across the court at all. At least you are not so heavily clad as many women."

"Yes, I wear my skirt above the ankle." She found herself wondering how many women he had played tennis with. "Do you play tennis often in America?"

"Not as often as I'd like."

"Is there a club where you play?"

"Yes."

"Are there many members?"

"Yes, it's a popular club."

"Do many women play tennis in America?" There, she'd asked as directly as she could. It shouldn't have mattered, but it did.

"Oh, yes, women are very sporty in America. They've taken up tennis with a will even though the game is much newer there than here."

"Do they play well?"

He regarded her over the rim of his glass before setting it back down, and she wondered how transparent she was being. "As I said, their progress is hampered in large part by the heavy clothing they wear. I don't know how more don't expire of heat prostration. I rarely play mixed doubles, preferring to play with a few of my male acquaintances who are very competitive at the game." He glanced away. "It helps keep me on my toes."

She smiled, feeling more comfortable. "I noticed your—ahem—competitive streak."

His gaze flickered back to hers. "I admit, when I play I play to win. I don't see much point in it otherwise."

Her smile deepened. "There is the benefit of exercise."

"I know, yet what makes the game exciting for me is to win." He shrugged, looking away again, as if uncomfortable. "It may be a failing of mine to want to win. I don't play with those I consider inferior to me. It would give me no pleasure to beat someone who wasn't a worthy opponent. That's why there are only a few I bother to play with."

She laughed nervously. "If I'd known that, I wouldn't have been so bold to play against you."

His brown eyes met hers immediately. "That was different."

She cocked her head to one side. "How so?"

"You are a woman, for one thing, and well…you first introduced me to the game." His lips curled up at one end. "Besides, you are a formidable player, despite your long skirts."

"I don't know whether to be insulted or flattered." She removed her straw hat with the narrow round brim and fanned herself. "I must confess, I have made some concessions in my attire. Besides, my shorter skirt I—" she lowered her voice "—I refuse to wear a corset to play. But it's a deep, dark secret, for if anyone should know, I would be excluded from any respectable tennis club, including Wimbledon."

She could feel her skin coloring under his scrutiny but his tone was light when he replied. "Well, you may rest assured I shan't let it be known."

His steady gaze hadn't left her face and she wondered why she'd told him such a thing. Just like fifteen years before when she'd dared him to kiss her, he brought out something uninhibited in her. "Sometimes, I feel as if we had seen each other only yesterday."

"You at least haven't changed outwardly."

She found herself blushing again. "Thank you, sir. I know it is mere flattery, but a lady of my age appreciates such remarks all the same."

His dark eyes remained serious. "I only spoke the truth. You appear as young as you did at—what was it you told me so emphatically? 'Almost seventeen'?"

She laughed. "I was desperate to grow up back then."

They sat in companionable silence, sipping their drinks. She felt at more peace than she usually did in London. "I want to thank you for taking time with Austen."

"You needn't thank me for something that gives me pleasure."

"Not everyone—especially a man busy with his affairs—would take the time with a young boy, especially one as shy as Austen."

"Perhaps he just hasn't had the opportunity to be brought out of his shell."

She rubbed the sweat beads on her glass, feeling on guard once again. "His childhood must seem very different from yours."

He emptied his glass in one long swallow, during which Alice found her gaze riveted to the strong contours of his neck. He set his glass down. "It is, yet those differences are more superficial than anything." A faint smile crossed his lips. "Boys will be boys."

"Do you—" it was hard for her to formulate the thought "—think he is too…timid?"

He seemed to be evaluating her question and she was grateful for that, unlike her brother and other well-meaning gentlemen, who were quick to point out all they thought was wrong with Austen.

Just as Nick had years earlier, he seemed to take her concerns seriously. "He is timid, but then lots of boys are at that age. He just needs to gain confidence in himself and his abilities. In the right atmosphere, surrounded by the right people, he'll do that, in his own time and way."

She poured him another glass of lemonade, as she pondered his words. "Do you think he's surrounded by the right people? I'm afraid sometimes I want to shield him too much." She set the pitcher down, afraid to meet his gaze as she said the last.

"You're his mother, that's your prerogative. I think any boy would be privileged to have you as a mother."

Her eyes locked with his. There was something unmistakably tender in both his look and tone.

He cleared his throat. "I wanted to ask your permission, actually, about something concerning Austen."

"Yes?" Wariness tinged her voice and she had to force herself to relax.

"I was thinking of taking him on a treasure hunt. You know, since you were reading him the book about pirates."

She smiled in relief. "Oh, yes! What precisely would you do?"

"Well, I could draw up a map, using the property around

here and its landmarks. We could make a morning or afternoon of it. I'd bury a little chest somewhere."

"Oh, it sounds delightful. Perhaps we can walk into town after lunch and look for a chest and some treasure."

"Yes, I thought about that." He grinned ruefully. "I'll probably have to go by myself, however, since you need to stay and distract Austen."

She smiled. "Of course. I'd been meaning to ask you if you'd like to accompany me to church tomorrow morning."

He didn't hesitate. "Of course."

"Would you like to go the chapel you attended before?"

His glass stopped halfway to his mouth. "Have you ever been there?"

She shook her head. "No, but I remember how I wanted to visit with you. We never had the opportunity."

"No, we never did." He continued regarding her and she looked away, remembering the end of that day.

He set the glass back down with a clink. "We can go tomorrow if you still wish to. I don't mind accompanying you to your church. I attended a number of different churches in America and found that God's presence in them had more to do with me than with the different buildings I was in."

She stared at this man who had made such an impression in a few short days so long ago and now again was amazing her with his insights. How many things he must have done since she'd last seen him. He made her feel as if she'd done very few brave things in her life, except for marrying Julian. How had she ever broken away from convention?

Nick watched Austen's face from the moment he entered the breakfast room the next morning, wanting to see when the boy noticed the map set beside his plate.

Alice looked up from her place at the table. "Good morning, darling."

"Good morning, Mama." The little boy glanced from his mother to Nick. "Good morning, Mr. Tennent."

"Good morning, Austen. How did you sleep?"

Nick had to strain to hear his low tone as the boy looked down. "Fine, sir."

"Anymore dreams of pirates?"

The boy's dark eyes came up. "No, sir."

"Pity." Nick said nothing more, but picked up his knife and fork.

The little boy carried his stuffed rabbit with him to his chair. First he set down the animal to one side, then as he moved to push his chair out, his gaze stopped at the roll of paper held with a string.

Nick's gaze darted to Alice. She, too, was watching her son. As if sensing his focus, she looked at him, and he winked at her. She gave him a barely discernable smile, and the two went back to pretending they were in the middle of their breakfast.

"What time should we leave the house?" he asked Alice.

"I was told the service begins at half-past nine. We should be all right if we leave at a quarter past. The chapel is a short walk from here in Richmond."

Austen had taken up the worn looking paper, unfurled it and untied the string. He was studying the map intently now. When he looked at his mother, a frown marred his brow. "What's this?"

"What's what, dearie?" His mother looked up from her plate.

He waved the paper. "This. It looks like a—map."

Alice reached out her hand. "Let me see it, Austen dear."

The boy brought the paper over to his mother.

She held it in her two hands and studied it, her coppery brown head bent over it, close to Austen's deep brown locks. "Hmm. It looks to me like—" she paused dramatically "—a treasure map."

Austen's eyes widened. "A treasure map!"

A sense of pleasure pervaded Nick at the thought that he had brought about the boy's wonder. The feeling left him bemused. He was used to dealing with business transactions in the hundreds of thousands of dollars, yet he was as anxious as a schoolboy to see how Austen would react. Is this what fatherhood was like?

Alice met Nick's gaze. "Why don't you take a look, Nicholas, and see if my guess is correct?"

"Certainly." He took the paper, which he had creased repeatedly to make it appear soft and worn looking, and spread it out on the table. He'd spent part of last evening with pen and ink drawing a detailed plan of the grounds around the house after having spent most of the afternoon looking for a good hiding place for the chest he'd purchased. After poring over it for a few minutes, he looked back up at Austen and then at Alice. "I think your mother is right."

Austen's dark eyes grew rounder. Then his mouth split open in a wide grin. "A treasure map! Do you really think so?"

He nodded. "It certainly appears to be. See the black X here?" He pointed with his forefinger. "I would say pirates usually mark the location of their treasure in that fashion, wouldn't you say so?" He looked to Alice.

"Oh, yes, I have heard it so. In fact, in all the pirate stories I've ever read, it's been that way. X marks the spot."

The boy's head was bent over the paper. "And look, this is our pond."

He followed Austen's forefinger. "Yes, you're right. The willow trees are surrounding it."

"Do you think this is our house?" His little finger pointed at another object.

"Well, it certainly looks like this house."

Now Austen looked from one adult to the other. "This map means there's a treasure buried near our house!"

Austen's large brown eyes stared up at him, enthralled by something it had taken Nick a moment to think of and only a few hours to put into place. He could see Austen wanted to ask him something but held back. He decided to make it easier for him. "Would you like us to go on a treasure hunt together?"

Austen turned to his mother and at her nod he turned his eyes back to Nick and nodded his head. "Yes, please." The words came out in a whisper.

"But first we must go to church," Alice told him.

"But we can go immediately after church," Nick said with a wink.

Austen gave him a big-toothed smile, revealing one adult tooth that had grown in and another which was only halfway in. "All right."

"Now, come and finish your breakfast," said Alice. "We don't want to be late."

Nick rolled the map back up and handed it to Austen. "Here you go, you might want to study it a bit more while you eat breakfast."

He took the map and continued looking at it as he walked slowly back to his place.

Nick sipped his coffee, content to watch Austen flatten the map under his mug of milk and his napkin ring.

"Austen, dear, finish your porridge."

The boy obediently took a spoonful, his eyes still fixed on the map. Nick smiled, unexpectedly looking forward to the afternoon's treasure hunt.

Nick enjoyed the service at the chapel. He was gratified that Alice had suggested going to his church.

He glanced at Alice over Austen, who walked between them. The three of them could have been a family. Maybe, soon they would be. He found himself wondering if Alice would ever want more children of her own.

"When can we go on the treasure hunt, Mr. Tennent?" Austen looked up at him under the brim of his straw hat.

Alice answered for him. "Right after lunch, sweetheart."

"Are we going to eat right away?"

She smiled. "Yes, I imagine so. Church has a way of making people hungry."

As they approached the iron gates at the bottom of the drive, Nick noticed a carriage pulled up in front of the brick mansion. Alice's footsteps slowed. "That looks like my brother's carriage. He and his wife sometimes come here for the weekend although I didn't expect them on a Sunday."

She quickened her step slightly and walked up the gravel drive.

Nick wasn't sure how he felt about seeing more of Alice's family. He'd seen Geoffrey only a handful of times at her father's office, but had never been formally introduced. He doubted the man remembered him.

When they entered the house, they heard voices immediately, coming from the rear.

"It sounds like they're on the terrace. Come, Austen, let's say hello to Uncle Geoffrey and Aunt Wilma." Alice took the boy's hand when he seemed to hang back.

Two couples stood on the wide porch, drinks in hand, talking and laughing. Nick recognized Geoffrey Shepard immediately, although the man had grown stouter and his light brown hair was gray at the sideburns. Nick stopped abruptly in the doorway when his eyes fell on the other man.

Victor.

The man stood as cool and self-assured as he had fifteen years ago when he'd played such a dirty trick on Nick.

Nick wasn't sure what he was feeling at the sight of the man who'd ultimately precipitated the course of action that had taken Nick away from England and across the Atlantic for so many years.

Victor's attention had gone from Alice to himself, the careless smiling fading, replaced with an insolent look which appraised Nick from top to bottom.

Alice leaned up and gave her brother a kiss on the cheek. "Geoff! I didn't expect to see you here this weekend."

"Hello, Allie." Her brother returned the quick embrace in a perfunctory manner. "That's because I didn't expect to be here, but Wilma was complaining of the heat and we decided to head out for the day."

One of the ladies sauntered closer. "And then Vic and I decided to tag along and make it a party. But we didn't know you had guests of your own." Her dark eyes swept over Nick and came back up to look boldly into his eyes.

"Oh." Alice's voice slowed as she contemplated the two of them. "I suppose we had the same idea." She turned back to her brother, her voice assuming its customary poise. "Geoffrey, I don't know if you remember Mr. Nicholas Tennent. He used to work in Father's firm."

Shepard lifted his prominent chin a notch and scrutinized Nick. "No, can't say that I do." He took a step forward and held out his hand. "Geoffrey Shepard, pleased to meet you. In what capacity did you work?"

Nick returned his look with a level stare. "I was your father's secretary for a few weeks."

The man paused for a fraction before releasing Nick's hand. "I see." As he turned away from him, he pursed his full lips. "Tennent, Tennent, the name sounds vaguely familiar."

Victor chuckled, approaching them. "You've probably heard my story of how Tennent here thought he could ride and took your old horse Duke out. Turns out it was the first time he'd ever sat on a saddle!"

The group erupted in laughter. Nick clenched a hand, restraining his inclination to wipe the smug smile off Victor's clean-shaven face. His glance flickered to Alice to see if she, too, remembered the account that way. Her eyes met his and he saw with relief that she was the only other one who had not joined in the laughter. Instead her blue eyes looked pained—and seemed to be entreating him.

He turned back to Victor Carlisle. His erstwhile rival was no longer a youth but had matured into a good-looking man in his mid-thirties, by Nick's calculation. His black hair was raked back from a high forehead and his gray-blue eyes challenged Nick to dispute the account.

"You were the one?" Shepard's tone held amazed disbelief. "Well, I never... At any rate, it looks like you survived." He took a sip of his drink. "Actually, I don't believe that's where I heard your name. You haven't any connection to Tennent & Company, do you? A distant family member?"

"I own the firm."

Shepard drew his thick eyebrows together, eyeing him

sharply. "You don't say." He shook his head. "Funny I've never run into you before."

Alice stepped next to Nick. "That is because Mr. Tennent has been residing in America. He's only recently returned."

"That explains it. I've heard a few things about your company."

"All naughty, I hope." The lady who had been watching Nick the whole time moved a step closer and smiled at him.

"This is Victor's wife, Cordelia," said Alice quietly.

Nick shook hands with her. Victor's wife held his hand a moment longer than was polite and gave him a coy smile. "You must tell me more about that horse ride." She glanced at her husband who was refilling his glass. "I'm sure there's more to the story than Vic is telling us."

He removed his hand from hers. "It happened so long ago, I hardly remember the particulars."

Alice touched him lightly on the elbow. "And this is Geoffrey's wife, Wilma." He turned with relief to the nondescript, prematurely stout woman with a haughty expression in her light blue eyes.

Mrs. Carlisle sidled back up to him. "If you've been with Alice, I assume you've been to church and must be parched. What will you have to drink?" She waved her glass in front of him. "Some champagne as the rest of us are drinking?"

"Thank you, no. I believe I'll wait for lunch."

Alice smiled at them, although her manner seemed unnaturally subdued. "We were just going in to luncheon. We have some plans for the afternoon." She looked toward Austen and smiled.

"Hello there, Austen." Victor went over to him and patted him on the head. "Cat got your tongue?"

The boy moved his head away from Victor's hand.

Alice put an arm around her son and propelled him toward Shepard. "Say hello to your uncle and aunt."

Austen did as his mother instructed, holding out his hand like a little gentleman.

Miss Endicott arrived just then and the company moved into the dining room. Nick noticed that Alice allowed Austen to remain with them at the table.

The group exhibited the high spirits due to drink and hardly included Nick in the conversation. Miss Endicott sat beside him and addressed him from time to time, but he found he preferred to observe Alice in this milieu. He'd made it a habit over the years to assess the terrain before making a move. It usually worked as well in business as in the social arena.

By the time luncheon was over, however, he'd drawn his conclusions. They were no different than most of what passed for society in San Francisco. Wealthy husbands bored with their own wives' society and wives who enjoyed spending their husbands' money and whose conversation consisted of empty-headed gossip and the planning of amusements.

He'd also had enough of observing Victor singling Alice out, while his wife kept Nick in her sights.

Austen had spent most of the luncheon hour playing with his food. Nick felt sorry for the boy and as soon as they had risen, he walked over to him. "All ready for the hunt?"

The boy nodded vigorously and went to tug on his mother's hand.

"Just a moment, sweetling."

Victor, noticing, asked with a smile, "Where do you want your mama to take you?"

The little boy looked down at his feet. "Some place."

"You must speak up, little fellow, if you want to be heard." His taunting chuckle gave Nick another desire to slug him.

Alice came to the boy's rescue. "Oh, it's just a little outing the three of us had planned."

Victor forgot the boy as he turned to Alice. "Oh, what a shame. I really was hoping to see you this afternoon."

"Oh?"

All mockery left his features and he said in a serious tone. "I needed to talk to you about something."

"Oh, what?"

"Well, it's private. As your solicitor."

She frowned. "Can't it wait until tomorrow? I can come by your office in the morning."

Nick strained to hear their words. What did Vic need to talk to her about?

He shook his head. "I'm afraid I'm all tied up tomorrow."

Her glance went from Austen to Nick and back to Victor as if helpless to know what to do. "In that case…" She turned to Austen. "Perhaps you can wait a moment, darling. Mama must see Mr. Carlisle for a few minutes."

Nick had had enough. Couldn't she see the man was deliberately putting her in a bind? "Why don't I take Austen along with me this afternoon? You go on with your business and Austen and I will have our adventure."

She bit her lip, again looking at her son. "I so wanted to go with you."

Nick cleared his throat. "It's all right. Come along, Austen. We'll have a grand time."

He was rewarded by Austen's wide smile.

Nick glanced at Alice. "We'll be fine."

She looked torn. "If you're sure…"

He held out his hand to Austen. "We'd best be going. We don't want anyone else to find it, do we?"

At the boy's look of alarm, he added, "You still have the map?"

The boy patted the side pocket of his sailor shirt and nodded.

"Good. You never know who might want to steal it. Come along."

Austen put his warm hand in Nick's. He enfolded it in his own, feeling the vulnerability in the small fingers that wrapped themselves around his. "We'll be back later this afternoon."

"Very well."

He tried to give her a reassuring smile, but he was feeling none too happy himself. The afternoon he'd planned with such care and thought had just been altered in the space of a few seconds. His mouth firmed in a grim line. By the same man who'd interfered with his life in such a malicious way fifteen years ago.

Taking hold of the boy's hand, he said, "Come along, treasure awaits." With more confidence in his tone than he felt, he left the house.

Once on the back lawn, he turned to Austen. "Let me see the map." He unfurled it and pretended to study it. "See, this is where we are. Now, if I'm reading this correctly, we must head south from this point…"

He had no great confidence in himself to entertain a shy, seven-year-old boy for the time it would take to find the buried treasure. He'd deliberately made the hunt challenging, even going off the property, because he'd wanted this to be a whole afternoon outing for the three of them.

Well, it was not to be. He'd have to swallow his disappointment and hope for a quiet evening with Alice when he returned. By then her brother and his guests should have tired of the country.

A burst of laughter from the dining room threw that hope to the wind.

Chapter Ten

Alice turned around when she heard footsteps, but it was only a servant coming to light the lamps in the drawing room. Where could Nick and Austen be?

"I'm sure they'll be along soon."

She turned on the sofa to Macey's soft tone beside her. "I know." She had thought Nick would be gone an hour, two at most, and then come marching triumphantly back with Austen holding a treasure in his hands.

But it had been—she glanced at the glass-domed clock on mantelpiece—five hours. What kind of treasure hunt had Nicholas devised for a seven-year-old that lasted this long? What could he have been thinking? Of course, he didn't have children of his own and might well forget that Austen would need to come home and have his supper on time. She tapped her foot and tried to contain her worry.

She pictured Austen exhausted, hungry, wanting his mother…

"They've no doubt forgotten the time."

She tried to smile at Macey but instead felt resentment grow within her. What kind of responsible adult forgot about the time when he was with a child—someone else's child at that?

"I say, Alice, how did you pick up with Father's secretary after all these years?" Geoff came over to sit beside her on the other side of the sofa, a champagne glass in hand. "I can scarcely remember the chap, but I hear he's making some noise in the city these days."

She turned her attention to him, glad for anything to distract her. "I met him at the gala I hosted last week. You were there."

"Yes, Wilma and I stopped in for a few minutes but I don't recall seeing Tennent. What was he doing there? Is he also taking the London social scene by storm the way he is the financial world?"

She glanced at her brother in surprise. "What do you mean?"

At that moment Victor and his wife came in, dressed for dinner.

Her brother swirled the bubbly golden liquid around in his wide, shallow glass. "I hear he's buying up companies right and left. What brought him to the gala?"

"He was interested in the charity work the Society is doing."

Geoff nodded and took a sip of his drink. "That would figure."

Before she could ask what he meant with the remark, Victor, helping himself to a glass of champagne from a tray, wandered over. "Discussing the prodigal returned?" He shook his head then regarded his glass as if pondering. "No, that wouldn't be quite accurate. The penniless made good?" Snide laughter followed. "Careful, Alice, I would watch my step with that one."

She started at the sound of footsteps at the door, but it was only the servant again, this time to wind the clock. As he turned to leave the room, she signaled to him. "Excuse me, William, but has Mr. Tennent returned with Austen?"

"No, madam, not to my knowledge."

"Please let me know as soon as they do."

Victor glanced down at her, a knowing smile on his lips. "Getting worried, are you?"

She looked down and arranged the folds of her skirt to avoid his interrogation. "Not at all. It's just, well, it is almost dinner time."

Geoff grunted at her side. "I know that look of yours. You fuss overmuch over Austen. The best thing for the little chap is to be sent off to school. It'll make a man of him."

She sighed. "Please, Geoff, I've told you before—"

"And I've told you before that if you don't send him off to school soon, he'll become a milk-sop holding on to your skirts until he's twenty-one. The little fellow hardly lets you out of his sight when you're in the room and he's scared of his own shadow. I've never heard him speak above a whisper."

Victor flopped down on a nearby armchair. "If you haven't persuaded her yet to let go of the apron strings, you're not going to do it this evening." He stretched his legs out before him and took a sip of his glass.

She pressed her lips together, still annoyed with him for delaying her on a silly matter that could have easily waited until they had returned to London. By the time she'd left the library, Nick and Austen had been long gone.

Mirroring her thoughts, Victor said, "I do think they should have been back by now. I wonder where Tennent has absconded with your son…" He glanced sidelong at her. "What do you know of this fellow, anyway? Appeared out of the blue from America and seems to have made himself cozy with you almost immediately."

Alice sat up. "Victor! How dare you say such a thing!"

He tilted his glass toward her. "For someone who worries about her only son so much, you were awfully willing to allow him to go off all afternoon with a stranger."

She felt her cheeks burn. "And whose fault is it that I was unable to accompany them?"

Geoff patted her hand. "Come now. It's too late now, though I do think Vic has a point." He shook his head. "One hears things in the city, don't we, Vic?"

Alice looked from Victor to her brother. Geoff didn't tend to blow things out of proportion. "Tell me what you heard."

Geoff pursed his lips as if deciding how much to say. It annoyed her that he still treated her like a baby sister when she was a full-grown woman of thirty-one. "He's said to be a Yankee shark." At her look of confusion, he added, "Swallows up companies right and left." He nodded at Victor. "He'll confirm it."

Victor set his glass down on the table in front of them and folded his hands in his solicitor's manner, all mockery wiped off his face. "In the few months he's been in the city, he's begun to wield a lot of clout. I represent companies. As soon as any show a sign of weakness, it's as if these investment companies are on the lookout. They come in and make an offer. They buy up shares and before he knows it, the owner has no more control." He gave a contemptuous laugh. "Next he'll be marrying a duchess or countess like any Yankee tuft hunter."

Geoff sniffed. "He may have been born a Brit but he's as crass as any American. And far more cunning. I wouldn't have anything to do with him if I were you."

Alice folded her hands in her lap, revealing nothing of the disquiet the words caused her. "I'm sure you're exaggerating."

He shrugged. "Ask anyone. They'll tell you Tennent & Company gets wealthy on the misfortune of others."

Geoff snorted into his glass. "The worst part is how he throws his money around to charities, like a typical Yankee, putting on that front of humanity when all along he is nothing but a greedy capitalist."

Her hands tightened. It couldn't be. Nicholas seemed too fine a man to stoop to such things.

A childish voice came wafting through the opened doors to the terrace. "Do you think it had been there very long?"

Forgetting all else, she jumped to her feet, hearing Austen's childish voice, followed by Nicholas's lower reply. Hurrying to the door, she saw them stepping onto the terrace.

Her son carried a wooden treasure chest against his chest. Alice rushed outside and knelt in front of him, her arms reaching out. "My darling, wherever have you been?" With an effort she kept her voice calm.

Austen held up the chest, a large grin splitting his face. Nicholas's hand rested lightly on his head. "Look what I found, Mama!" He looked up at Nicholas. "Didn't I find it all by myself, Mr. Tennent?"

Nicholas winked at Austen before turning to Alice with a smile, which she found she couldn't return at that moment. "You certainly did," he replied to Austen, his eyes still on Alice. Didn't he know the anguish he'd put her through?

"Look what's inside, Mama." Austen stepped away from her and knelt on the floor before the wooden chest. He dug into his pocket and pulled out a large key. "We had to find the key first. It was buried under a tree." He stuck the key in the lock and lifted the lid. Inside lay a pile of jewels—glass and paste that Nick had procured at a shop in the village the day before. "Aren't they beautiful?" He smiled proudly at her.

She touched a strand of pearls. "Yes, dear, they are beautiful. But, dear, you were gone so long." She smoothed back the hair from this forehead and picked a dried leaf from his hair. "Goodness, look at you. Your face is smudged with dirt and—" Her glance traveled down the length of him.

His short pants were streaked with dried mud, his stockings had fallen, showing red scratches on his thin legs. "Where on earth have you been?"

Nicholas cleared his throat. "We ran into some rough country, eh, Austen?"

She frowned up at him. "Indeed? Wherever did you two go?"

"Mama, we went up to Richmond Park, we had to go through a forest, and we had to ford a stream, and then we had to climb a tree. There was another clue there—"

Nicholas had taken him off the property! Alice stood and took Austen by a hand, keeping her voice steady with an effort. "You can tell me all about it, but let's get you upstairs and cleaned up. Nanny Grove will be frightened when she gets a look at you."

For the first time, Austen hung back from her outstretched hand. "But, Mama, I want to stay with Mr. Tennent."

Nick touched him on the shoulder. "Run along with your mama. I'll come up and say good night to you if you'd like." He lifted an inquiring brow toward Alice. "Perhaps read you a story?"

She turned away from him without answering. Austen beamed up at him. "Yes, I should like that very much. May he, Mama?"

"We'll see." She tugged on his hand once more. "But we'll have no story tonight if you don't wash up and have supper first."

She walked back into the house, not sparing Nick a parting glance. Her brother's words came back to her. How much did she really know about Nicholas? How could she be so gullible to think he'd be the same man she'd met fifteen years ago? She'd scarcely known him then, and yet she'd built her dreams on him.

She was no longer that lovesick girl. Her fingers tightened on Austen's hand. Her son was too precious to her to trust to anyone but herself.

Austen walked alongside Alice, carrying his treasure chest under his arm. At the door of the drawing room, she couldn't help one last look back. She regretted the impulse when she saw Cordelia sauntering up to Nicholas, two glasses in her hand.

Cordelia was known for her flirtations. Was Nicholas a womanizer as well? Was that why he hadn't ever married? Alice turned away from the sight, feeling sick inside.

"Mama, you should have seen where the treasure was buried. It was under some tall reeds. We had to dig with our hands and bits of sticks and stones."

She lifted the hand tucked into hers. "Goodness, your nails are filthy." She frowned. "Didn't you get hungry all day? You missed teatime."

"Oh, Mr. Tennent brought along some biscuits. He had them tied up in a handkerchief—the way real explorers carried their food, he told me—and a flask of water. Did you know in the desert they look for 'oases'? Those are places where's there's a little lake and usually date palms. He said that's what we'd snack on if we'd been in the desert—"

In the moments that followed, she heard "Mr. Tennent said this" and "Mr. Tennent did that" countless times as Austen continued telling her about their afternoon together. Alice listened, injecting the appropriate sounds of wonder at intervals as she helped him strip off his clothes and sponge the dirt from his body. Moments passed before she realized the anguish in her heart. She never remembered her little boy showing such enthusiasm for life. And she hadn't been there for his most exciting day.

Why did it have to be a near-stranger who'd enjoyed it and not his own father? Why hadn't she ever thought to plan such an outing for her son herself?

Austen stuck his head through the neck of his nightshirt and poked his hands through the sleeves. "Mr. Tennent told me ever so many stories of when he was a boy. Did you know he had a little brother and they did everything together?"

"Yes, I knew…" She remembered the day she'd asked him all about his family. The day she'd demanded a kiss from him. Shame filled her now at her brazen behavior.

She combed back her son's damp hair, disquiet filling her at how in only one afternoon, this man had succeeded in winning over her son so completely. Would Nicholas Tennent succeed in displacing Austen's father from her son's tenuous memory?

Austen crouched down and retrieved his treasure chest. "I wish I had a little brother like that."

"Darling, it's a bit dirty. I don't think you should take it with you to bed."

He brought it to his table instead. Alice had dismissed Nanny Grove after she'd brought up his supper tray, preferring to do things herself this evening. "Now, come eat up your porridge and drink your milk."

He bent his head and said grace then picked up his spoon. "Mr. Tennent's mama used to give him a cold potato she'd baked for him the night before, and he'd put it in his pocket the next morning to take with him to the mill." Austen's dark brown eyes stared up into hers. "When he was seven, he had to go out to work." His tone was solemn.

"Did he indeed?" How much had he resembled her little boy at that age? She realized with a pang that in coloring—even in slimness—Nicholas could have looked a lot like Austen at his age. She searched for similarities in her son to his father. But his face resembled her own more from his little pointed chin to his slim nose.

"He'd eat his potato on the way to the mill. That's where he worked. There were big machines there that made loud noises. He said at first they scared him. They were always moving the way he imagined the octopuses in the ocean would move about in the stories his mother read to him. Only on Sundays were they still."

Touched by the stories, she had to resist the urge to soften toward Nicholas. "Now, eat your supper."

He took a sip of milk. "His mama used to read him bedtime stories at night just like you do, Mama, and he heard all about jungle explorers. She didn't have many books, though, but he said she remembered ever so many stories and would tell them out of her head. He says he thinks she made lots of them up. Did you ever make up stories?"

She glanced at the row of beautiful books that ranged her son's bookshelf. "No, I guess I don't need to."

"We caught a frog at the pond today."

"Goodness, you seem to have done a lot of things today." She looked back down at the trousers. "I shall have to mend these."

His gaze followed hers. "That happened when I slid down the tree. Mr. Tennent said we had to go and have a lookout, to make sure none of the pirates were following us.

"He showed me how to catch the frog. We had to sit ever so quietly for the longest time at the edge of the pond. I got tired sitting there, but then a frog came hopping to sit on a rock near us, and Mr. Tennent swung his hands out like this—"

"Careful with your glass—"

She caught his glass before it went over. Austen resumed demonstrating, cupping his hands around a make-believe frog. "He held him like so and showed him to me. I wanted to bring him home."

"Where is the frog now?" She glanced at the treasure box nervously.

"Mr. Tennent made me let it go after a bit. But I got to hold it." He sighed and took another sip. "I wanted to show it to you, but Mr. Tennent said the frog probably had his own family to go home to."

"Yes, indeed." Grateful at least for that, Alice sat back. "All finished?"

"Almost." He was quiet, and she was glad to see he ate with relish. Most nights he picked at his food. She wondered what he was thinking—reliving his adventures with Nicholas? She felt more disappointed than ever that she had not been along—even a little jealous, she had to admit. But she couldn't ignore the fun her son had had in a man's company.

How could she reconcile the two images of Nicholas Tennent she'd received this evening?

Her experience with her father had seared her for life against men whose sole ambition was to gain wealth. She sighed, focusing on her young son once again. "Would you like to go away to school, like your cousins?"

He stared at her, his bowl tilted toward him, before shaking his head. "Mr. Tennent never went away to school. But he did go to Sunday school every Sunday."

She stood. "All right, let's brush your teeth and you can pick out a storybook."

"I thought you said Mr. Tennent could tell me a story tonight?"

She bit her lip. "Very well. But he needs to eat his dinner, too."

"Can he come up afterward and say good night to me?"

"Very well." She tucked her son into bed and bent down to kiss his forehead. "And perhaps he can tell you a short story out of his head, the way his mama used to tell him."

He smiled up at her. "I should like that."

She pulled over a stool and picked up his book. "If you don't mind your mama's storytelling, I shall read a little bit from the book Mr. Tennent gave you and then go down to my guests."

Satisfied with the arrangement, he settled back against the pillows and waited for her to begin.

Nick was aware the moment Alice reentered the drawing room. After changing for dinner he'd rejoined the company on the porch and waited for her, wondering if he had imagined the displeasure in her expression and tone when he'd returned so late with Austen. He needed to explain how time had gotten away from them.

"Well, here is our hostess at last," murmured Cordelia, who hadn't moved from his side since he'd reentered. "Playing at nanny again, Alice, darling?"

Alice glanced her way, her eyes skimming past Nick's.

As usual, Alice looked beautiful in a pale green gown of shimmering satin. She shook her head at the servant's tray and ignored Mrs. Carlisle's remark. "I'm sorry I'm late. Shall we go into dinner?"

Miss Endicott rose from the settee. "Yes, dear, we were just waiting for you." She turned to Nick. "Come, Mr. Tennent, would you like to escort an old lady to the table?"

Disappointed not to be able to escort Alice, he offered Miss Endicott his arm with good grace. "I shall be honored to do so, although I must take exception to your calling yourself an old woman. You are nowhere near that."

She chuckled as they walked toward the dining room. "Thank you. My, I haven't seen Austen looking so happy since I've known him."

Noticing Alice's sharp glance, he shrugged off the remark. "I just took him to do the kinds of things little boys like to do."

She smiled. "You both looked a little the worse for wear when you came in. I hope you had as enjoyable a day as Austen seems to."

His lips crooked upward. "Indeed I did. I haven't had the chance to be a little boy myself in many years."

He watched Alice lead the way into the dining room and then stand in the background as the guests seated themselves. Assuming she would sit at the foot of the table, he made his way there, but instead, Mrs. Shepard took the hostess's chair, her husband at the head.

Having no idea where Alice would sit, he was forced to seat Miss Endicott first, where she indicated, and then take the place beside her. Mrs. Carlisle promptly took the seat on his other side. Alice took a seat too far removed for comfortable conversation and he wondered if it had been deliberate. Why was she acting so reserved? His jaw tightened with annoyance when Victor sat down beside her.

Dinner proved long and tedious with Shepard dominating the conversation and Mrs. Carlisle addressing almost all her remarks in low asides to Nick. The only one genuinely friendly to him was Miss Endicott. To her credit, Alice did not seem on the same friendly terms with Victor as he with her. She spoke little and ate little. Only once or twice did he catch her looking at him, but instead of smiling, she quickly averted her gaze.

What had gone so wrong?

When at last they all retired to the drawing room, he didn't know how to speak with Alice alone. If he singled her out, all eyes would be on them. He didn't care what any of them thought, but how would Alice feel? This was her world, and once before he'd made the mistake of underestimating it.

The two couples lit cigarettes and the room was soon filled with smoke. Miss Endicott sat down to the piano and began to play softly.

Nick turned with relief when Alice came up to him but his joy was quickly tempered by her serious look. "If you wouldn't mind going up to see Austen, I told him you would tell him a bedtime story. One of those you know out of your head."

He narrowed his eyes at her. Was there a tinge of sarcasm in the last words? Her tone sounded too polite. "Of course not. I'll go now."

"He might have already fallen asleep. He was quite exhausted. If he is, please don't wake him."

Although she seemed to be avoiding his gaze, he waited until she was forced to look up. "You can trust me. I won't disturb him." He made his tone deliberately gentle. She gave him a quick look before nodding her thanks and moving away from him.

With a sense of relief at leaving the tense atmosphere of the drawing room, he walked up to the little boy's room. He truly had enjoyed himself this afternoon, and only wished Alice had been a part of it. He'd wanted to tell her that if she'd given him the chance.

Austen was already half-asleep and he remembered his promise to Alice, but at the sight of him, the little boy sat up. "I thought you'd never be done with dinner."

He took the stool beside the bed. "It was a rather long meal. Now, lie down. You need to get your sleep if you want to have more adventures."

Austen settled back down under his covers. "Will you tell me another story about when you were a boy?" he said through a yawn.

"All right. Let me think." He rested his chin on his fist, pretending to ponder. "Ah, here's one. When I was—"

"Did you know my father?" Austen's brown eyes looked at him solemnly.

Nick's thoughts stilled. "No, I didn't, but I have heard that he was a very fine gentleman."

Austen sighed. "I don't remember Papa. I have a little picture of him. I'll show you tomorrow if you like."

"Yes, I should like that. I'm sure he was a father you could be proud of. I don't remember my father too well, either, but I know he was a fine man, too."

The little boy folded his hands atop the bedcovers, his thin wrists jutting out from his striped nightshirt. "What do you remember best about him?"

Nick thought back. Ever since receiving news of his mother's passing, he had thought a lot about his youth and childhood. "I remember someone dark-haired, like myself, and smelling kind of funny, like the coal that always covered his clothes. He worked down in the coal mine, you see. And then I remember the smell of soap, once he'd washed up and came to kiss me good night, just like your Mama does with you every night."

Austen picked at his bedcovers. "I don't remember my papa at all."

The forlorn tone touched him. He reached over and covered the little hands with one of his own. "You were very young when he passed away. It's all right. He remembers you. That's what's important."

Austen turned one of his hands around and took hold of Nick's. Nick enfolded it in his own, feeling an odd spurt of emotion at the trusting gesture. The boy's large brown eyes met his. "Do you think so?"

He nodded. "Absolutely. And you have your mama to tell you all about him, so you won't forget the kind of man he was, even though you don't remember the details yourself."

Austen nodded and smiled. "What story are you going to tell me?"

Nick sat back although he didn't let the boy's hand go.

"Let me see…where was I…" He pursed his lips, as if searching his memory, before beginning again. "This one is about a man who rode the rails. That means he'd hop on a freight car and go wherever he wished…"

He hadn't even gotten halfway through the story when Austen's breathing slowed and his hold on Nick's hand loosened. Nick fell silent and waited another minute to see if the boy would awaken.

Assured that he slept peacefully, Nick slowly pulled his hand away. He got up from the stool and yawned, wishing for a moment he didn't have to go back downstairs.

But he wanted to see Alice. That thought alone propelled him back to the drawing room.

The murmur of voices reached him before he entered the room. Miss Endicott had stopped playing and sat in an armchair reading. The others lounged on the sofas and chairs. After a pause when he stepped in, the low talk resumed. Cigarette smoke hung in the lamplight like thin cotton strands, its acrid smell reminding Nick of the gin mills in the lower quarters of San Francisco. His gaze roamed over the room, narrowing when he saw Alice on the couch with Victor sitting too close beside her. She looked up as soon as he entered. He half-expected her to avert her gaze, but instead she straightened and rose, excusing herself from Victor.

She reached him before he'd taken more than a few steps into the room. "How is Austen?"

He blinked at her lack of greeting. "I expect off somewhere dreaming of pirates and freight cars and—"

"Frogs," she finished for him.

Was that the beginnings of a smile at the corner of her lips?

"Yes, likely frogs figure in there somewhere."

"I wanted to thank you for spending the afternoon with him." She knotted her hands, looking down, her tone low. "I just worried when you weren't back after a couple of hours. I'm sorry if I overreacted."

His hurt at her earlier coldness dissipated at her halting words. He wanted to reach out and take her hand, but didn't dare with the company around them. "I'm sorry we were gone so long. The time flew by and he didn't seem tired. If I'd seen his energy flagging, I would have brought him back immediately, I hope you believe that." He smiled. "Even if it'd meant carrying him."

She seemed to search his face but didn't return his smile. "I appreciate that."

"What are you two up to with your private murmurings in the corner?" Victor sauntered over to them and draped an arm around Alice's shoulders.

A look of annoyance skimmed her features, and in a deft movement, she sidestepped his embrace. "I'm just asking about Austen."

"You'll never let the boy grow to a man the way you coddle him."

Her face flushed.

Nick eyed Victor. "I found him like any boy of his age."

Victor's insolent gaze swept over him. He sported one of the thin mustaches beginning to be seen on young men both in England and America who fancied themselves swells. "How many seven-year-old boys are you acquainted with?"

Nick's ire rose. "I have nephews." Whom he'd only just seen at his mother's funeral.

"As the father of two boys, I think I speak with more expertise than a bachelor."

Alice put a restraining hand on his arm. "Please, Victor. I think I know my son better than anyone." She then took a step away from them. "I believe I shall retire for the evening. Good night, everyone." She gave him a fleeting look. "Good night, Nick. Thank you for taking care of Austen."

"Good night, Alice." He'd hardly gotten the words out of his mouth when she was gone, almost as if she were running away from him.

He hesitated a moment in the room, but not liking the stifling smell of cigarette smoke, and seeing Mrs. Carlisle eye him, he bowed to Victor. "If you'll excuse me."

He wandered back out to the porch and from there onto the lawn. Tomorrow they'd be leaving this country house, and he didn't know what precisely had gone wrong. He hoped he'd have a chance to talk to Alice, but knew from the trip coming down that the train compartment would afford little privacy with Austen, Miss Endicott and the nursemaid along.

Well, he consoled himself, he still had the endowment to her charity. Perhaps in London he could make another appointment with her at the Society to discuss the gift.

"It was stuffy in there, wasn't it?"

He swirled around at the husky female voice. Mrs. Carlisle stood at the edge of the verandah, silhouetted against the light from the drawing room. Unlike Alice's more modest gown, Mrs. Carlisle's silk sheath had a low v-neck, leaving most of her shoulders and upper arms bare.

He knew her type well. Bored and needing attention. As he debated how to decline her advances, she sauntered down the steps onto the yard where he stood.

"A lot of hot air."

She chuckled, a low-throated sound and looked up at him, knowing undoubtedly how it showed her creamy neck to advantage.

"I was on the point of retiring," he said.

"What a pity. The evening is young." She eyed him. "You don't like my husband, do you?"

"Let's just say I had a brief acquaintance with him in his youth."

"How droll. Sometimes he seems to be still in his adolescence."

Nick took a step away from her. "Well, if you will excuse me, Mrs. Carlisle—"

"I shouldn't hold out much hope for Alice, if I were you."

Her words stopped him. "No?"

"I pity the man who fancies himself in love with her. She is the kind of woman who appears weak and will always have some poor gentleman in tow, but her heart will never be his."

He stood silent, unwilling to hear the words, but powerless to move away.

"She'll always hold up Julian as a standard, and the poor man will never live up to the dead paragon." She gave a bitter laugh. "The living can never compete with an ideal."

The words, so like his own thoughts, chilled him. He merely inclined his head. "Good night, Mrs. Carlisle."

Her throaty laugh followed him. "Good night, Mr. Tennent, and sweet dreams."

Chapter Eleven

Alice reread the note in the masculine scrawl:

Alice,
Thank you for the weekend in Richmond. It was most
enjoyable to me, not least for the time spent in your
delightful son's company.
 I hope that I can see both of you again.
 The reason for the present is to make an appoint-
ment to further discuss an endowment to the Society.
I could come to your office or residence, or you can
come to my office. I leave it up to you whatever is
most convenient to you.
 I remain, as ever, your servant,
Nicholas Tennent

Her glance strayed to the bottom of the note where he'd
written his address on Threadneedle Street. His business
no doubt. Or, *businesses*. She remembered Geoff's and
Victor's remarks and tried to push them away as merely
masculine envy.

She turned over the envelope that lay on the desk. The Savoy Hotel was embossed on the back flap. The image of the hotel as his residence conjured up a transient with no permanent home.

Did Nicholas plan to remain in London or was he here only temporarily? How little she still knew of him.

Her son had done little but talk of Nicholas since their return. Was she jealous of Nicholas's success with Austen? The ugly thought lodged in her mind and she couldn't brush it aside so easily. Was she such a terrible mother to begrudge her only son some masculine companionship?

She'd always been protective of Austen, but now she realized how difficult it was for her to trust her only child to someone else. Julian would gently admonish her to trust their son to the Lord's care. Tears welled in her eyes, blurring the note before her. Despite her trust in other areas, she felt little able to relinquish control in this area. Austen was all she had left. All that was truly hers.

She wiped at her eyes and picked up the note from Nicholas once more. When she'd first seen the envelope in her stack of mail, she'd felt a spurt of anticipation. Now, her confusion returned. And if she were honest with herself, did it not include disappointment as well?

He'd written that he hoped to see *both of them again*. When Nicholas had bid them goodbye at Victoria Station the day before, he'd taken her hand in his and thanked her for the weekend. Then he'd stooped by Austen and shaken his hand.

She'd watched, touched by their exchange. Nicholas treated him like a miniature adult. He'd promised her son they would be seeing each other again.

Yet, here in the note he expressed only an intention to

see her regarding a charitable donation. What did she want? Staring out her rain-spattered window, she chided herself. It was she who had pushed away any friendly overtures on Nicholas's part.

Shaking aside her own foolishness, she focused on the latter part of the note. The only reasonable thing to do was reply to his request and meet with him to discuss the particulars of the charitable donation.

"Mama."

She turned with a smile to her son. "What is it, Austen? Why aren't you with Miss Grove?"

"I told her I left Moppet down here and had to get him."

"Of course. Then you'd better hurry up to your lessons. If you finish early, we can go to the park together."

"Is Mr. Tennent coming, too?"

She turned away from him, feeling sudden guilt. Had she driven her son's only friend away? Or, had Nicholas's interest in the boy already waned? "No, dear."

"Why not?"

"Mr. Tennent is a busy man. I imagine he is at his office working right now."

"When is he coming to visit? He said he'd see me soon."

"I don't know exactly when. We've only been home one day." She glanced down at the note. Should she say anything to her son about the note? Or would that be raising his hopes unfairly?

Austen located his stuffed rabbit behind a sofa cushion and came to lean against her. "Mama, will you write to Mr. Tennent and ask him to visit us? Tell him we could take my sailboat to the Basin."

She put her arm around his shoulders. "You and I can take it with us today. We don't need Mr. Tennent for that."

"But I should like it if he came with us."

She touched the strands of hair that had fallen against his forehead. "You don't want to be with just your mama?"

"I should like it better if he came with us," he repeated stoutly, unaware how the words cut her. Why did Julian have to die and leave Austen fatherless? There had been no confusion in her life then.

"Very well, we shall see what we can do. I'm sure you'll see Mr. Tennent very soon. Now, run along and finish your lessons." She kissed his forehead and gave him a little shove.

"All right, Mama." He ran off, but at the door he paused. "Don't forget to write to Mr. Tennent."

"I won't."

When he left, she sighed and turned back to her desk. After rereading Nicholas's letter, she picked up her pen and let it hover over her stationery a second more, debating her opening. Before she could decide, she heard the front door ring. Her heart began to pound. Could it be Mr. Tennent? Of course not, she scolded herself for acting like a silly schoolgirl.

At the soft knock on the parlor door, she twisted around in her chair. "Yes?"

The maid poked her head in. "It's Mr. Carlisle, madam."

Victor. She dismissed the slight annoyance at his un-announced visit so soon after seeing him the day before. He was her solicitor after all—at Geoff's insistence. "Show him in."

Victor strolled in, presenting his usual dandified appearance in a black broadcloth coat and finely checked trousers. "Hello there, Alice."

She stood and smoothed her gown. "Hello, Victor, what brings you by today?"

He leaned down and planted a kiss on her cheek and she had to brace herself against flinching. His cheek smelled of bay rum, a scent she'd never cared for. Ever since he'd become her solicitor, he'd become excessively attentive.

She'd spoken to Geoffrey about it, but her brother had pooh-poohed her concerns. "He's like a brother to you! It's nothing but a little harmless flirtation. Don't be such a prude, Allie."

Victor glanced down at her desk, and she had to refrain from moving in front of it to prevent him from seeing the note from Nicholas. "I was in the neighborhood and thought I'd stop by and see how you made it back."

"How thoughtful of you." She deliberately moved away from her escritoire and took a seat in an armchair, motioning for him to do the same. He sat down on the adjoining sofa and smoothed his brightly colored four-in-hand tie. "Been corresponding with that chap Tennent? You seemed a bit tight with him for such a short acquaintance."

Deciding silence was the best defense, she sat straight, her hands folded in her lap.

Victor leaned back against the velvet upholstery and seemed to study the ceiling. "Curious how he suddenly popped back into London after all these years." He shook his head and chuckled. "From lowly clerk to head of a company. Only in America does one see such things."

"I think it shows his talent and energy."

He lowered his face to gaze at her sidelong. "Or ruthless ambition."

Alice swallowed, wanting to refute the allegation. Instead, she asked through stiff lips. "What do you mean?"

"A man with nothing doesn't get to where he is without some cold-blooded maneuvers. I've heard he buys out any company that shows the least weakness, fires all the principals—'restructuring' he calls it—then incorporates it into his vast enterprise of Tennent & Company." He shook his head. "One can't help admiring his tactics, in a Neronian sort of way."

"I don't know how you can compare him to a ruthless Roman emperor, Victor. Just because he has made something of himself. I think it's admirable."

Victor let out a skeptical sniff. "Making something of himself is one thing. To go from a penniless young man to one who throws his wealth around—"

She gave a laugh, which came out sounding sharper than she'd intended. "Oh, come, you're exaggerating. These things happen all the time in America."

"Poor Allie, you've lived a sheltered life in the north with your curate. A man who puts up at the Savoy, installs himself in an office building in the heart of the city, drives in a newly purchased coach, and buys up companies as if they are weekly groceries doesn't strike me as an innocent lamb. Even in America business is a ruthless affair."

"If you've come to criticize Nicholas, you needn't bother—"

"Ah-ha. So it's like that, is it?" He sat up, eyeing her with his customary cynical amusement.

She blinked. "Like what?"

"*Nicholas,*" he mimicked. "Be careful, sweet Alice. You've been alone some time now and are vulnerable. Be careful you don't give your heart to someone whose heart is as hard as granite."

She stood up and walked away from him. "You are fancying things which are not there. I merely admire Mr. Tennent if he has made something of himself, and wished to make him feel welcome since his return." She fingered the lace on her collar, keeping her back to Victor.

"Of course, dear, if that's what you say. Anyway, I came by today to tell you that Cordelia and I wanted to have you over for dinner some evening this week."

"I don't know…" She hated those evenings, filled with a lot of worldly society couples whose interests were so far removed from her own. At the same time, she knew how valuable such connections were to the charity. It was her duty to continue to make these people aware of those less fortunate than themselves. "Let me look in my engagement book." She crossed back to her desk. "Which evening were you thinking of?"

He came to stand behind her, so close she had no space to move away. "I'm not sure which evening Cordelia has in mind. Let me have her confirm with you."

"Oh, very well." She stifled her annoyance that he didn't have a definite date in mind. Had he only come by to criticize Nicholas?

"There's one other thing."

She glanced at him, then quickly away when she found his face inches from hers. "Yes?"

"Your portfolio has taken a plunge lately. Bit of a recession on the market, you know. I'm afraid your income will be going down this quarter."

"Oh." She chewed her lip. Why did it always seem Victor took pleasure in being the bearer of bad tidings where her finances were concerned? "Well, it only means I shall have to be more careful of my expenditures."

"Yes." His hand came up to her face.

She jerked her head back. "What are you doing?"

"Just brushing away a stray lock." He tucked the

supposed strand of hair behind her ear, while she stood rigid. Despite that they had known each other as children, she was tired of the liberties he took. Lately, he was going too far.

She took a deliberate step back. "Well, if that is all, Victor, I have some things to attend to."

"As do I, as do I." Before she knew what he was about, he leaned in again and planted a soft kiss on her cheek.

She flinched, and his low chuckle vibrated against her skin. "My, you are getting jumpy these days. Sure it's not that Tennent making you so nervous?"

With a wave, he moved away from her. "I'll see myself out. Cordelia will be in touch." He sauntered away from her before she could think of a retort.

After he'd left, she took up Nicholas's note once again and reread it. Then she picked up her pen.

Dear Mr. Tennent, Why not "Nicholas," she asked herself? She decided she was letting herself go too quickly. There had been no one since Julian and there wouldn't be.

She needed time to get a proper perspective on her newfound friendship with Nicholas Tennent.

I received your kind letter. There was no need of thanks. Both Austen and I enjoyed our weekend in Richmond and we thank you for your company.

If you would like to discuss a donation to the Society, why don't you visit here at my residence later in the week? I suggest Thursday or Friday afternoon—

She deliberately set the date as far to the end of the week, and in the latter part of the day, denying herself the pleasure of seeing him sooner. With distance, her own feelings would have a chance to settle. And give Austen's memory of his weekend adventures with Mr. Tennent an opportunity to fade as well.

> *You may let me know the date and time convenient to you by return post.*
>   *In the meantime, I remain, sincerely, your servant,*
> Alice Lennox

There, that was sufficiently businesslike without being unfriendly. She perused it one more time and before giving herself a chance to question or reword it, she quickly folded it and put it into an envelope. It would go out in the afternoon post. Or, perhaps tomorrow morning's was better. She didn't want to appear too eager. This was strictly about business.

Yes, tomorrow's post was soon enough. He'd receive it by mid-morning and still have plenty of time to decide on seeing them by week's end.

Nick frowned as his eyes skimmed down the contents of the brief note, beginning with "Mr. Tennent." His disappointment deepened as he read "Thursday or Friday."

He'd waited until late Monday afternoon, expecting an immediate response to his note to her. It was not until almost noon Tuesday that he'd received her reply, and now she was postponing a meeting until the end of the week.

Wasn't she interested in a donation for her charity?

Or was it that she didn't want to see *him?* He considered the various possibilities. Perhaps she didn't want him to see her son?

Their ride back in the train from Richmond had been pleasant enough. As he'd foreseen, there had been no time for any meaningful conversation. Austen had taken up most of his attention, but the more the boy had chattered away with him, the more Nick had sensed Alice's withdrawal. Could she possibly resent the boy's attention?

He couldn't fathom it and wanted to talk to her about it. But, he looked down at the note again; it seemed he would have little chance until Thursday or Friday. At least she wanted him to come to her house. He'd see Austen again. Funny how much he'd missed the little fellow.

He'd leave the entire afternoon free to spend with him. If Alice allowed him to.

He sighed and picked up his pen. He would request a meeting on Thursday at half-past two. That should still qualify as afternoon and not interfere with the lunch hour.

Alice paced the front parlor from a quarter past two onward. She stopped in front of the mirror hanging over the mantelpiece and adjusted the ruffled collar of her gown for the third time.

She tucked a stray strand of hair into her coiffure.

"Mama, I think I see him."

She jumped at the sound of Austen's voice. Her son had stood at the bow window for the last half hour. He craned his neck through the foliage of the potted plants, peering into the street below. One small hand held back the gauze outer curtain.

"Austen, please get away from the window." She couldn't help going over and glancing over his head.

He sighed. "No, it's not him. I thought it was him." The gentleman with the bowler hat and dark suit walked briskly by, swinging his walking stick back and forth over the pavement.

"Now, come away from the window."

"Yes, Mama." He let the curtain fall and walked beside her, dragging Moppet in one hand.

"Come, let's read a storybook while we wait for Mr. Tennent. Now, remember, he is here to see Mama on business, so after greeting him and speaking a few minutes, you must excuse yourself. When he is ready to leave, I shall summon you again and you may say goodbye to him."

His solemn eyes looked into hers as he settled beside her on the sofa. "Yes, Mama," he said with a sigh.

Since their return to London, nothing she'd tried to engage Austen in could compete with his memories of the treasure hunt.

She picked up the edition of *Coral Island,* which she had hoped would assuage his desire for adventure. "Now, remember, when we last left Jack and Peterkin, their ship had been wrecked. Let's see what happens when they awake."

He settled beside her, putting a thumb into his mouth. She frowned at the habit he'd almost given up until this week. "The ship struck at the very tail of the island," she read.

"Mama, you have to speak like a pirate when you read it."

She looked down at Austen's serious gaze and smiled. "Very well."

But just as she turned back to the story, they both heard the doorbell ring.

Austen immediately scrambled off the sofa. "I know that's Mr. Tennent. Mama, may I go out and greet him?"

She was about to impress upon him that one awaited one's guests to be announced, but at the sight of his eager face, she didn't have the heart. "Very well."

She closed the book slowly as he ran off. Then she stood and smoothed her skirt, deafened to all sound but the hammering of her heart.

Nick was giving his name to the maid when a door opened to the side of the corridor and then Austen was running toward him. "Mr. Tennent!" The boy suddenly stopped short and hesitated, as if unsure at the last moment how he would be greeted. Nick smiled at him, feeling happier than he'd have imagined a moment ago at seeing the young boy, and squatted down.

Before he knew how it had come about, his arms were around the young boy, and Austen's arms were about his neck.

"I didn't think you'd ever be back," he said against Nick's collar.

Nick squeezed him a second before sitting back. "Of course I would. I told you I would." He stood slowly and handed Austen the package he'd brought.

The boy's eyes grew round. "Is this for me?"

He nodded.

Austen just stood staring at it.

"Well, why don't you open it?"

The boy pulled at the string, then growing bolder, tore through the brown wrapping. He took out the navy blue captain's hat with the gold anchor insignia at the front.

"Put it on and see if it fits."

With wonder in his eyes, he set it on his head.

"Well? How does it feel?"

Austen's mouth curled into a smile. "Just right. Is this a real captain's hat?"

"It is. If we're going to go sailing together, you've got to look the part."

"Are we really going to go sailing?"

"Certainly." He coughed softly. "That is, if your mother gives you permission."

"Let's ask her now."

"Wait a minute. I have something for her, too." He picked up the parcel he'd set down and took Austen by the hand. "Tell me what you've been up to since you returned to London." With a glance at the maid, he crossed the threshold.

Austen tugged on his hand. "Mama is waiting for you in here."

The maid shut the door behind him with a nod, and Nick allowed Austen to lead the way. She was waiting for him? That perhaps boded for good.

Alice stood by the sofa when he entered, her glance going from Austen to him and back again.

Nick advanced into the room, letting go of Austen's hand when he reached Alice. He handed her the bouquet of roses he'd brought. "Hello, Alice." Would she address him as Mr. Tennent?

"Oh, goodness, what's this?"

He gave a nervous laugh. "Well, I hope their scent gives them away."

She carefully drew aside the paper and gave a small gasp.

He cleared his throat. "I hope you like pink."

"Oh, yes, indeed, I do." She bent over the dozen pink roses and breathed in deeply. "They smell wonderful." Her eyes lifted and she smiled. "Thank you."

He felt the tension in him easing at her shy smile.

"Let me ring for someone to put them in water. Please, have a seat."

Nick took a seat on the chintz sofa, listening to Austen show off his new cap to his mother.

Alice came back and took a seat in a nearby chair. She turned to her son, who'd come to sit beside Nick. "Austen, darling, Mama must talk with Mr. Tennent for a little bit. You may come back in a few moments and have your own visit."

Nick bent and touched him on the shoulder. "Do as your mother says. Perhaps—" he spared her a brief glance "—we can do something together afterward."

She pressed her lips together, as if the idea didn't please her. Was she still holding the treasure hunt against him? They were silent as Austen dragged himself off the sofa and walked slowly to the door.

When it closed, Nick turned back to Alice. She sat with her hands folded primly on her lap. Before he could say anything, she said, "Mr. Tennent, thank you for coming."

He felt a stab of disappointment—mingled with irritation—at the formal name and tone. Hadn't they just enjoyed a weekend of getting reacquainted? "What happened to 'Nicholas'?"

She averted her gaze. "I thought since we were meeting to discuss—uh—business, it was more businesslike."

He quirked an eyebrow. "Business? Since when is charity business?"

She met his eyes once more. "Isn't it for you?" There was something in her tone.

"No." When she didn't reply, he said, "Thank you for—" he paused imperceptibly "—agreeing to see me."

She looked down, so he was sure the inflection was not lost on her. "Well, yes, you said you wished to discuss a donation to the Society."

He leaned forward. "Yes. I had in mind a donation to be able to build a row of terrace houses such as you showed me last week."

She pursed her lips. "That would be a substantial cost."

"I understand. It would only be an initial donation. I would like to see several such dwellings constructed in time."

"I don't know what to say."

He smiled slightly. "You could ask how much the initial donation would entail."

"Very well. How much did you have in mind?"

"One hundred thousand pounds."

Her mouth fell open, as if she'd never heard of such a sum. "I beg your pardon."

He repeated the sum.

Her eyes began to light up, realizing he was serious. Before Nick could feel the pleasure of the giver, the light faded. "You must be very wealthy to be able to afford so large a donation."

"The Lord has prospered me in my time away from England."

"Has he?"

He drew his eyebrows together at her tone. "You sound doubtful."

"They say you are...aggressive in your business dealings."

"I see." What had she heard? Rising, he walked toward the window. "When one is successful in business, one makes enemies. One gets used to slander."

She rose as well. "Is that all they are—rumors?"

He swung around to her. "Who have you been listening to?"

She made a vague gesture. "Businessmen."

His jaw hardened, not liking the fact that she was so quick to doubt him. "Let me guess. Victor or your brother?"

"I trust Geoffrey's judgment."

His jaw hardened. So they were back to that. Her family against him. "Are you interested in the donation or not?"

"I shall have to discuss it with my board of trustees."

His annoyance grew. "Then I shall let you get on with it." He took out his pocket watch and snapped it open. "If you will permit me some time with Austen, I think we've concluded our business."

She drew back and he had a moment's remorse at the hurt look in her eyes. "I shall call for him."

While she went to the bell pull, he turned away from her again and waited by the bow window, his hands clasped behind his back. Perhaps he'd been too hasty in his anger. But if she doubted him so quickly, what hope was there for them? And by that brother of hers, who'd probably rejoiced when she'd been disinherited. He shook his head in disgust.

The two waited in uneasy silence until the maid came. "Please send Austen to me."

"Yes, madam."

When Nick felt the tension couldn't increase anymore in the room, the door finally opened and Austen walked in, his sailboat already in his arms. "Hello, Austen. That didn't take too long, now, did it?" His tone was gentle and friendly. No one would suspect he had a hard lump of anger in his chest.

He grinned. "No, sir." Ignoring his mother, he walked over to Nick.

"Now, what would you like to do this afternoon?"

"May we go sailing?"

Nick's glance went immediately to Alice. "If it's all right with your mother."

She twisted her hands together, clearly on the spot. Well, he felt no pity for her this afternoon. "Why don't you do something here at home, darling?"

Austen looked down and didn't say anything.

"I don't mind taking him to sail his boat. Where do you usually go sailing, Austen?"

Nick's quick words drew a smile from the boy. "The Round Pond."

His mother frowned. "But that's all the way in Kensington."

"We can go in my coach," put in Nick quickly. "It's parked right outside."

Her gaze went from his neutral one to her son's, visibly torn. Nick hid his impatience and waited. If anyone was going to disappoint this boy, it wouldn't be he.

"Please, Mama, mayn't I go with Mr. Tennent?"

She drew in a deep breath. "Very well, but don't be too long."

Nick exhaled in relief. "We shan't," he promised with a small smile as a peace offering. "Come along, let's be off."

At the door, he patted Austen on the shoulder. "Wait for me at the front door."

As soon as Austen had left, Nicholas turned to Alice, wanting to reassure her. "Thank you for trusting Austen to my care."

She pressed her lips together, and he suddenly realized she was near tears. "He's all I have," she whispered.

The words tore at his heart, and he almost entreated her to go along with them. Instead, he reached his hand out and patted her awkwardly on the shoulder. "I won't let him out of my sight."

She nodded wordlessly.

"We'll be back soon. I shall await your committee's decision."

Nick put his disquiet aside and concentrated on helping Austen up into the landau. The little boy scrambled onto the seat at the front and bounced up and down on the red leather upholstery a few times. "Oh, I can look all around me."

Both sides of the top had been folded down for the fine weather. Nick smiled up at him before addressing the coachman. "Take us through the park to the Round Pond."

The coachman tipped his top hat at him. "Yes, sir."

Nick climbed into the carriage and sat facing Austen. "Tell me what you've been up to since you returned from Richmond."

The boy's smile disappeared and shrugged. "Nothing much. Mama has engaged a governess to give me lessons and Nanny Grove takes me for a walk every day." Austen's gaze didn't stay fixed on him but roamed over the parkland as they entered Hyde Park through Stanhope Gate and rode under an alley of plane trees.

As the boy chattered on, Nick allowed his thoughts to return to Alice. She seemed deeply distressed about allowing her son in his company. What had her brother been telling her about him? Nick intended to get to the bottom of it. His frown deepened, not liking the things his secretary had begun discovering about her father's company.

"Do you think there'll be enough wind to sail my boat?"

He forced his attention to the boy in front of him. "If

not, we'll go another day and today make do with towing her along by her string."

"May we really go again another day?"

"Of course, why shouldn't we?"

The little boy shrugged and looked out the side. "I don't know. I've been asking Mama since we arrived home when you were going to visit."

His deep sigh stirred Nick. Why hadn't Alice replied sooner? He'd contacted her the day they'd returned. He remembered his own yearnings as a boy, how little they were ever satisfied until he'd become resigned to be content with his lot in life.

But why would Alice not want to indulge her son, when clearly the boy was lonely and in need of some male companionship?

His concern grew, and he had to strive to keep his tone light whenever he spoke.

Alice attempted to catch up on her correspondence while Austen was away. She usually reserved this time for Austen, and now found the time weighing heavily on her hands.

At the sound of carriage wheels, she rose from her desk and looked out the window, but it was only a passing coach. She forced herself to sit back down and pick up her pen again, determined not to behave the way she had over the treasure hunt.

Austen was in good hands, she repeated to herself. Nicholas, whatever he might be in business, seemed to genuinely care for her son. Her eyes drifted to the large bouquet of roses in the corner of her desk. She touched a soft petal, moved by the thoughtfulness of his gifts to both her and Austen.

Letting her pen drop, she bowed her head. *Dear Lord, Forgive me for this worry. Help me to be unselfish toward my son.* She thought of Julian and his gentle example of selfless love. He'd taught her to put her trust in God above all. She'd thought she'd succeeded as they lived always on the edge of poverty and had had to face death constantly with Julian's illness.

It was only now that Austen's affections were straying beyond the safe boundaries of his home that she was beginning to see how much she clung to him.

Forgive me, Lord. Grant me your grace. Show me who Nicholas Tennent really is. Is he the ruthless tycoon they tell me he is? Is he the best example for my Austen?

About an hour later, as soon as she heard a coach pull up in front of the house, she rushed to the window, careful to keep behind its lacy veil. She watched the two descend, Nick helping Austen down, then holding his hand and carrying his sailboat in the other. Austen chattered up the whole walk to the front door, exhibiting more animation than he did at home.

She couldn't see them when they entered under the portico. The dim sound of the door penetrated to the parlor, and she held her breath, wondering if Nicholas would ask to see her. What would she say? Part of her wanted to run out into the hallway and see him again, part of her wanted to remain hidden.

But no one came. A few minutes later, she saw him return to his coach. Only then did her breathing return to normal. With a sigh, she turned to go to Austen, feeling more lonely than she had for a long time.

Chapter Twelve

Alice spent the next week immersing herself in her work. After receiving a formal letter from Nicholas's firm about the intended donation, she truly began to believe it.

Overwhelmed with what the Housing Society would be able to accomplish with such a sum, she wanted to do something to show her appreciation to him. She decided to plan a special dinner with the entire board of trustees. Nicholas would be given a chance to address them and outline the vision he had for the donation, and they in turn could honor him with a special plaque.

Perhaps they could name the first terraces after Nicholas? On a burst of inspiration, she jotted down the various ideas she had.

Keeping herself busy with work helped assuage the disappointment she felt at not having seen Nicholas on a personal level. He'd been to see Austen three times, usually taking him to sail his boat, but always when she was at her office.

She bit the end of her pen. Nicholas knew where her office was located, so if he had wanted to see her, he certainly could have done so. He even had a legitimate pretext with the pending donation.

It was for the best, she told herself, looking back down at her notes. Wasn't it what she'd wanted? Simple friendship and nothing else. She should be thankful things had resolved themselves so satisfactorily. Austen was happy and thriving. And she had peace.

"Hello, are you busy?"

Alice started up at Macey's voice. Her friend stood at the door of her office. "Oh, hello, come in. I'm never too busy to see you."

Macey entered the room, pulling off her gloves and smiling broadly. "I mustn't stay long. I've too much to do, but I wanted to say goodbye before I left."

She looked at her friend in bewilderment. "Left? Where are you off to? What about the dinner I'm organizing?"

Macey sat down opposite her and undid the ribbons of her bonnet. "Oh, I shall be back in time for that. It isn't for at least a fortnight, isn't it? Tell me how the plans are coming."

Alice brought her up to date, still disconcerted that she wouldn't have her friend's help in organizing it.

"But you've got everything pretty much settled," Macey said in reply to this. "It's just a matter of ordering things and securing the ballroom."

"Where are you going, anyway?"

Macey removed her bonnet and smoothed down her hair. "Didn't I tell you last week? I'm sure I meant to. I'm off to catch the steamer to Le Havre. I'm taking a holiday in Deauville."

"Deauville! Goodness, Macey, when did you decide to go to Deauville?"

"A few weeks ago. Elizabeth Wilcox raved about it when she came back."

Alice made an effort to inject some enthusiasm in her tone while she tried to suppress her dismay. "Well, it sounds lovely. When are you off?" Macey always left London in the summer, but it was usually not far from the city, where Alice could visit on the weekends.

"Tomorrow, my dear. I'm sure I must have told you."

Alice stared at her. "Tomorrow?" Why did she feel suddenly abandoned? She shook her head with a wan smile. "I don't remember. It must have slipped my mind, what with going out to Richmond last week and planning this and all…" Her voice dribbled off as she glanced back down at the papers on her desk.

Macey placed her bonnet on the seat beside her. "How is Mr. Tennent, by the way? I've been meaning to ask about him. Have you seen him since we came back from Richmond?"

"Yes, once. He stopped by when he first broached me about the donation."

Macey frowned. "Only once?"

Alice shuffled her papers around. "Yes. But he has taken Austen out a few times—close to home," she added. "I know he is a very busy man."

"Taken Austen out, but not you?"

Alice's gaze shot up. "I beg your pardon?"

"I know he is a busy man, but I shouldn't think he was too busy to stop by and see you." Macey folded her hands in her lap.

Alice made a point of arranging her papers in a pile. "Oh, well, I'm busy, too."

"I liked him."

"You did?" Why did Alice have the urge to burst into tears and tell her friend all about her wayward heart?

The older woman looked at her in surprise. "Yes, why? Don't you?"

"Yes, of course. I mean," she added, not meeting her friend's gaze, "you are usually so critical of men. Why are you championing Nicholas Tennent?"

Macey sat back. "There's something forthright about him. He appears a strong, yet not overbearing, person. I don't get the impression with him that he would be afraid of a woman who knew her own mind." She nodded, warming to her view. "A woman could form a true partnership with a man like that."

Alice stared at the older woman. She'd never heard her talk like that of any man.

When she said nothing, Macey asked gently, "Has something happened between you two?"

"Oh, no," she said quickly, too quickly. "Why should it have?"

"Then what is it?"

"Nicholas and I are…only acquaintances," she began.

"But I thought you two had known each other years ago."

Alice studied the neat words on the stationery before her. "Yes." That magical period of hardly more than a week. "It was so long ago. He was with Father's firm for a very short time. Until Father dismissed him."

"Oh, that's too bad. He struck me as someone who would have been an asset to the company."

"It was all my fault."

Her friend gave a small gasp then she leaned forward. "I'm sure you did nothing so terrible."

Alice had never told anyone about that day. Only her father had known. Long minutes passed before she was able to speak. "I fancied myself in love with him."

"Oh, my dear…"

Alice swallowed. "I was a foolish young girl looking for attention. Mr. Tennent seemed to notice me. For the first time, someone was genuinely seeing who I was." She held up a hand before her friend could say a word. "Don't misunderstand. He did nothing wrong, nothing improper. It was I who pestered him." She pressed her lips together, finding it difficult to tell the rest. "It was I who threw myself at him, until one day—" her voice lowered to a mere whisper "—I demanded a kiss from him." Her face flamed with the recollection. After a few seconds, she continued. "Father caught us."

"Oh, no!"

"He immediately dismissed Nich—Mr. Tennent." She shook her head, still grieved by that act. "The poor man was completely innocent. He was out of a job, with no references, just because of my silly schoolgirl behavior. That's why he was forced to emigrate. Father sent me away to live with relatives." She said softly, "I never saw him again, until the other evening."

"Your father could be quite harsh."

When Alice made no comment, Macey reached across the desk and patted her hand. "What an awful thing you both went through. Young love can be very painful. But that's all in the past. Your Mr. Tennent has returned and you've been able to renew the acquaintance. It sounds like a storybook."

Alice put a hand up to her mouth to stifle her emotions.

"What is it, Alice?" Her friend's low tone was filled with concern.

Unable to sit still, Alice got up and walked to the window overlooking the street. "I don't know." She hugged her arms to herself, wishing she could understand what she was feeling.

Macey came up behind her and touched her on the elbow. "Did he say something to you—or Austen?"

She shook her head. "No…no, it's just me. I don't know what I'm saying. Don't mind me," she said with a nervous laugh. "I'm just tired and confused," she added under her breath.

"Don't be afraid of your emotions, my dear."

Alice pressed her lips together, trying to regain her composure. After a moment, she said, "I have never sought anyone since Julian. I loved him. I can't…" She shook her head, unable to say anything more.

Macey put her arm around her. "There, my dear, don't fret. Your heart won't be betraying your late husband if you still feel something for Mr. Tennent."

"But I don't know what kind of man he is!" She didn't voice her greatest fear. What if he was a man just like her father?

Her friend patted her arm and stepped away. "Well, perhaps you need to take the time to find out."

Alice turned slowly to look at her. "What do you mean?"

"I mean just that. Get to know him."

She swallowed back a bitter laugh. How was she to do that when he wasn't even around? He was too busy with his business concerns. "It's for the best if we leave whatever was in the past, in the past," she finished with more firmness than she felt inside.

Alice turned back to her desk. "Come, I'll ring for some tea. Tell me more about Deauville before you leave. I envy your being able to just take off at a moment's notice."

"Well, why don't you come with me?"

Alice laughed as she went toward the corridor. "Yes, I'll just run away from all my responsibilities for a few days and not tell a soul where I am—"

"I'm serious, Alice. Take some time off for a proper holiday and come along with me. You know I'll pay all your expenses. You don't have to worry about a thing. It will do you the world of good."

Alice shook her head at her friend. "You know I can't go anywhere right now. What about the dinner I'm organizing?"

Macey took her seat once again. "You have a good staff here. They can carry out your instructions, we'll be back in plenty of time for the finishing touches. If you need, I can put off my trip another day or so to give you time to get your things together."

Alice walked slowly back to her own seat after requesting the tea. "Are you serious? You know how busy I am. I couldn't possibly just leave for more than a few days."

"Yes, you can."

"What about Austen?"

"What about him? Take him along. Children love the seaside. Think of it. A sandy beach and plenty of sunshine and fresh air, just what he needs." Macey nodded at her for emphasis. "And you, too. You look tired, my dear. If you continue as you've been, you'll work yourself to exhaustion and then where will your son be?"

"Hush, Macey. Don't say such things, even in jest."

Her friend's tone softened. "There now, Alice, I'm not trying to frighten you. I just want you to get away from things here for a little bit and take some time to enjoy yourself. The time alone with Austen will do you good. What do you say?"

Get away from things here for a little bit. Alice focused on those words and, suddenly, the plan sounded all too agreeable. If she left London, she wouldn't have to think about Nicholas Tennent. Wouldn't have to wonder why she was missing those dark eyes looking into hers, demanding something from her which she was afraid to respond to.

Nick paused in the letter he was dictating to his secretary and stared out the window. Would Alice be in her office at this time of day? It had been over a week since he'd last seen her. He'd kept away from her deliberately, sensing she needed time. He'd also needed the time to get over his anger.

The anger had long since dissipated. He'd thought by keeping away longer, he'd hear from her, if only on the subject of the donation.

But all he'd received was silence. Any communication about the donation had been from the treasurer of the society.

His strategy clearly had not worked. He gave a derisive snort. Was she really glad to be rid of his presence? Perhaps she'd believed even more slander from her brother or that sly Victor.

A soft cough interrupted him. He glanced at his secretary, who sat with pencil poised over his pad. "I'm sorry?"

"You were saying?"

"Oh, yes, where was I?"

The young man looked at his notes. "The share price of Henderson Limited fell two points yesterday."

"Yes." He cleared his throat and continued. He needed

to stop dwelling on Alice and concentrate on his business concerns.

Two sentences later, he snapped open his pocket watch. Perhaps he could stop by to discuss the housing project. He knew she was planning a dinner where he would present his ideas to the board of trustees.

Four o'clock. Was it too late?

He turned abruptly to his secretary. "Excuse me, we'll have to finish this tomorrow. I'm going out."

The man blinked at him. "Oh. Very well, Mr. Tennent. Do you want me to continue when you return?"

"No, I probably won't be back at the office until late." With some final instructions, he bid the man goodbye and left the office.

A young woman sat at the front desk of the Housing Society.

Nick presented her with his card. "Is Mrs. Lennox in?"

She looked at him in surprise. "No, sir. She's away."

He eyed her more closely. "Away?"

"On holiday, sir."

"To Richmond?" She'd probably left early for the weekend, he thought, stifling the sense of disappointment he felt that this time he'd not been asked along.

"Oh, no, sir. She's gone to France."

He stared at her. She might as well have said to China.

"Is there some message you'd care to leave for her when she comes back?"

Nick collected his thoughts. "Er, no. That is, can you tell me how long she will be away?"

"A fortnight, sir."

Another tremor jolted him. "Do you know where she went exactly?"

"I'm not at liberty to say, sir. I'm sure her family can inform you if you are a friend of theirs."

Nick replaced his hat on his head. He was no friend of the Shepard family, that was certain. It looked like someone was trying to separate them again. "Thank you. Good day to you."

"Good day, sir."

When he returned to his office, his secretary hadn't yet left.

"You're back, sir?"

Nick sighed heavily. Another long evening behind his desk awaited him. Although he'd told himself it was time to make some changes in his life, he found he had no heart to go to concerts or to the theater by himself.

"I'm glad you returned, sir." His secretary laid an envelope on his desk. "This came by the late afternoon post."

"Thank you." He didn't recognize the neat script on the front. "Why don't you get on home?"

"You don't wish to finish your letter?"

He shook his head knowing he'd not be able to concentrate on figures now.

"Very well, sir, good night."

After he'd left, Nick looked at the envelope more closely. It was postmarked *Deauville*. His pulse quickened. Could Alice have written him? But it wasn't her writing. He turned the letter over. On the flyleaf was written M. Endicott.

He picked up his letter opener, more puzzled than ever, and slit the envelope open. Could something have happened to Alice?

Dear Mr. Tennent,
Greetings, or should I say "bonjour," from the coast of Normandy. At the last minute, I invited Alice and Austen to accompany me on my annual holiday. The

outing has really done wonders for both of them. The weather has been wonderful and this lovely resort village is perfectly charming.

I am writing to suggest that if you can spare a few days from your business—or if you can perhaps find some business to do in France—that you come to Deauville. I recommend the Grand Hotel. It is very pleasant.

I look forward to your arrival.

A bientôt!

Macey Endicott

Nicholas reread the letter two more times before it began to sink in. Alice's friend was on his side.

He stuffed the hotel stationery back into its envelope and stood. Glancing at the wall clock, he saw it was only five o'clock. But he mustn't waste any time. He had a lot to do before catching a boat across the Channel.

"Mama, may I go back on the beach after tea?"

Alice looked at her son across the wide wicker table on the hotel veranda. "It's a little late in the day. Perhaps tomorrow."

Austen was distracted by the waiter who set down a platter of pastries and teacakes in the middle of their table.

"Oh, don't those look delicious," Macey said. "Which one would you like?"

Austen examined them carefully, his brow scrunched up in indecision.

Alice smiled then allowed her gaze to wander beyond their table to the ocean view on her right. She hugged her teacup in her hands. Macey had been right to urge her to take this holiday. In the few days she'd been here, she already felt a calming of her spirit.

The excitement of the journey across the English Channel and their location by the sea had also distracted Austen enough so that he hadn't mentioned Nicholas more than a few times. As for herself, she'd managed to push him to the recesses of her mind, at least during the daylight hours.

Nicholas. As she said the name to herself, she suddenly saw him walk out onto the terrace from the hotel lobby.

She blinked. Was she dreaming? How could she suddenly be thinking a name and conjure up the person in question? She lowered her cup, barely aware when it hit the saucer.

He was surveying the hotel guests on the veranda. In a few seconds he'd see them. Her heart sped up. She wasn't ready to face him. At the same instant she felt a burst of elation and longing so acute, it laughed to scorn all her illusion of having forgotten him. What was he doing here?

His eyes met hers and she had to clench her hands together to keep from springing up from the table and running toward him.

He made his way across the other tables to them.

Then he stood before her. "Hello, Alice." He gave her a brief nod, before turning to Macey, breaking into a smile. "Miss Endicott." His smile widened as he came to Austen. "Hello, Austen, fancy seeing you here."

Austen jumped up from his chair, almost sending it toppling backwards. "Mr. Tennent! How jolly to see you here. I've been bathing. Can we go into the ocean together? Mama won't let me go beyond the very edge."

Nick glanced briefly at her before turning his attention back to Austen. "I should like that very much."

Macey extended her hand to Nicholas. "I'm so glad you could come. Please, sit down."

Nicholas glanced back at Alice, as if asking her permission. "Yes, yes, of course, please sit down. What are you doing here? Did you know we were here?"

As he pulled out the chair, Macey touched her hand, drawing her attention away from Nicholas. "Mr. Tennent is here because I invited him here."

Alice stared at her friend. "What?"

"I thought it would be nice if Mr. Tennent joined us here at the hotel for a few days, so I wrote to him."

Nicholas cleared his throat. "I was so glad to receive Miss Endicott's note and decided to combine a short holiday with business. I have been meaning to cross the Channel to look at a few firms I've had my eye on."

"I see." She nodded, understanding. Of course, business had brought him. "Well, I wish you success then."

"I came principally to enjoy a holiday, if you don't find my presence an intrusion to your own."

"N-no, of course not." She looked away from his keen observation.

Macey signaled the waiter for more tea and an extra place. Alice was able to compose her thoughts somewhat as Nicholas turned his attention to Austen.

She sighed, listening to Austen's chatter. Nicholas was remarkably patient with him. It was hard for her to believe the picture of him as a ruthless business executive. Her father had never exhibited the kind of attentiveness Nicholas was showing her son.

Was it all a front? Would it endure after Nicholas obtained what he wanted?

What did he want? Did she want to know?

The question left her full of expectancy and fear.

Mid-morning the following day, Alice emerged from a beach hut and stood a moment, shading her eyes from the bright sun, as she searched for Austen and Nicholas along the crowded seashore.

The Normandy beach was a wide, flat expanse of sand, the sparkling water lapping softly at its edge. Shouts of children came to her from the water's edge and she strained to hear her son's voice.

She squinted at the two figures far out in the water, and she felt a momentary rise of panic. Austen had never ventured so far out. Her worry eased only slightly when she saw Nicholas standing right beside him. Her son was splashing around, clearly showing him he could swim.

Alice and Macey had only been on the female beach up to now. But today, with Nicholas's appearance, they had chosen the mixed beach so that he could teach Austen to swim. Alice had been reluctant at first until Nicholas had convinced her that there was less danger in the water if he knew how to swim.

Alice smoothed down the hip-length skirt of her dark blue wool serge bathing costume, hesitating to join Nicholas and Austen out in the water. Here in France, she'd noticed the beaches were less formal than across the Channel. Even some of the newer bathing costumes of the women had shocked her at first with their bloomerless skirts above the knee.

Still, she felt self-conscious appearing before Nicholas

in the outfit. It was short-sleeved, with narrow bloomers beneath the skirt. Dark blue hose and espadrilles laced around her ankle and calf completed the suit.

Finally, seeing no help for it, she began walking over the hot sand, skirting the holiday goers. Family groups sat together on canvas chairs on the sand, and dozens of children played along the water's edge. Others, fully dressed, wandered through the crowds.

She reached the edge of the water and allowed the mild surf to sweep over her toes, cringing a bit as the cold water seeped into her shoes.

"There she is!" Austen waved both arms at her. "Mama!"

She ventured farther in, allowing the water to swirl about her ankles.

Nick and Austen begun running toward her, their legs kicking up the water. She hugged her arms to her chest as the water splashed her. "Stay away from me! You're getting me wet!" she scolded in mock anger.

As their intent became clear, she screamed, "Oh, no, you don't!" Before she could back away far enough, they grabbed her hands and pulled her into the water.

She cried out at the shock of cold water. "No!" It was useless to struggle against their firm tugging. Her feet stumbled in the wet sand but Nicholas's strong grip didn't let her fall.

"Oh, it's too cold!" The next second, Nicholas lifted her from behind and threw her into the water. She was plunged in up over her head and screamed as she went in.

She came out, spluttering and dripping, determined to exact her revenge. "How dare you throw me in!" Laughter mingled with outrage in her voice.

"You'll soon warm up." Nick laughed, but before he

could say another word, she lunged toward him, toppling him backwards. "Hey!" he went under, his legs pulled out from under him.

He easily fought free of her grasp and came up from the water, shaking the water from his hair. Austen laughed with glee. "You both went under!"

Nicholas began walking toward her again, a glint in his eye. "Does she realize the penalty she must now pay?" The words brought back a flash from that day over the chess board and its dire consequences. A part of her thrilled as it had then when she'd ventured such a daring challenge.

Seeing his intention, she backed away, shaking her head. "No, you don't! Now we're even."

Austen began clapping his hands. "Mama, you've got to swim away!"

But before she could make another move, Nick lunged for her and, grabbing her by the waist and plunging her under. Alice struggled to loosen herself but he only tightened his hold around her. She grabbed him by the arms and attempted to push herself upward and him down, but he moved his arms around her, bringing her against his chest. Although she kicked her feet, he held her fast.

He rose, bringing her head out of the water but not loosening his hold.

Austen came up beside them. "Mama, Mr. Tennent has caught you!"

Alice's hands were flattened against his chest. He gazed down at her and chuckled. She felt the sound resonate against her palms.

"Yes!" she managed breathlessly. Before drawing away from him, she looked up into his eyes and found herself captured by the look in his eyes. It both frightened and exhilarated her as nothing had since that long ago day above the chess board. She felt as daring as the girl she'd been then. If they'd been alone, she would have reached up on her toes and kissed him.

"Mama, he won't let you go!"

Suddenly she became aware of their scandalous position. She pushed herself out of his embrace and was almost surprised—and a little disappointed—when he let her go immediately. He turned abruptly to Austen and pulled him out of the water by the armpits and splashed him back down again. "And now I've got you!"

Austen shouted with laughter. Nicholas repeated the dunking. As if hiding herself, Alice crouched down in the water up to her neck and watched them. Nicholas stood waist-high in the water, and she couldn't help noticing his muscular upper arms and shoulders through the short-sleeved suit whose dark wool material clung to his skin. When he glanced her way, she turned quickly toward the beach.

Her eyes scanned the crowds until she spotted Macey holding her bright blue parasol.

Alice whirled around when Nick approached her from behind. "Oh—!" She gave a nervous laugh. "I was afraid you'd try to drown me again."

"Drown you? What are you talking about?"

"I'm not lowering my guard around you and Austen again."

He smiled, standing tall above her. "All right, let me see your stroke."

She adjusted her oiled silk bathing cap. "I told you, I'm a very poor swimmer."

He frowned. "How is that, growing up in Richmond?"

She averted her gaze, feeling self-conscious under his

scrutiny. "Well, the river has too strong a current, and there was nowhere else appropriate. Remember, I grew up in London."

His next words took her by surprise. "I can teach you the basics."

"Oh, I'm too old—"

"Nonsense, I didn't learn until I was out west in the States." His dark brown eyes held a teasing light. "Think of it as recompense. There's finally something I can teach you."

A flutter began in her stomach at the thought of his holding her the way she'd seen him hold Austen.

"Mr. Tennent is going to teach Mama to swim!" chanted Austen, jumping up and down in the water. The ocean reached his upper chest, and Alice admonished him to be careful.

"He'll be all right." Nicholas turned to Austen. "Show your mother what you can do already."

Austen promptly flopped onto his back and floated on the surface, the soft swells carrying him. "See, Mama, I can float!"

"My goodness. That's wonderful."

She turned to Nicholas with a smile. "So quickly!"

"Now, it's your turn."

"Oh, I don't think—" she said, backing away.

He stepped toward her. She backed away some more, but that only brought her into deeper water.

Before she knew what he intended, he bent to lift her. She yelped and circled his neck with her arms, afraid he was going to dunk her into the water again.

"Relax," he murmured, holding her above the water and cradling her body against his chest. "I won't let you go. I'm just teaching you to float."

"All right," she stuttered, letting go of his neck.

"We'll go where it's shallower. Come along, Austen."

Austen splashed along beside them.

Nicholas began to ease her into the water. She couldn't help grabbing one of his arms, feeling the rock-hard biceps beneath her fingers. She bit her lip to keep from crying out.

"Don't worry, I've got you. Besides, the water is only about three feet deep here."

She glanced up at his amused tone. "Just don't let me go, yet."

"I won't, I promise." His eyes met hers and she felt for a few seconds that the threat of drowning didn't presently come from the water beneath her. As if unaware of the sensations he was awaking in her, he drew his glance from hers and said in a calm voice, "Your body will naturally float, if you let yourself relax."

She marveled how anyone could sound so normal when her whole body had gone rigid from the feel of his arms under her and his body so close to hers.

"You must relax." His tone became soothing.

She tried breathing deeply, looking beyond him at the puffy white clouds overhead.

"Put your head back and stretch your arms out." As he spoke, he pushed her torso upward, so she felt as if her head were going to sink into the water. She resisted at first but then as the soft swell of the water beneath her bore her up and down, she began to marvel at the ride atop the gentle waves.

He was soon able to let go and she gave a little laugh. "It feels wonderful, just floating."

"Mr. Tennent, let's build a sandcastle!"

She started at the sound of her son's voice, she'd felt so tranquil.

"Very well, let's ask your mother." Nicholas's dark eyes loomed over hers again, his head blocking the sun. "Are you game?"

"All right." She smiled into his gaze, wondering at the feelings this man was reawakening in her. She felt like an adolescent once again.

"Come on!" shouted Austen.

They followed Austen out of the surf and chose a location near the water's edge, where the sand was hard-packed and wet.

She retrieved her straw hat from beside their beach chairs, trading her beach cap for it, and went to kneel beside her son, who was already busy digging in the wet sand with his two hands. "You know, when the tide comes in, the castle will disappear."

Nick looked up from where he was beginning to heap up sand into a mound. "That's all right. The tide is going out now, so it'll be hours before that happens."

They worked together for a good while, the shouts of other children on the beach floating around them.

Soon, a small crowd of children had gathered round. Some began to build their own castles nearby, chattering in French as their sturdy hands heaped up the sand.

Alice was decorating crenellated walls with seashells. She glanced over at Nick, whose head was bent near her son's, both concentrated on their side of the now sprawling edifice.

She felt a pang at the sight of the two dark-haired heads, one whose straight hair flopped over his brow, the other, whose crisp waves glinted in the sun.

It gave her a good feeling to see her son so active and normal. She paused over the word, realizing how worried she'd been about him since Julian's death, and her own move back to London. How would Julian view the scene?

He had been such a gentle man. She was sure he would be happy that his son had someone he could look up to. But could he? Once again, her brother's and Victor's warnings came back to her.

She pushed their ugly words aside. Her thoughts returned to what she'd felt earlier held against Nicholas's chest. How different from what she'd known with Julian. She pressed her lips together, resisting a comparison. Julian had been so good to her. He'd offered love and solace to a lonely, unloved young woman. But he'd been sick much of their married life. She'd never undergone a sense of wanting to abandon all moorings to an unknown, unfettered experience as she had in Nicholas's arms. It frightened her. It meant a letting go of all that was safe and calm.

She glanced over at Nicholas now, remembering he was the one who had first kindled these yearnings in her so long ago. He looked up at that second, and her cheeks grew warm. He lifted his brows in inquiry but she shook her head and bent over her work in the sand once more.

Why had Nicholas come to them now and why was he being so kind? What did he want from this friendship? The questions she'd thought to escape by leaving London resurged and she saw only danger ahead with a man who'd awakened her once before and was doing so again. Once before her heart had known devastating heartbreak because of this man.

Could she trust it to him again?

Chapter Thirteen

Nick stood in waist-deep water, watching Austen flail his thin arms in the water, creating more splashing than movement but little by little, his small body began mobilizing away from him.

Alice clapped her hands. "Very good. You'll be a champion swimmer soon."

Nick came up beside her. "Are you ready for your lesson?"

She took a deep breath before plunging into the water and beginning the breaststroke he'd been teaching her.

"That's right, bend your knees and kick hard. Very good, bring your face up with each stroke." He kept his tone impersonal, although each day it was becoming more and more difficult to keep his distance. She swam a bit farther, keeping parallel to the beach as he'd taught her. When she finally stopped and stood to look back from where she'd started, she asked, "How did I do?"

"You're a remarkably quick learner. Come, swim back now."

While she complied, he glanced down at Austen who

was tugging on his arm. "Look at me dive!" The boy held his nose and ducked under the water, no longer afraid of submerging his head completely.

When Alice stood next to him again in the water, she said, "I'm going to sit with Macey a while."

He glanced at her wet bathing costume, steeling his features to betray nothing of what he felt inside at the revealing silhouette. "We'll be out soon," he told her.

"We're going to build another sandcastle," Austen added.

Nick watched Alice leave, wondering if he had scared her away. He'd tried his best in the preceding days to be nothing more than an attentive friend to her and an uncle figure to her son. Since his arrival, they had regained much of the friendliness they'd first enjoyed in Richmond, but he still sensed a reticence in her that he hadn't been able to break through.

Later that evening after dinner, he waited on the veranda, hoping she would come down after bidding Austen goodnight. They'd spent most evenings with Miss Endicott and in the company of some of the other guests, sometimes crossing the bridge to the neighboring town of Trouville or strolling down the long lit pier between the two towns.

He breathed a sigh of relief when he saw Alice entering the verandah by herself this evening. He turned to her from his view of the ocean when she came to stand beside him by the railings. "Where's Miss Endicott?"

"She decided to stay upstairs tonight. She asked me to give you her excuses."

Was his ally helping his cause along this evening? "Is she feeling unwell?"

Alice shook her head. "I think she merely wanted a quiet evening to herself."

Before Alice could suggest anything with the other guests, Nick said, "Would you like to walk along the beach?"

Instead of replying immediately, she stood a moment, gazing out at the black sea. To avoid a refusal, he said, "We can see the remains of today's sandcastle."

She smiled. "I imagine the tide has washed it away."

The steady rhythm of the waves beckoned them. The murmur of other holiday guests came over the verandah, but the beach was wide and empty.

They descended the shallow wooden steps onto the grassy sand dunes. Before leaving the steps, she halted. "Let me take off my shoes so we can walk on the sand better."

He held out his hand and she put hers in it while she bent to remove her heeled slippers. Holding them by the straps, she straightened. "Thank you."

"Ready?"

"Yes."

"Come." He offered his hand again and after a second's hesitation, she put hers in it.

The dune grasses shifted in the breeze. A lacy cloud drifted over the half-moon overhead.

He enjoyed the feel of her soft hand in his, realizing he'd never allowed himself this kind of companionship with a woman.

They walked in silence until they neared the spot where they had built a sandcastle earlier. The water now swirled around it. What had been sharp edges before were only shapeless mounds.

"So much work," she murmured, taking care not to step too close to the encroaching waves.

"Yes, like everything in life."

She glanced at him, as if surprised. "Do you see your own work that way?"

"In a sense. I hope it will outlast me, but I know I have only a season to accomplish what I wish."

"You have no one to leave it to?"

His dark eyes surveyed her over the sandcastle and he shrugged. "I have my brothers and their offspring, but I've provided well for them over the years."

She disengaged her hand from his and hugged her light cashmere shawl closer.

"Cold?"

She shook her head. "My wrap is sufficient." After a few minutes, she asked, "Why haven't you ever married?"

He gave a deep sigh, breathing in the sharp, salt-laden night air, having known this question would eventually come. He paused, deciding how to answer. She was waiting attentively.

"When I met you, you were too young." He didn't flinch from the surprised look in her eyes. "I had nothing to offer you, even if your age had not been an issue. Your father would never have countenanced anything between us."

He gave an embarrassed laugh. "I don't know if you'll believe me when I tell you that when I sailed for America, I had every intention of working hard until I had enough to come back and declare myself to you."

"I never knew," she said softly, her gaze roaming over his features as if seeing them for the first time.

He shook his head. "I was confident I would make a fortune virtually overnight. It didn't work out that way. The years went by and fortune seemed to elude me despite my efforts. I realized after a while that it had been a vain notion to think I could come back to England and win you.

After several years had passed, I imagined you married with children."

She looked down at the sand at her feet.

He shoved a hand through his hair, finding the next part the most difficult. "Five years ago, I decided it was time for me to marry and settle down, begin to build a dynasty and all that rot." Again, he gave a shame-faced laugh.

"I had had no time for romantic entanglements up to then. All my time and resources had gone into building up my company. But then I felt I had reached the place where I could begin to enjoy the fruits of my success. I began to look around me at what San Francisco society had to offer."

"You met someone?" came her soft voice.

"Yes." When she said nothing more, he continued. "I fancied myself in love. I should have known what she fancied was my pocketbook."

"No—"

He looked up at the swiftly spoken word.

"How can someone have treated you so shabbily." She sounded angry.

"Do you really think all women are as selfless as you?" he asked gently, touched by her obvious outrage.

"But, you have so many other assets than material wealth. I'm sure there were many women who would look beyond that."

"Do you think so?"

"I'm sure of it."

"You are as kind as you always were."

"I'm sorry if she hurt you."

He gave another cynical laugh. "I think if anything was hurt, it was my pride. I know now I was not really in love with her, if the state of my emotions are anything to be judged after I found her giving herself freely to another man."

Her sharp intake of breath caused him another bitter smile. "I don't know how anyone could be so cruel."

He ran a hand through his hair, looking away. "She was young, and I cannot say I blame her now for not falling in love with someone more interested in his work than in her."

"You cared more for your work?"

He chanced a cautious glance at her, gauging her tone. "At that time, yes."

He wanted to take her hand again, but she stepped away from him. "Shall we continue?"

"If you'd like," he said, sensing her withdrawal.

He led her beyond the high water mark to where the sand was dry and still warm from the day's sun. They passed another couple strolling along arm-in-arm. They had walked about a quarter of a mile when he halted again to gaze out at the dark ocean and listen to the sound of waves. The surf had risen a little and small white caps were visible in the moonlight.

She stooped to pick up a piece of driftwood and tossed it into the waves. It disappeared in the dark. "I wonder if I'll find it washed up tomorrow."

"Like me after fifteen years."

She glanced up at him and smiled. "I'm glad you decided to return after so long."

Her softly spoken words encouraged him. "When you tilt your head like that, you look just like the sixteen-year-old you used to be."

She gave a nervous laugh. "I'm far from that girl."

"I want to kiss you."

Her gaze shot upward at the abrupt statement.

She swallowed. "Perhaps that's not a good idea."

He lifted a tendril of hair that had blown across her cheek. "Why not?"

She looked away. "I'm not that girl you knew, nor are you the man I knew." She ended in a tone so low he had to bend to catch the words.

He stroked her cheek with the back of his hand. With one step she'd be in his arms, but he sensed she was as skittish as the strands of hair tossed about her face.

"Perhaps who we are now is better," he murmured, his fingers continuing their caress. Her skin was velvety soft.

"I don't know." Her voice was breathless although she tilted her head back a fraction, as if seeking his caresses. "You scare me sometimes."

"Scare you?" He narrowed his eyes at her, her words throwing him. "How do you mean?"

"You seem so sure of yourself, of what you want." Were those tears glinting in her eyes?

"I've never forgotten you, Alice," he murmured, his voice growing husky as he came to the end of the words, "and I've wanted you for a very long time." His gaze roamed over her, seeking some sign that she wanted him as much as he wanted her.

Not allowing her a chance to move away, he circled the nape of her neck with his hand and drew her closer. "Kiss me, Alice," he whispered against her, his lips hovering just over hers.

And then he touched them with his own.

He kissed her slowly, savoring the moment. He dug his fingers into her hair, bringing it tumbling from its loose knot. It was as silky as he'd always imagined.

Alice gasped as his mouth came down and covered hers.

His lips felt warm and soft against hers. Had he truly wanted her all this time? Her body and spirit thrilled at the thought. As she leaned closer to him, her arms inched upward, her hands clutching his lapels.

He kissed her thoroughly and she got the sense he knew exactly what he was doing. The way she imagined he did everything.

She couldn't help responding. Giving herself as she'd never done before, she felt like a bud that had only begun to open before its development had been arrested. Her petals unfurled at last, stretching out towards the sunshine.

Moments later they broke apart slightly. She felt dizzy with the sensations swirling through her and was glad of his hands on her back. She murmured against his shirt front. "You must have kissed a lot of women."

"I've had little practice."

She looked up at the words to find a frown creasing his brow. He loosened his hold enough to peer into her face. "I've just dreamed of this one for a very long time."

His answer stunned her. He couldn't mean he'd thought of kissing her for so many years.

She gave a nervous laugh. "I hope I didn't disappoint you, then."

He brought a finger up to touch her cheek. "No, you didn't disappoint. On the contrary. You've made me want you more."

The answer frightened and thrilled her. Yet, he spoke only of wanting her. "Does this mean that you are pursuing me the way you do a business enterprise?" Although she spoke the words lightly, she searched his eyes, fearing the truth.

"Is that what you think?"

"I don't know what to think."

With a sigh he let her go and stood a few feet away from her, looking out at the ocean. Had her answer displeased him?

He took up a piece of driftwood of his own and threw it into the surf. "I've learned over the years to go after what I want. Sometimes it takes me years before I get what I want, I'll admit." He turned to her again, and she stepped back, his words chilling her more than the breeze.

She drew the shawl tighter around her. "Do you always know what you want?"

"Generally speaking."

"Do you always get what you want?"

His mouth twisted. "As you have heard, no." After a moment he spoke. "What do *you* want, Alice?"

"I don't know," her answer was almost lost on the sound of the surf.

"Are you sure about that?"

She struggled to discern the meaning of his words. Did he think she was playing a game with him?

Before she could find a suitable reply, he said, "What are you so afraid of?"

How could she tell him it was the feelings he awakened in her that she feared most of all?

Abruptly, he turned away. "Come, you're getting cold. I'll take you back before you get a chill." His voice sounded almost harsh.

Had she disappointed him so much with her response? Would he again go without a word, leaving her unfulfilled, yearning…brokenhearted?

He began walking back toward the hotel—a distant

glimmer in the dark, not bothering to offer his hand or arm this time.

She followed silently after him, unsure whether she felt anger or disappointment.

Nick plodded through the sand, her accusation still smarting. Did she truly think he was as cold-blooded as to equate her to a business? He'd told her he'd never forgotten her and dreamed of their kiss—had that meant nothing to her?

The kiss he'd dreamed of for so many years had finally materialized. Manna in the desert, elixir to a dying man, the taste of her lips lingered in his memory—and made him wish for more.

He'd restrained himself, unsure if she'd welcome his kiss. But she'd given herself to him in a way that had emboldened him to hope that perhaps she could someday give him her heart.

Chancing a glance in her direction, he could read nothing from her expression in the dark. Unlike the young girl who'd kissed him inexpertly so many years ago, Alice was now a widow, someone who'd known the love of a man—a most worthy one from all reports. Was she comparing his kiss to her late husband's—a man who'd had the advantage of enjoying years with the woman he loved?

He dug his hands into his pockets, swallowing the bitterness that rose in him and threatened to spoil the recent intoxication of Alice's embrace. Clamping down on his emotions, he quickened his step, when all he wanted was to stop and grab Alice once again and crush her to himself until his kisses obliterated her late husband's.

By the time they reached the hotel and he put a hand to her arm to help her up the steps, he had no idea how to proceed.

He knew very well Alice was not like a business— although he'd faced plenty of complicated situations in the latter, situations requiring careful proceedings and lots of finesse. But his fiasco in San Francisco had taught him how little he understood women.

He was a different man now, and Alice was a completely different quantity from the young woman who'd jilted him. At the moment he had no idea how to read her. In the light spilling out from the wide doors of the hotel, she looked coolly elegant and not like a woman whom he'd so recently ravaged with his kisses.

"Thank you for the walk," she said in the well-bred tones of a lady being returned from a concert. "It was lovely."

Lovely? The moment he'd waited for for fifteen years relegated to a description one used to describe blancmange or a bouquet of flowers?

She looked away from him. "I think I'll retire now."

He nodded. "Let me walk you to your room."

"Very well."

They walked silently up the stairs. At her door, she held out her hand, not meeting his gaze anymore. He took her hand in his. At the last moment, he found he didn't have the control necessary to merely shake her hand and leave. Tentatively, feeling as unsure as a schoolboy, he leaned down and kissed her on the cheek.

He felt her stiffen a fraction. Feeling rebuffed, he bowed his head. "Good night. Sleep well."

Was he destined to destroy whatever he reached for in

the emotional realm? Was he the man Alice thought he was—nothing but an avaricious, ambitious, ruthless business tycoon?

How could he convince her otherwise?

Alice stood a long time at the narrow balcony in her room, staring out at the sea, hearing the relentless swish of waves, in and out. The sound mirrored her feelings, which swung from exhilaration at the remembrance of Nick's kiss to the doubts and fears rising to displace it.

She remembered the last time in her life she had allowed herself to feel like this. Only Nicholas had ever touched the deepest places in her.

But she'd paid a high price for reaching for what she'd wanted without weighing the consequences.

Banished from home, she had had to endure the strict atmosphere of her austere aunt and uncle and endure the taunts of their offspring. She hadn't been allowed to return to London until her twenty-first birthday.

That had been a turning point for her. A large party had been planned, of course, at a hotel ballroom. At the last moment, her father had absented himself. It had been the loneliest day of her life—swarmed by acquaintances and few loved ones.

Acquaintances. It had been Nick who'd first taught her the difference between them and real friends.

That day, Alice had realized her father would never change. She would always be waiting for him to come home, and something more important would always keep him away or give him only enough time to come in and leave before she'd have a chance to do something to capture his attention.

A week later she'd met Julian. He was a young divinity student visiting a relative in Richmond. She'd met him at church one morning. He'd called on her the next day.

His dreams of his own church and helping the poor in his community had inspired her. During the six weeks he'd been at his relatives recuperating from an illness, she'd grown to admire the young man.

But she'd never felt with him what she'd experienced with Nicholas.

Her mind went over that summer before her seventeenth birthday when she'd first met Nick. He'd fascinated her then as he did now. His strength of mind, strength of purpose, his ability to focus on her and make her feel like the most special creature on earth.

But he'd disappeared and crushed her youthful heart.

Why hadn't he ever written to her? Not even a note to tell her he could no longer see her? Day after day she'd waited for a line, one word from him. She would have run away with him then.

But she'd heard nothing. Her world had been ripped apart by him. She'd even gone back a few days later to Richmond Park where they'd ridden and found their two handkerchiefs still lying on the rock, stiff and dry.

She still had them folded away in a drawer.

And now?

Did Nicholas love her? He had said nothing of love. Only want. Did he want her as a possession, like owning a business? She'd vowed long ago never to marry a man like her father.

She gripped the iron railing under her hands, knowing she should go in but knowing she would only toss and turn in bed. She had loved Julian, she was sure of it, but the tumult she felt around Nicholas threw what she'd felt for Julian in doubt. It reawakened all her girlhood longings.

She put her head in her hands, hating the direction of her thoughts. Why did her love for Julian now seem so pallid in contrast to what Nicholas stirred in her?

But she'd been a good wife! She'd supported her husband in his work and nursed him through his illnesses and been with him at the end. Nothing else could compare to that.

Why did Nicholas have to reenter her life now and confuse her so? And what of Austen? Would he think so little of his mother if he thought his father was being replaced? She thought of how good Nick was with Austen. Her son was finally emerging from his shell and behaving like a normal, active seven-year-old. Would Nicholas cause him to forget his father?

Would Nicholas always be there for Austen?

Her son had already lost one father. She would not let him lose two.

The next morning, Nick was down early, having woken at dawn and watched the sun rise over the Normandy coast. He entered the dining room, impatient for his first sight of Alice to see how she would greet him. Would she repudiate him? Ignore what had happened between them? Ask him to leave?

He heard Austen's cheerful voice soon after he had sat down. The boy came over to his table, followed by his nanny.

"Can we see if my sandcastle is still there this morning?" was his first question as he took his place.

Nick nodded to Miss Grove and pulled a chair out for

her. "I'm afraid I checked on it last night, and it didn't survive the tide." At the look of chagrin on the boy's face, he added, "We'll build another one."

"After breakfast?" He lifted his chin as his nanny tied the napkin around his neck.

Nick smiled and sat back down. "I thought we might visit the hippodrome. Have you ever seen horses race each other around a track?"

Austen shook his head.

"It can be quite exciting." He signaled a waiter over and ordered breakfast for the boy. His French was rudimentary—taught to him by his mother when he was a boy. He turned to Miss Grove, who had a better command of the language. "I'm afraid you'd better order your own."

She smiled and turned to the waiter.

At that moment, he saw Alice and her friend enter the dining room together. They spotted him and made their way to the table.

He stood before they reached it and waited for them.

He nodded to Miss Endicott and turned immediately to Alice.

"Good morning," he said, trying to read her expression.

She lifted her blue eyes to him, the corners of her mouth lifting in what seemed to him a tentative smile. Was she, too, unsure how to proceed? It gave him hope. It meant she was not rejecting his suit out of hand.

His own smile grew and he pulled out a chair for her.

"Thank you," she murmured.

She looked so fetching today in a white gown all ruched up the front, with big blue bows matching the deep color of her eyes going up the length of it.

He turned reluctantly away from her and to Miss Endicott.

"Thank you," she replied when he'd pulled out a chair for her as well. "It's a fine morning, is it not?"

He made an attempt to join in the casual pleasantries as they ordered their breakfast and he mentioned his idea for visiting the famous hippodrome. They seconded the idea enthusiastically.

"Perhaps we can take a ride around the countryside afterwards," suggested Miss Endicott. "I've heard there are some lovely chateaux and apple orchards to be seen."

They continued planning their day as they ate.

When they broke up after breakfast, planning to meet again in a short while, Nick arranged for a trip back to Le Havre to follow up with a company which looked promising. He could work some this evening to catch up.

He didn't have a chance to talk alone with Alice until late that afternoon. During their outing, they behaved as if nothing had happened to them the night before. He took his cue from her, although he caught her looking at him a few times, and he was hard-pressed to keep from gazing at her.

When they returned from their long drive, they all separated to freshen up and take naps. Nick spent the time working in his room. He descended to the hotel lobby as soon as he could and looked about for Alice, hoping she might, too, want a word alone with him.

He stopped at the entrance of the veranda. Several guests were there and he'd almost turned back in disappointment when he saw her at the far end chatting with a couple. When she spotted him across the verandah she nodded and smiled. Encouraged, he walked over to the group. After a few pleasantries, they excused themselves from the couple.

When they were out of earshot, he turned to her. "Where's Austen?"

"He's still upstairs with Nanny Grove. I told her to put him to bed early this evening." She smiled at him. "He had a full day today. Thank you for planning such a lovely outing."

"You're welcome. It was nothing too extraordinary."

"You are good at organizing things."

He looked at her quizzically, not sure if she was complimenting him or not. He'd thought long and hard last night about how he should approach her. "I think we need to talk. Would you care to take a short walk before dinner?"

He waited, not realizing he was holding his breath for her answer. She looked at him steadily. "Yes, I think we do."

He didn't know if her reply signaled good or ill for them, it was said so seriously. At least, it meant she hadn't dismissed his kiss.

This time, they walked along the boardwalk on the grassy sand dunes above the beach. The surf had continued rougher than in the preceding days and there were no bathers in the water nor many people on the sand.

They walked until they came to a small pavilion overlooking the ocean. Thankfully, it was deserted at the moment, most people having gone in to dress for dinner.

He motioned to the wooden bench set under the pavilion and took a seat beside her after she'd sat down.

Suddenly, all his neatly prepared speech deserted him. He cleared his throat. "I—"

"Wha—" she began.

They both stopped and then said, "I'm sorry—" at the same time.

"You first," she said quietly, clasping her hands on her lap like an obedient schoolgirl.

"I merely wanted to beg your pardon if I offended you last night. Was it presumptuous of me to—" he paused "—kiss you?"

He watched the color rise in her cheeks. Slowly, she raised her eyes and looked into his. Their deep blue pierced him anew and he wanted nothing more than to lean forward and kiss her again, this time showing none of the restraint he had last night. "No." The word was so low a whisper he would have lost it if it hadn't been so clearly apparent from the shape of her rosy lips.

Instead, he dared reach out and cover her hands with one of his. "I—that is—" Why was he acting so unsure of himself? He cleared his throat anew and began again. "I would like to court you, Alice."

The warmth grew in her eyes and then it slowly faded and she looked away from him at the ocean in front of them. "I thought about you last night, that is, about us. I didn't know what your intentions were."

He wanted to protest that his intentions were very clear but he remained silent sensing she needed to speak. He watched her profile and waited.

"I loved my husband and am not sure—"she bent her head and looked down at their hands "—if it's right to think of giving my affections to anyone else. Part of me feels as if I'm being disloyal to him."

He could see the words were difficult for her. They were no less difficult for him to receive. Would she ever love him the way he loved her? The irony was that he'd known her before ever Julian had met her.

He schooled his features to show nothing. "I don't want to compete with your late husband," he said, looking toward the ocean, whose whitecaps reflected his turbulent emotions. "I met you many, many years ago, and regret now that I didn't speak for you then."

"I never knew what our kiss had meant to you."

His hand reached out for hers again and he clasped it. "It meant the world to me. You were too young, and I left, thinking I would never have the right to pay my addresses to you, not if I remained in England. When I saw you upon my return, it was as if I'd been given another chance."

He squeezed her hands gently beneath his. "I would like to marry you, Alice."

She drew in her breath and he saw wonder in her eyes. Did it really come as a surprise to her? Before he could formulate any words, she tilted her chin the slightest degree upward and he found himself leaning down to her.

Once again, their lips met and he could think of nothing else.

She was the one who drew away first. "We mustn't here—in a public place like this…" Her breathing was rapid and she didn't quite meet his eyes.

"I'm sorry." He struggled to keep himself in check.

She moved a little apart from him and he felt a sense of loss.

He gave a deep sigh. "The Lord has allowed me to prosper and has given me the chance to come back and claim you. I don't ask you to know your mind now. All I ask is if you would permit me to call upon you when we return to London."

Slowly she nodded.

For now, it would have to be enough for him.

Chapter Fourteen

Alice felt sad to leave France. It had been a wonderful interlude, a time in which she wasn't required to think about anything back home. But she knew it couldn't last. Her work required her back in London. But she feared what a return to their normal lives would bring to the growing closeness between her and Nick when each returned to their work.

She was afraid to depend on Nick's attentiveness and thoughtfulness. What would he be like when he was pulled by the demands of his business? Would he even have time for her, much less a little boy, who'd grown dangerously fond of him?

As soon as she returned to her office, she put the final touches to the gala dinner for Nick, which was to be held that evening.

Even the lord mayor was going to be present. She smiled in satisfaction as she eyed the acceptance she'd just received in the post. It would be a grand event, a fitting event for Nick. No one deserved it more than he, who'd worked hard to achieve the success he was enjoying now.

She was looking over the menu in her office when she heard a throat clearing. She looked up to find her brother in the doorway.

"Hello, Geoffrey, what brings you here?" Her brother never came to the Housing Society office.

He walked into the office with barely a nod and took the chair opposite her desk. "I thought it the best place to find you this time of day."

She frowned at his grim tone. "What is it, Geoff? You sound as if you'd had some bad news."

The chair creaked under him as he leaned forward and removed his top hat and placed it on his lap. As usual he was impeccably dressed in a black frock coat and charcoal trousers. He fiddled with the brim of his hat.

"Are you still seeing that Tennent chap?"

She put down the pencil she'd been holding. "If you mean Nicholas Tennent, he is a friend of mine."

He frowned at her. "Is it true he showed up in Deauville at the same hotel you and Macey were at?"

"Yes." Who had told him? And why did she feel defensive as if she were still twenty-one?

He nodded at her as if he knew something she didn't. "You'd better have a care. Elizabeth Raleigh and her husband said they saw you there in his company quite a bit."

A British couple she'd seen one afternoon there. She shook her head at how quickly gossip traveled. "Mr. Tennent was very good company. He made himself very useful with Austen."

Geoffrey's lips thinned. "Careful he doesn't start looking at him as if he's his papa."

She looked down at her pencil, considering how she would answer. "Would that be such a bad thing?"

He made a choking sound. "I cannot believe you are even contemplating such a notion."

She looked at him steadily, her irritation changing to real anger. "Geoffrey, in case you've forgotten it, I am a full-grown woman who needn't consult with you about whom I am seeing."

"Except when it's an upstart scoundrel who is trying to muscle in on our family's firm."

"What are you saying?"

"He's bought out Steward."

She stared at him, the words making no sense. "Old Mr. Steward?" That was Father's principal partner, a silent partner who'd always left her father in full control of the day-to-day business of the company.

He nodded grimly. "Alistair was a trusting simpleton. Tennent seems to have charmed him at his club and convinced the doddering old fool to sell him his partnership. You know what this means?"

She didn't dare hazard a guess.

Geoff rubbed a hand across his chin. "He now owns fifty percent of our company, the firm our grandfather established and our father built up to what it is today."

She looked down at her desk, the papers she had been studying before her brother had walked in making no more sense to her. "I don't believe it. There must be some explanation."

Her brother gave a dry bark of a laugh. "Oh, Alice, don't be so naïve. There's an explanation all right. Tennent wants to get back at us for some slight that happened over fifteen years ago."

He jumped up and began to pace. "He'll stop at nothing until he destroys this family. Well, I won't have it!"

"What are you talking about?" Now, she was truly alarmed. Her normally stolid brother was acting positively choleric.

"Father sacked him. For what I don't know. Probably incompetence." He stopped in mid-stride and looked at her, thrusting his hat at her to drive home his point. "I spoke to Father's old secretary, not Simpson, but the man he hired to replace Tennent when he up and left Father."

She waited, dreading what her brother might say to destroy her newfound hopes for happiness.

"He says Father gave Tennent the boot without so much as a reference. It was right after that accident. He was in his rights to do so, since Tennent had only been with him a few weeks." Geoffrey shook his head in disgust. "It was then he took off for America. Now that he's made good, he probably wants to get back at Father."

Alice sat back in relief. "He already told me about Father. But he was almost thankful for it now. It was the reason he emigrated." She waved a hand. "My goodness, he's amassed a fortune. He doesn't need your company!"

Her brother wasn't listening to her. "It's clear Tennent has had it in for us since he has returned the wealthy American. He's out to prove something. He's got to be stopped or he'll destroy all our family has worked for for three generations—as well as your heart and reputation if you let him."

"You're wrong, Geoff."

Geoffrey pinioned her with a look. "This concerns you as much as it does me. This is Austen's future. Do you want some upstart secretary muscling his way in and stealing your son's inheritance?"

She gave an outraged laugh. "Nicholas would never do that!"

"So, it's *Nicholas* now? Gone as far as that, has it?"

She clamped her mouth shut. Seeing her brother's grim look, she relented enough to say, "Mr. Tennent wants to marry me."

"Hah! He not only wants to take over our firm, but he wants to have you, too! The filthy scoundrel. How dare he!"

Alice stood. "I won't have you saying such things about him!"

He leaned over the desk. "He doesn't care a whit for you! He just wants to humiliate us! He's out to prove a point!"

She put her hands to her ears, not wanting to hear any more.

"Don't you see, Alice? He just wants you in order to steal control of Father's firm."

"But you still have half the company. There's nothing he can do to buy you out!"

He leaned closer, his knuckles white atop the desk. "*You own ten percent in the company.* All he needs to do is marry you and *he'll control the firm.*"

"What are you saying?" she whispered. "Father disinherited me."

Geoff moved his head slowly from side to side like a pendulum, his gaze never leaving hers. "Not entirely. Victor persuaded him to allow you ten percent. It was small enough not to make a deal of difference. Victor said we would merely invest your profits and keep them for Austen when he reached his majority. That's the only way Father would be satisfied to change his will."

She fell back in her chair, feeling numb. "Why was I never told this?"

"You can't let yourself be used like this!" Geoff jabbed a hand through his hair, his voice cracking with desperation. He'd never been so distraught, not even when she'd married Julian.

She stared at her brother. "Why didn't you tell me?"

"Because it was the only way Father would agree! You disobeyed him. Be thankful for Victor who championed you. Besides, the shares have made nothing this past year.

"All that's neither here nor there now. You've never lacked for anything. I've given you Father's house, you've a houseful of servants. What's of concern now is Tennent. He wants to ruin us, I tell you. He's bought up the company behind a front."

"What are you talking about?"

He gave a harsh laugh. "While he woos you, he's quietly bought the shares using another company, so none of us—least of all *you*—will know he's behind it."

It couldn't be. "There must be some explanation."

Geoffrey continued pacing. "Now all he needs is your ten percent, which he'll get as soon as he marries you. You haven't gone as far as agreeing, have you?" he asked, swiveling around to her.

She didn't bother answering, but continued trying to sort through it. "B-but Nicholas wouldn't know about my shares. How could he know?"

"Oh, doesn't he?" he barked out a grim laugh. "He's made sure to find out everything about our firm."

Her world was cracking under her and she had no idea how it had come about. She leaned her head into a hand, trying to think clearly.

Geoffrey's voice grew quiet. "One of the board members

came to tell me this morning. They're going to force me out as president and chairman of the board."

She drew in her breath. "How is that possible?"

"All he needs is full control and he'll demand my full resignation. I know it." He ran a hand through his hair, his eyes darting left and right.

"Why should he want to do that?"

He pressed his lips together, a sheen of perspiration covering the top of his lip. "Because he's a ruthless scoundrel. You've got to stop him."

"Me? What can I possibly do?"

"Don't let yourself be tricked by him. He can't think he can take us all over. He only wants you to solidify his hold on our business." He grabbed her hand. She'd never seen desperation in her brother's eyes. "You've got to help me. It'll mean my ruin otherwise." He looked away from her. "I've made some poor decisions.

Then his bloodshot eyes focused on her again, and his hand squeezed hers painfully. "Don't let him use you! He only wants to take you as the crowning achievement to his insatiable greed. Don't let yourself become his trophy! He cares nothing for you, only what your name represents. It's only his pride because Father thwarted his ambitions so long ago."

She broke away from her brother's hand. "Leave me, please leave me." Her voice cracked and she turned away from her brother.

She had to see Nick. That's all she knew after her brother left and the office grew quiet, broken only by the ticking of a clock on a shelf nearby. She didn't know how much time had passed as she sat there staring at her desk, unseeing.

Could Geoff's accusations be true? Was Nick only interested in getting back at her father through her? Had he pretended some attraction to her, was his kiss only pretense? Thinking back to it now, had what she took for expertise been in truth the carefully controlled performance of someone proceeding with his calculations, weighing everything as he did in business? Had he been playing a role, a role he may indeed have found distasteful?

She stood from her desk, unable to bear her thoughts.

But what need had Nick to stoop to feign an attraction? He was rich and powerful. He could have any woman he wanted. Why bother with her family?

She stood at the window looking through the film of curtain at the street beyond. Her thoughts went back to that summer she'd first met him. How infatuated she'd been.

All the fears of abandonment following his disappearance, of thinking herself unlovable, came to flood her now.

Oh, dear Lord, show me the way. Show me the truth. Is this man worthy of my love? she prayed.

She had to know. Like an automaton, she picked up her gloves, hat and handbag, glancing down at her bare finger before donning her gloves. She'd removed her wedding band when she'd come back from Deauville.

Had she betrayed Julian's memory for someone so wholly opposed to his values? No, she wouldn't think it. It couldn't be.

She stumbled toward the omnibus stop by sheer instinct, her thoughts all consumed by Nicholas Tennent.

The omnibus was crowded with people and she squeezed onto the wooden bench between two women, a heavy-set one whose clothes reeked of sweat, and another who barely moved to make room for her. Alice held her lawn handkerchief to her nostrils, feeling sick as the omnibus began to rattle and sway over the cobblestones.

Bitterness and doubt crept into her thoughts, try as she might to suppress them, not least because of Nick's absence from Austen. Austen had asked for him every day. They'd seen little of Nicholas since their return from Deauville. He'd sent her a note the day after their arrival in London that he'd found several things pending at his office which would take him a few days to clear up. Had one of them been the takeover of her father's firm?

When she arrived at the number on Nick's business card, she glanced up in surprise at the imposing office building. Expecting a modest office within the building, she was further taken aback to discover the whole five-story building housed Tennent and Company.

She opened the polished wooden door, its brass plaque glowing. Inside, clerks bustled to and fro, others bent over their high desks, all looking important. It reminded her painfully of her father's firm. The few times she'd stepped across its threshold, she'd been confronted by the same hum of activity—of money being made, she'd always told herself. Now, it gave her a feeling of foreboding. Had she really stopped to think about what gave Nick's life meaning? All that she'd repudiated.

A young clerk cleared his throat beside her, and she jumped. "May I be of service, madam?"

"Yes. Yes, please. I should like to see Mr. Tennent." She handed him her card.

He glanced at it and gave her a slight bow. "Very well. Would you care to wait in a more private chamber?"

"No, thank you. I shall wait here." She clasped her hands over her handbag and edged against the wall.

"Very well, madam."

In a few minutes, he returned. "Mr. Tennent will see you, if you'd care to follow me."

He led her to the lift and held the door open for her. With a bang, he slid it shut and the brass cage began to rise with creaking sounds. She was calm enough by then to notice it went to the top floor. Up here, everything was hushed. The building featured more modern devices and more opulence than her father's. Oil paintings lined the corridors on the top floor and a thick Turkish carpet covered the anteroom floor. They stopped before a heavy mahogany door at the end of the corridor.

The clerk knocked and immediately entered. He stayed at the door and motioned her in. "Mrs. Lennox to see you, sir."

When Alice entered, Nick had already risen from the large desk and was advancing toward her, his hand held out. "Alice, how good to see you." He gave the clerk a curt nod. "Thank you, Jeffries, that will be all."

She heard the heavy door click behind her and felt at a loss as to what to say. The sight of Nick overwhelmed her. In the scant few days she hadn't seen him, she already missed him unbearably, and she realized in that moment she didn't want to feel this way about a man. The risks were too great.

He took her hand in his and she fought the impulse to draw back. But she detected a look of puzzlement in his features, and for a second she thought he would stoop down and kiss her. But he let go of her hand and stepped back.

"I was going to stop by Park Lane this evening to call on you." He ran a hand through his hair and half-turned away as if embarrassed. "I bought something for Austen."

"You needn't buy him things to assure his affection. He

already adores you. Indeed, he has been asking for you every day since our return."

A frown formed at her words. "I'm sorry. I've been meaning every day to stop in at least for a few minutes, but it seems I've been tied to the office until late each night."

She looked down. "Yes, I understand." She'd grown up with such a father.

Suddenly, she didn't want to confront Nicholas. She wanted him to confide in her. She shouldn't have to be questioning him. He should be open and honest with her. There should be nothing hidden between them if they were to have a future together. She didn't realize the pleading look in her eyes as she looked at him silently, clasping her hands in front of her.

He took a step toward her. "What is it?"

She shook her head.

"You must have come by for a reason."

She gave a short laugh. "Do I need a reason?"

He touched her arm. "Of course you don't. But you seem, I don't know. Something's happened." He scanned her face. "Is it Austen?"

At the shake of her head, he continued. "Something with the dinner? It's still set for eight o'clock?"

The gala dinner. She'd forgotten all about it. What was she going to do about that?

His sharp tone penetrated her confused thoughts. "What's happened? Has there been a hitch?"

"No." She swallowed. Before he had to ask anything else, she said, "How is your business these days? You said you had much to do since your return."

"Yes." He gave a shrug and embarrassed laugh at that.

"I've never taken a holiday before and didn't realize how much I'd find piled up at my return. Not that I wouldn't do it again. Not to worry, though, I'll have everything up to date in a few days and will have more time to spare."

She looked at him sadly. Would this be her future? Living with a man whose priorities were just like her father's? Without thinking, she found herself saying, "Geoffrey came to see me today." This was his chance to tell her.

He raised an eyebrow. "Is that unusual?"

She shrugged and approached his massive, oblong desk, its ebony surface like a mirror. So much like her father's. "It is when he comes to my humble office."

"Maybe he missed you while you were away."

Was that cynicism in his tone? She glanced back at him. He hadn't moved and he reminded her of a silent statue, his features as if carved in stone. "Perhaps." She turned to study his desk once again. Lots of papers covered it but they were all neatly arranged. Were some of them concerning Shepard and Company? Now, Shepard & Tennent. "You seem to be very busy."

"Yes."

"Do you have much to do with my father's firm?"

He said nothing until she was finally forced to turn to him once again. She was struck by the intent way he was looking at her. "Why do you ask?"

She shrugged imperceptibly. "No reason, merely curious."

He walked around his desk to stand by his chair. "Shepard and Company and Tennent & Company are competitors, and in that sense, would have little direct involvement with each other."

"Yes, I see," she murmured, looking down at his papers

again, feeling a disappointment so profound it almost wounded her.

She took a deep breath and looked up with a bright smile. "Well, I must be going. I have much to do and… and…you're busy." Her voice broke and she turned away quickly and hurried to the door.

Nick stared at Alice. What had happened? Before she had a chance to turn the door knob, he realized she was going to walk out without telling him.

"Wait!"

The word came out a brusque command. It succeeded in stilling her hand. In a few strides he was at her side before she had a chance to tighten her hand on the knob once again.

"What is it?" he asked, hardly daring to touch her sleeve.

She lifted stricken eyes to him. "Why didn't you tell me?"

What was she referring to? Was it because he had scarcely been to see her or Austen since their return? He wanted to make it up to her.

He searched his brain, but the only thing that came to him was his maneuver with her father's firm. She couldn't know about that. Could she? As the seconds ticked by, a sick suspicion spread in his gut. How had it been discovered?

"Tell you what?" he asked steadily.

She turned away from him as if she'd received a physical blow from him. He dropped his hand. "You know," she whispered.

The feeling in the pit of his stomach grew. "Does this have to do with your brother's business?"

The look in her eyes as she raised them to his gave him the answer he needed.

He shoved a hand through his hair, wondering how to explain. "Who told you?"

She gave a strangled laugh, turning away from him again. "*Who told me?* Does it matter? Isn't it more important that I didn't hear it from you? When exactly were you planning to tell me?"

He stared at her, finding it hard to believe—and yet, all too easy to believe—that she was doubting him. "Sometime after we were married."

She stared at him open-mouthed then began shaking her head. "You were going to calmly put my brother out of business and tell me about it after we were married? You are a worse scoundrel than Geoffrey claims."

He gave a short, bitter laugh. "I should think he would know what it takes."

Her voice rose. "You go behind his back and plan to take over his firm and you have the temerity to call *him* a scoundrel?"

He stared at her, hardly believing she was so quick to judge him against her brother.

"You'll swallow him up with no thought to how it might affect me?" she whispered, eyeing him as if he were a monster.

He kept his voice deceptively soft. "Careful you don't draw the wrong conclusions."

"What other conclusion can I draw if I'm not given any?"

"You could trust me."

"A man who was treated badly by my father? A man who might be courting his daughter in order to gain full control of his business?"

Each word was like a slap in the face. He felt the accusation hit deep.

"Is that why you looked me up, Nicholas? Is that why you bothered to befriend Austen?" Her voice began to quaver. "You could have done anything to me, but why— why—" she wiped angrily at her eyes, her voice breaking "—why did you have to gain Austen's trust? It wasn't worthy of you!"

She turned back to the door. He planted his palm against it, not believing she would really leave him like this.

"Do you really think I would hurt you and your little boy?"

Her tear-filled eyes looked up into his, but she said nothing. "It's too late to cancel the gala, but I must tell you I shan't be present. I can't bring myself to honor someone who would stoop to dishonor my family in such an underhanded way."

He dropped his hand from the door, staring at her. Could she really doubt him to this degree? If that was the case, there was nothing left for him to say.

"Why, Nick, why?"

He stepped away from her. "I'm a ruthless businessman, remember?"

He watched her leave the office.

As the echo of the door faded, Nick continued staring at it, not believing the woman he'd waited for so many years had truly thought so little of him.

The image of her first husband, a saintly man, came to taunt him. She must have been measuring Nick against the curate all along, and finally found he couldn't measure up.

He felt his eyes begin to fill, and he stepped back, aghast to find himself crying—over a woman. He never cried, not since he'd been a lad of about four and seen how little time his poor mother had for sympathy for such things as scraped knees and cut fingers.

He swiped at his eyes angrily.

When he reached his desk, he stood staring down at the papers lying there before sitting down. The evidence before him was irrefutable. Shepard and Company owned and had owned for years—behind the front of other firms—a number of housing blocks in the slums, of the kind Alice had pointed out to him, of inferior quality.

Complaints had been pouring into the city officials of sinking floors, flooding, leaking roofs—without much response from the government, since the tenants were people of little political or economic clout. But a few conscientious journalists had taken up the cause of the tenants and written about some of the worst complaints.

Nick sighed and rubbed the back of his neck. He hadn't yet decided how to break it to Alice. She'd caught him unprepared. He'd wanted to gather all the evidence before presenting it to her—and show her how he planned to rectify the faults of her family.

He sat down and slumped over his desk, all energy leaving him.

Since the day he'd seen Alice again, he'd allowed himself to believe their love might have survived over a decade, that there was a woman worthy of his trust, a woman like no other, who was willing to forsake all for their love.

She'd declared she'd been willing to forsake her family for him fifteen years ago.

But, now that her trust had been put to a test, she'd proven incapable of believing in his honor and integrity. Whatever she'd felt for him had not been strong enough to withstand her brother's poison.

He hadn't realized until this moment how much he'd wanted her trust. Did he want anything less of his future wife?

* * *

Alice spent the rest of the afternoon frantically seeking Macey. Now that she'd renounced her attendance at the dinner, she needed to inform someone. After all, she was the hostess.

When she finally found her at her small flat, Macey stared at her. "You're what?"

"I can't be at the dinner tonight. You'll have to do the honors for me."

"Tell me what this is about."

"I'd rather not." She turned away from her, unwilling to talk about Nicholas to anyone else yet, when she, herself, was still too hurt and confused.

Her friend sat down. "I'm sorry, my dear, but I will do nothing for you unless you tell me the real reason you can't be there tonight."

Alice finally sat down next to her with a long sigh. "I can't talk about it. Suffice it to say, I just found out something disquieting about Nicholas. It involves Father's firm."

Macey remained serious. "Who told you?"

"Geoffrey came to see me today."

"I see." Her friend was quiet a long time. Then she turned to her. "I don't know what it might be about. I know nothing of your family's firm. All I know is are you quite certain what he has told you about Nicholas Tennent is the truth?"

Alice searched her friend's eyes. "I don't know. But he wouldn't lie about something so serious. I would soon know the truth. Besides, you didn't see him. He sounded desperate. I've never seen him in such a state."

"Have you talked to Mr. Tennent about it?"

Alice looked away. "I went to his office. I've just come from there. I had to know from him if there was any truth to it."

"Well?"

"He as good as admitted it! What am I to do?" She squeezed her eyes shut. "All he said was to trust him!"

"Maybe you ought to, my dear."

She turned to look at Macey. "But how can he ask that of me? I have Austen to think of, too. What if Nick is no different than Father was? How can I think about joining my life to his—to someone who stands for everything that I find so unworthy?"

Her friend covered her hands. "Only you can answer that. But be careful you don't misjudge Mr. Tennent. He seemed an honorable man to me."

"I don't know…" Alice rose. "I must think…"

Macey joined her. "Yes, think and pray. I'll be at the gala. I'll do anything you need me to do, but think long and hard before you leave him there. It would be a terrible humiliation for someone like him."

Nick sat at the head table, ignoring the buzz of voices around him and the clink of silverware on china. Miss Endicott sat beside him, in the place that had been reserved for Alice.

He eased his standing collar away from his neck with his finger, wondering how much longer before this cursed event would be finished. The meal was finally over and now the meeting would convene.

Miss Endicott patted his hand. "You're doing fine. Now, you'll just have to sit back and listen to a number of items being presented before we'll discuss the donation. Then after a few more speeches of appreciation and acknowledgement, I will present you the plaque and only then may you abscond." She said the last with a smile.

"All this for the privilege of having a donation accepted?"

She smiled sadly. "We Brits like to stand on ceremony. You must indulge us in this. You are the prodigal returned home—well, if not the prodigal, then the boy who made good."

"Where is Alice?"

His abrupt question gave her pause. "I don't know. She had a lot to think about."

He looked away, saying in an undertone, "Only one thing as far as I'm concerned."

"What is that?" she asked softly.

He turned back to her. "Would I do anything to hurt her?"

"Maybe you are asking a lot of someone who was abandoned by you once before."

He frowned at her. "I never willingly abandoned her."

"She might know that with her head, but her heart might still feel the pain of abandonment."

The words caused him much thought.

After that they spoke no more.

The speeches began, business colleagues speaking about the needs of the growing city, others lauding him for his contribution to the business world. Finally, he was presented with his plaque.

It should have filled him with joy, but it left him cold. The one who would have made the evening truly meaningful for him was absent.

He would have long since left, but Miss Endicott had proven a true ally and he wouldn't dishonor her that way.

Afterward, people crowded around him, all vying for his

attention. He answered as many questions as he could, smiled at people's expressions of gratitude until he felt his lips would crack.

"Excuse me, Mr. Tennent, would you answer a few questions for *The Daily News?*"

He braced himself for the journalist's questions. "Yes, of course."

"This is a sizeable endowment to one single charity. What made you select the Housing Society?"

"I was acquainted with Mrs. Lennox years ago and felt confident that any charity run by her would be a worthy one."

He continued asking Nick questions about his time in America and his decision to return to London. Nick answered each one in as general terms as possible, not disposed to have all his personal reasons in print for all to read.

"My invitation stated that Mrs. Lennox, as head of the Housing Society, would present the plaque to you herself. If she was the main reason you decided on this charity for your donation, may I enquire why she was not present this evening?"

The question only made him more aware than ever what others must be asking themselves about Alice's pointed absence.

"I don't know. You shall have to ask her. If you'll excuse me, I need to speak to some others." He turned away and made his way out of the room, ignoring any more requests for his attention.

Chapter Fifteen

Alice sat in her drawing room staring at the papers laid out on the table before her.

It was the day after the dinner. She'd heard nothing except for a brief note from Macey telling her everything had gone off without a hitch. She gave no other details.

Alice had lain awake most of the night by turns staring dry-eyed at the dark ceiling and tossing this way and that, wondering, worrying, fretting.

She hadn't had the energy or heart to go to the office this morning. It was almost too much to keep up a front before Austen at breakfast. It was with relief that she'd bid him goodbye as he went off to the park with Nanny Grove.

Then as she'd sat in the drawing room, her hands idle, her maid had brought in a large, thick envelope in the morning's post.

Not recognizing the writing on it, but seeing the name of Nick's firm on the return address, she quickly opened it.

Instead of any kind of letter, a thick sheaf of official looking documents fell out on her lap. Only a small white square of notepaper clipped to the top contained Nicholas's writing. She grabbed it up eagerly.

It only held one sentence:

I was saving these for your wedding gift. Seeing that is no longer a possibility, I am giving them to you now.

No closing, only the scrawl of his name: *Nicholas.*

Feeling a sharp jab of disappointment that there were no explanations, no apologies, nothing, she finally turned to examine the papers.

At first they made no sense. But her heart began to pound when she saw the fancy scroll of the name of Shepard and Steward, Ltd. across several.

Many of the pages seemed to be shares made out to her. She continued reading, growing more confused as she saw articles and documents about the London Building Society, among other building firms. Newspaper clippings she'd read herself detailed the problems and complaints with their substandard building practices. Further on she found numerous documents with the names of other companies. Little by little she began to decipher the information.

It listed all the companies that had invested in these building societies and described the amounts of their investments. It was like following a maze, so many companies seemed to be owned by others, making it difficult to track which company had invested in which building society.

Her head ached from reading so much fine print. But she didn't stop until she had succeeded in following the path of one, whose investment in the building societies was indubitably clear. Shepard and Steward, Limited.

The papers fell to her lap, as she stared before her.

What had her father been responsible for?

* * *

"Well, you see, I need to go away for a bit." Nicholas sat on the park bench facing the Round Pond at Kensington Gardens, his head bent toward Austen.

Alice held her breath, trying to catch his next words.

Austen swung his legs back and forth on the bench. "Where do you have to go?"

"Back to America. It's where I came from."

"Maybe I can come, too?"

Nicholas draped his arm across the back of the bench. "Maybe some day. But now you have your lessons, and your mother, and Moppet."

Before Austen could reply, Alice stepped forward. They both turned around.

Austen smiled brightly at her. "Hello, Mama."

"Hello, Austen. I'm glad you are still here." She'd taken a chance that perhaps she'd find Nicholas with him. She turned stricken eyes to him, afraid he'd get up and leave.

But he only watched her, his expression unreadable. Taking a deep breath, she walked around the iron bench to face them.

Austen's face turned serious. "Mama, Mr. Tennent has told me he has to go away. Why can't we come with him like he did with us to France?"

She moistened her lips, clutching her handbag in front of her. "I don't know. Perhaps he'll be very busy with his work."

Austen immediately turned to Nicholas. "Will you be very busy?"

She closed her eyes, too afraid of hearing his reply.

"I'll never be too busy for you."

She bit her lip, her eyes filling with tears at the reply.

Trying to compose herself once again, she approached Austen and knelt down in front of him. "Austen, darling,

Mama needs to talk to Mr. Tennent. I want you to go home with Nanny Grove now."

"But Mama, Mr. Tennent just came."

"I understand. But this is a serious talk."

"Are you going to say goodbye to him?"

She swallowed, finding it hard to speak. "I don't know… Perhaps—" she chanced a glance at Nicholas before looking away as quickly "—he can stop by and see you a bit later."

Nicholas's hand squeezed Austen's shoulder. "I'll do so, I promise."

Her son nodded his head to him then slid off the bench.

She stood and motioned for Miss Grove who sat knitting on another bench a bit farther away. "I'll see you in a little while, Austen." She leaned down and kissed his cheek.

He turned to Nicholas. "You'll come soon?"

Nicholas ruffled his hair and smiled. "Yes, very soon."

The two watched Austen walk away with his nanny.

Alice braced herself when Nicholas turned back to her. "I received the documents you sent me."

When he made no reply, she cleared her throat and looked down. "I came to ask for your forgiveness." She took another deep breath. "You see, before yesterday, I had no idea I owned a share of my father's company."

"Your brother didn't inform you?"

At his sharp tone she looked up and shook her head. "My brother and father never saw fit to involve me in the business." She gave a bitter laugh. "Especially once my father disinherited me." Moistening her lips she continued. "I was hit with a few too many surprises yesterday afternoon."

"I'm sorry I had to be among them." Nicholas shifted over on the bench. "Why don't you sit down?"

She complied, her knees feeling shaky.

He cleared his throat. "I began investigating your family's firm when I first returned. I admit I probably did it mostly out of curiosity. Your father was no longer around to give me the satisfaction of showing him I'd made good. The next best thing was to see how your father's firm had done over the years compared with my own." He paused. "I was also astounded to discover your father had disinherited you. I think this most of all prompted my investigation."

She watched his profile as he spoke. Her hand ached to reach out and touch his beloved face, to smooth his hair, but although he sat only a few inches from her, she felt he was miles away.

"What I found was that your brother had not only mismanaged your family's firm, but the types of investments were also unsound. The deeper I went, the more concerned I grew. Your brother is close to bankruptcy."

She shook her head. No wonder Geoffrey had been so frantic the day before.

He looked down at his loosely clasped hands. "I didn't know how to tell you, perhaps that's why I kept silent. Your father's firm was responsible for some of the shoddy housing of the kind you were showing me that day.

"One of the companies responsible for investing in some of the building firms has another name, but your brother is the principal behind it, your father before him. They put up the money, hoping for a quick return on their investment."

She hadn't been wrong in her interpretation of the documents. "You should have told me."

His dark eyes gazed into hers and she wished with all

her heart that she'd never distrusted him. "I didn't want to hurt you. I thought instead that I could put a stop to it by buying out your father's partner. When I discovered you also owned some shares, I saw my way clear to gaining control of the company, as well as shore it up before your brother ran it into the ground completely. It is, after all, your son's inheritance."

She shook her head sadly. "As Geoffrey pointed out to me."

"I was going to present you the shares I'd purchased on our wedding day—that is, if you'd ever agreed to marry me." His lips twisted. "I had no interest in running your company—as long as you discharged Geoffrey as president—and got rid of Victor as chief counsel. His advice has not aided your brother in making sound decisions."

"So, he, too, has been privy to Geoff's mismanagement?"

"Yes."

The silence stretched out before them. "I'm sorry, Nicholas, for not trusting you." She looked down at her hands. "I was afraid to."

"Why?" he asked softly.

"I was afraid to feel what I had for you before."

"Was it because your father sent you away?"

She put a hand to her mouth, unable to stop the tears. "Because it hurt to love you. When Father dismissed you, I didn't understand that it would be for good. I kept expecting to see you, that somehow you'd come back—" Her words became incoherent.

"I'm sorry I left you the way I did that day, without a word. Believe me, it was not my intention."

She couldn't stop weeping. "I waited for word from you—some word, anything. My father said only that he had sent you away." She swallowed. "I cried and cried. I had nothing from you…and then I remembered that afternoon we went riding in Richmond Park—"

She dug frantically in her handbag. "After you left, I went back there and found these." She pulled out the two handkerchiefs they'd used that day. "You probably don't even remember, but you'd given me your handkerchief to dry my face. They were still there, lying on the rock where I'd spread them out to dry."

He took the two handkerchiefs from her. They were wrinkled but neatly folded in squares. His monogram was clearly visible in the corner of one. "Yes…I remember that day very well," he said softly, fingering his initials.

"It was all I had of you. Then Father sent me away in disgrace. It was so awful," she sobbed. "Being with those relatives was like being a prisoner. I never felt more alone in my life. I didn't understand being punished so cruelly just for loving you. Every day I expected you to come back, to contact me somehow. I dreamed of how you'd come back and rescue me…"

Somewhere in her incoherent speech, Nicholas had put his arm around her. He stroked her hair and murmured soothing words. "Don't fret yourself, Alice."

"I loved you so much…I would have gone anywhere with you—"

"Dear, sweet Alice, it wouldn't have been possible. I was penniless."

"I wouldn't have cared—"

She sniffled and Nicholas handed her her old handkerchief. She took it and blew her nose and wiped her eyes.

In a calmer voice, she continued. "For a long time I felt abandoned by everyone, even God. It wasn't until I met

Julian a few years later that he helped me find solace. He showed me that the Lord loved me and hadn't abandoned me. Through His grace I was able to forgive Father—and you—for never coming back."

She sat up and looked at Nicholas. His dark eyes had softened. "I thought I was fully healed until I saw you again." She pressed her lips together, afraid she would begin to cry once more. "You showed me how fearful I still was. I was afraid of losing Austen, afraid of what you made me feel again…"

She clutched the handkerchief in her hand, ashamed of looking at him. "Can you ever forgive me for not trusting you?" she whispered.

He covered her hand with his own. "If you can forgive me for not trusting your feelings for me enough to confide in you."

"Oh, Nicholas, I was so afraid you would choose your business concerns over me."

He looked down, and for a moment she was worried she had offended him again. Then he said, "I love you and Austen more than any material thing I own. When my mother died, and I couldn't be here in time to say farewell, I realized how futile everything I'd striven for was without having someone to love."

She drew away enough to say, "I love you."

"I'll never replace Julian."

She placed her hand against his cheek wanting to erase the bleak look in his eyes. "You never will because you have no need to. You were in my heart first."

A smile began to warm the dark depths of his gaze. "Does this mean you will marry me?"

"If you'll have me, and Austen."

He nodded. "I love both of you and hope I can be the husband you want me to be, and the father Austen needs."

"Oh, Nicholas, will you promise to always tell me what is closest to your heart?"

He drew her toward him and she came willingly, at long last feeling she was in the right place. "I will trust you with my deepest dreams and fears," he whispered against her hair, "and never fear your love won't be strong enough to bear it."

She leaned toward him, her fingers tunneling his short hair, and he drew forward, his lips finding hers.

Long minutes later, she asked, "Are you still leaving for America?"

"Not immediately—unless you want to go. When I came back to England, I meant to come for good."

She smiled. "I'm glad you've come home, although it would be nice to see America."

"You shall."

Some time after, he murmured against her cheek, "I hope you'll get rid of Victor as your solicitor now."

"Of course."

"I'll take care of the matter if you wish."

She laughed against his chin. "That's all right. I've known him all my life. I'll do it."

"Only if I'm present," he growled, his lips nibbling her earlobe.

She smiled in gratitude and understanding. "Thank you. I hope I shall always have you around to face all unpleasantness."

"Your wish is my command," he chuckled.

"You are indeed a man most worthy."

Epilogue

September 1891

Nick breathed in the sharp tang of sea breeze and watched the view of the harbor coming in sight. Soon they'd be home again. Home.

He put his arm around Alice's shoulder and whispered in her ear, "Excited?"

She turned to him with a smile. "Yes. But it was worth crossing the Atlantic. I loved every minute of it."

"Especially the fact that we're not coming back empty-handed."

They both looked down at the bundle she held in her arms. "We're bringing home our own little Yankee," she said, her voice filled with tenderness.

"How's our little princess doing?" he asked softly, gazing down at their three-month-old daughter.

"Sleeping peacefully." Jean Anne Tennent, named for his mother, lay swathed in pink blankets, her shock of hair as dark as his. At that moment she stirred and stared up at them, her eyes as blue as Alice's. She yawned, her little bud of a mouth opening wide.

Nick felt a mixture of pride, deep humility and overwhelming love well up inside him, as it did each time he looked at the perfect little creature. He could still scarcely fathom this outcome of his and Alice's love.

When Alice had told him she was expecting, he'd gone past the hope of ever knowing the joys of fatherhood and was grateful just being able to share in Austen's upbringing. Alice had confided that after her first husband's death, she too had never thought to be blessed with more offspring.

Little Jeannie was truly a gift from God and they both thanked Him every day for her.

Austen's clear voice rang out, "Papa, look at all the ships!"

The name on the eight-year-old's lips still filled him with another sense of awe. Only a few weeks ago, the boy had taken him by surprise during their nightly bedtime story to ask permission to call him Papa.

"Of course you may…son," Nick had answered in a quiet tone, trying to mask the catch in his throat.

"Dear, be careful!" Alice's voice warned as she glanced at the boy, who leaned out far over the rail.

Nick reached for his daughter. "Here, let me take our Yankee while you grab our son before he falls overboard."

Alice chuckled as she relinquished her precious baby to her husband. She watched for a second as he cooed over his daughter. Alice never worried about Nick with either child anymore. He was an extraordinary father.

"Mama, look, we're getting closer!"

Alice moved to stand behind Austen and hold him

by his suspenders. He'd grown a couple of inches in the last year.

His bond with Nick had only deepened over their year in America. When Alice had discovered her pregnancy, Nick had insisted they remain in San Francisco until the baby was old enough to travel. She hadn't let her confinement stop her activities, however. She'd seen and toured many benevolent societies and Nick had named her chairman of his entire charitable trust.

She took a deep breath, as they drew near the harbor. She was looking forward to their new life back in London and Richmond, and wherever the Lord would lead her with her beloved companion.

She turned to glance at her husband once again and caught his eyes. The warmth grew in them, as she returned the smile of the man whom the Lord had brought back to her life. The man who'd been her first—and last—love.

* * * * *

Dear Reader,

Sometimes life offers a second chance at love with an old flame. I had an enjoyable time imagining what it would be like for a young girl on the brink of womanhood to fall in love with a man who enters her life for only a few days. The timing and circumstances are all wrong then, but fifteen years later the two are given a new opportunity. Will they be brave enough to take it, or has life taught them caution?

Perhaps this story was inspired by my 30th high school reunion (which alas, I was unable to attend), but seeing pictures on the Internet of some of my former classmates convinced me I'd probably *not* be attracted to former boyfriends if we met again!

Wishing you all a happy read,

QUESTIONS FOR DISCUSSION

1. What is it about Alice's home life that makes her vulnerable to falling in love with a virtual stranger at the tender age of sixteen?

2. How is Nicholas Tennent different from the other men in Alice's life?

3. What makes Nick throw aside his usual caution around Alice when he first meets her?

4. When they meet again fifteen years later, their roles are reversed. Why has Alice now become the fearful and cautious one, emotionally speaking? How is this reflected in her attitude toward her only son?

5. Despite her caution, what attracts Alice to Nick again after so many years? What repels her?

6. What has made Nick return to England? Although on the surface Nick seems to have forgiven (and even been thankful to) Alice's late father for having dismissed him, has Nick truly overcome this past slight?

7. What about Nick resembles Alice's late father? How is he different? What does he have in common with Alice's late husband, Julian?

8. How has Alice's faith over the years helped her come to terms with her feelings for her father?

9. Why is it that sometimes when one has matured spiritually in an area, the emergence of a situation or person will reveal there is still a weakness to overcome in this area? How does Nick's reappearance in Alice's life reveal this in her case?

10. Why is it so important to Nick that Alice trust him unconditionally? How did his past treatment by her father contribute to this? Is this fair to ask of Alice?

11. When Nick and Alice meet fifteen years later, both are older and wiser. How does this make them less willing to take chances with their hearts?

12. How does the testimony of his handkerchief (kept by Alice all these years) soften Nick's heart toward Alice when she proves she cannot trust him unconditionally, and enable him to forgive her?

Love Inspired

Widower and former
soldier Evan Paterson
invites his five-year-old
daughter's best friend
and her friend's single
mother to the ranch for
the holiday meal. Can
these two pint-sized
matchmakers show two
stubborn grownups
what being thankful
truly means, and help
them learn how to
forgive and love again?

Look for

A Texas Thanksgiving
by
Margaret Daley

Available November 2008 wherever books are sold.

Steeple
Hill®

REQUEST YOUR FREE BOOKS!

2 FREE INSPIRATIONAL NOVELS
PLUS 2
FREE
MYSTERY GIFTS

Love Inspired.
HISTORICAL
INSPIRATIONAL HISTORICAL ROMANCE

YES! Please send me 2 FREE Love Inspired® Historical novels and my 2 FREE mystery gifts (gifts are worth about $10). After receiving them, if I don't wish to receive any more books, I can return the shipping statement marked "cancel". If I don't cancel, I will receive 4 brand-new novels every other month and be billed just $4.24 per book in the U.S. or $4.74 per book in Canada, plus 25¢ shipping and handling per book and applicable taxes, if any*. That's a savings of over 20% off the cover price! I understand that accepting the 2 free books and gifts places me under no obligation to buy anything. I can always return a shipment and cancel at any time. Even if I never buy another book, the two free books and gifts are mine to keep forever. 102 IDN ERYA 302 IDN ERYM

Name	(PLEASE PRINT)

Address	Apt. #

City	State/Prov.	Zip/Postal Code

Signature (if under 18, a parent or guardian must sign)

Mail to Steeple Hill Reader Service:
IN U.S.A.: P.O. Box 1867, Buffalo, NY 14240-1867
IN CANADA: P.O. Box 609, Fort Erie, Ontario L2A 5X3

Not valid to current subscribers of Love Inspired Historical books.

Want to try two free books from another series?
Call 1-800-873-8635 or visit www.morefreebooks.com

* Terms and prices subject to change without notice. N.Y. residents add applicable sales tax. Canadian residents will be charged applicable provincial taxes and GST. Offer not valid in Quebec. This offer is limited to one order per household. All orders subject to approval. Credit or debit balances in a customer's account(s) may be offset by any other outstanding balance owed by or to the customer. Please allow 4 to 6 weeks for delivery. Offer available while quantities last.

Your Privacy: Steeple Hill Books is committed to protecting your privacy. Our Privacy Policy is available online at www.SteepleHill.com or upon request from the Reader Service. From time to time we make our lists of customers available to reputable third parties who may have a product or service of interest to you. If you would prefer we not share your name and address, please check here. ☐

LIH08R

Love Inspired.
HISTORICAL

TITLES AVAILABLE NEXT MONTH

Don't miss these two stories in November

CALICO CHRISTMAS AT DRY CREEK by Janet Tronstad
Alone in the Montana Territory after the death of her
husband and child, Elizabeth O'Brian sees no hope for the
future. Jake Hargrove needs someone to help him care for his
two young part-Sioux nieces. It would be just a marriage of
convenience. But as Christmas approaches, the two may find
themselves getting more than they could have hoped for—
a new chance for love.

REDEEMING GABRIEL by Elizabeth White
A life of deception has eaten away at Gabriel Laniere's soul.
Being a spy for the Union army is a noble cause, but it's kept
him from getting close to anyone, even God. Yet Camilla
Beaumont, daughter of the Confederacy, might just be the
exception. Hiding a dangerous secret of her own, she may
well offer the love Gabriel needs to heal any conflict.

LIHCNM1008